OPEN DANGER

By

Ceige Templar

WOLFCREST PRESS
UTAH

This is a work of fiction. The events and characters described herein are imaginary and are not intended to refer to specific places or living persons. The opinions expressed in this manuscript are solely the opinions of the author and do not represent the opinions or thoughts of the publisher. The author has represented and warranted full ownership and /or legal right to publish all material in this book.

ACKNOWLEDGMENTS

I'd like to thank my beta readers and my editor for the encouragement, and keeping me focused on my writing.

Dedicated

To my fans, and my family, for never letting me quit. I love you all.

PRELUDE

My name is Alexandra Kendall. I work at the corporate headquarters of Oshler & Marsh Construction in Omaha, Nebraska. I started in the mail room when I was eighteen, working my why through numerous departments until I reached the age of twenty-eight becoming the youngest Vice President in Logistics of the Pipe Line Division. I had many good mentors to learn from, giving me the ability to work in a man's world, and have the respect of many. I hated being called beautiful as men looked at me like the cover of a book, not expecting to find intelligences inside.

At work in the office, I wore my dark chocolate hair in a bun, black frame non-prescription glasses with a grey tint to distract from my sea-green eyes, and thick black lashes, and tailored suits. In the field I wore jeans, tee shirts, and a suite jacket. I spoke frank and to the point, not taking any of their shit.

I had worked hard to reach my position and had sacrificed a lot in my private life. Only once had I come close to marrying, and that had been to Joe Larkin. Joe owned Galvestone Steel in Galveston, Texas, a company we did business with regularly. I put my career first and broke it off. That was seven months ago.

I'd ignored Gary Spindle's advances for six months after my breakup with Joe. But after the party hosted by my company, I found myself dating Gary, breaking one of my own rules of not dating anyone at the office. Gary had been hired two years prior as line draftsman. He'd also put in his application for the job opening as my assistant, as my current assistant left unexpectedly after seven years with the company.

Right now, we we're working on the Company's largest pipeline that would last three years, unusually long for a pipeline job. The Pipeline would come down from Alaska, split in South Dakota, one line going east the other going west. The company celebration for the contract closure of all land right-a-ways had been a two-year struggle meeting stringent demands. Invitation to the black-tie event had gone to all contractors wanting a chance to bid on sections of their expertise. There was big money to be made on this job and not only did it bring out our general contractors, but had drawn out others like ants from the woodwork.

When I think I have all the time in the world, it takes a life and death situation for me to take a second look at my decisions.

CHAPTER 1

"Good evening Miss Kendall," the bellman greeted me as he pushed the button for the elevator to come down. "You're looking mighty lovely this evening," he added. Alex had left the black rimmed glasses home and let her hair down, falling gracefully over the corner of me left eye. The backless jade dress molded to my body and intensified the green of my eyes.

"Thank you, Martin. Have many guests arrived?"

"Yes Ma'am. I talked to Mr. Kierbow, and his daughter. He always stops to chat when he's in town." The doors were closing when I heard someone yell.

"Hold those doors please!"

"Yes Sir, I'll do that, Mr. Spindle. Good evening Sir," Martin responded pushing the door stop.

"Thank you, Martin," Gary replied as he stepped inside. "Wow, aren't we queen of the ball tonight," he said, smiling at Alex. "Wouldn't know you were the same gal from the office, this must be Cinderella's night out?"

I gave Gary a quick smile. "Thank you, Gary. Even Cinderella gets a night out occasionally. You also look very nice in your tuxedo. Oh, and by the way, congratulation on the new job. I was told you were the best qualified for my assistant."

"Thank you, I know Sharon did an excellent job for you."

"Yes, she did. You could say she was my right arm. I'm going to miss her," I said, watching the buttons in the elevator light up each floor.

"I'm sure I can fill her shoes, and perhaps much more," he said, smiling devilish at me.

Looking at him directly, I spoke deadpan serious, "Gary, I'm sure you would like to work your job before you lose it. I have declined your advances in the past. If you just do your job, we'll get along fine."

The elevator doors opened, and I walked passed him into the reception area. Looking around the crowd, I caught sight of Lester Kierbow and his daughter Ateara at the Hors d oeuvre table. Lester's tight, curly silver hair against his black skin was easy to find. Ateara, was beautiful with flawless skin that I had always envied. Her large dark eyes, ebony shoulder length hair, and voluminous figure always turned heads. Easing my way through the crowd, I picked up a plate and took a small portion of caviar and shrimp before walking up behind Lester.

"Excuse me Sir, but could you hurry up a bit?" I teased, winking at Ateara. Lester turned around grinning from ear to ear when he saw who was speaking to him.

"Miss Alexandra. It's always such a delight to see ya child. Joe be with you tonight?"

"No. Not tonight Lester." Lester's smile always shone in his eyes. He was a strong, but a gentle man. Also, a man respected by his crew. "Please, won't you both sit at my table? It's reserved, and the first one on the left at the front." Lester nodded, following me to the table with the large place card that read, reserved Kendall. I took a seat where I could observe everyone in the room.

In the convention hall, there were fifty tables and each one-seated eight. Each setting had a large white envelope on the seat of the chair, and a name card of the contractor above the dinner plate. Most contractors escorted wive's, while others their secretary. Earlier in the day, I had placed the name card for Lester and Ateara along with three contractors I'd worked with in the past.

They were all seated except for one contractor who sat down at another table. The contractor would have sat directly across from me. Rising to go speak to him, a tall, dark, gentleman walked over to the table and pulled out the chair.

"Good evening, Miss Kendall. Excuse me for changing tables, but I couldn't resist sitting across from the most beautiful woman here tonight. I'm Nick Salva from Louisiana."

"Mr. Salva let me introduce you to the rest of those at the table; Lester Kierbow and his daughter Ateara."

"I do know Lester and his beautiful daughter. How are you this evening?" Nick shook hands with Lester and took Ateara's but instead of shaking hands, he put her hand to his lips kissing it lightly.

"How you be Nick? I'm surprised to see ya here." Lester answered his tone a sharp edge. Ateara smiled politely but said nothing, while quickly taking her hand back feigning interest in something across the room.

"Aren't surprises nice," Nick said.

I looked between them, the tension palpable.

"Roger Harris, Rickland Jones, George Haight, Recardio Martinelli; Nick Salva, I finished with the introduction. A moment later the waiter approached with their salads. The conversation was light through the meal, and I found myself several times looking at Nick. Nick Salva was in the range of six foot three, wavy black hair, and dark eyes. You could tell he spent a lot of time outdoors as he was incredibly tan for this time of the year, but then again he did live in Louisiana. He was an excellent conversationalist, had a beautiful smile and I guessed he was in his late thirties. But there was something, perhaps more of a feeling; I couldn't put my finger on.

After desert, they listened to Mr. Oshler give instruction to the contractors and an overview of the project that lay ahead. I couldn't help noticing when glancing at Salva, he was watching me.

After the speakers had finished talking, all were invited to stay for dancing. Also, a bar had been set up at each end of the room for those who wished to partake of spirits. When the music started, I turned to speak with Lester. Moments later Nick Salva was standing behind me.

"May I have this dance?" he asked, holding his hand out to me.

"Yes, thank you." Taking his hand, he led us onto the dance floor. They were playing a tango and I was hoping my feet would remember the steps.

Nick placed his hand on my bare back and brought me so close, breathing felt impossible. His muscled legs pressed against mine, and when he dipped me, the strength in his arms as though I weighed no more than a feather. Nick's eyes, those beautiful dark eyes, sent chills down my spine sending off a warning signal inside. When the music ended, Nick had danced them out onto the terrace.

"You dance very well Alex. Not many women can tango with such fire."

"Thank you. You dance very well yourself," I said, backing away from Nick.

"Do you do everything with such fire?" Nick took a step closer to me, my back against the iron railing. He wrapped his arm around my waist, pulling me against him away from the rail before sliding his hand down to caress my buttocks. His other hand closed on the back of my neck, lips claimed mine in hungry desire. Feeling his arousal against my stomach, I struggled to back away only to back into the railing again, his body leaned into mine.

"Stop, Nick!" I managed to say.

"You know you want it as much as I do. I saw it in your eyes," he said, moving his hand down my neck.

"Alex, are you, all right?" Gary asked, walking over to us. Nick let me go, and as he backed up, I slapped him across the face.

"I am now Gary." Moving to Gary's side, he walked me back into the ballroom. Nick's redden face glared at me. Walking away I didn't turn back around to look at him.

When Gary and I arrived at my table, Ateara was sitting alone. I sat down beside her.

"Would you ladies like something to drink?"

"Yes Gary, rum and coke; Ateara?"

"A glass of wine would be nice, thank you."

Gary strolled away to get our drinks, I sat back in the chair letting out a heavy sigh.

"I'm sorry Alex. I didn't have a chance to warn you about Nick. Are you okay?"

"I'm all right. Nick just took me by surprise is all?" I looked at Ateara with interest. "You mean to tell me you know him?"

"Yes, we grew up in the same town, went to the same school. Nick has been sweet on me for a long time, but I've managed to keep him at a distance. I've seen the other women Nick has kept, and I wanted no part of him."

"It is hard to believe that someone as handsome and intelligent could have such a dark side. I'm glad Gary came out to the balcony, or Nick would have been picking himself up off the floor. With all the traveling I do, I've taken martial arts, and that has been useful."

"Gary watched Nick dance you out to the balcony. He stood by the door watching you."

"Gary, really!" I pushed the remark to the back of my mind to dissect later. "How have you been Ateara? It's been awhile since I've seen you."

"I be good. Looking after Pa, be keeping him out of trouble. I think I've talked him into retiring after this job."

"This job would set him for the rest of his life. If he does retire, I will miss him. He's become a good friend, you both have."

"That doesn't mean you can't come to Louisiana for a visit, girl."

"You're right. Are you still dabbling in the craft?" I asked, giving Ateara a sly grin.

"I never dabble," Ateara said, smiling back. "You need a spell? My mammy taught me good."

"Oh no, I don't get into Voodoo. I've seen your work, and I'll pass."

"Alex, in the realm of voodoo, that was nothing, just a tip of an iceberg of what I can do," Ateara laughed.

"Well, I'll pass on your nothing," both of us laughed. "It's good to see you again. I'm glad you came with your father."

"Ladies, your drinks, and I did remember them right." Gary put the glasses on the table and sat down next to Alex. A few minutes later Lester returned. The four of them talked about one thing, the pipeline.

"Alex, would you like to dance?" Gary asked, putting his hand out to me to take. I took it tentatively as they stepped out onto the dance floor.

"Thank you, Gary for rescuing me," Alex said, looking around the room.

"He left, if you're looking for Salva."

I relaxed enjoying the dance along with the rest of the evening mingling with the other contractors besides the Kierbow's.

"Well, I think I'm going to call it a night," I said, before standing to give Lester and Ateara a hug. "I'll be talking to you soon."

"I'll walk you to your car Alex. I won't take no for an answer," Gary said.

I smiled as Gary walked me out. We didn't talk until we were out of the building.

"I'm parked across the street, over there, the red BMW," I motioned pointing across the street. I can't believe all this traffic for this time of night." Cars sped past them as they waited to cross.

"You're looking at the traffic, and I'm looking at the stars. Amazing some nights, the sky is so illuminated."

"Yes, the sky is beautiful tonight."

"You mean morning? I see you traded in the pumpkin for a carriage."

I started to laugh, thinking of the image. "I don't always drive my truck. What's with this Cinderella thing?"

"That's the way you look tonight." Gary gave my hand a light squeeze. "You're completely opposite from the way you look at the office."

"That doesn't stop you from hitting on me."

"You can't hide your beauty behind those black rimmed glasses, and your hair pulled back in a tight bun," Gray said, smiling sheepishly.

We hurried across the street. Standing beside the BMW, Gary took my keys opening the door. Taking my hand, helped me into the car.

"I'll see you on Monday." Turning the key in the ignition the only sound was sputter, sputter. Trying again, the same noise was heard, sputter, sputter. "I don't believe this. I've never had trouble with this car before."

"Try it again, but give it a little gas first." Sputter, sputter. "Come on, I'll give you a ride home. I would look under the hood, but I am no mechanic. However, I am a great rescuer," Gary chuckled.

"Well, you certainly have been tonight. Maybe I should call a tow truck," I said, hesitantly. Getting out of the car looking up and down the street I wasn't sure.

"Alex, with the traffic on this road your BMW will be okay until tomorrow. Come on, I'm only half a block up." Taking my arm, he guided us to the sidewalk, and we strolled toward his car. "I believe tonight was a great success. I didn't know there were so many contractors," he said, placing his hand over mine on his forearm. "Did you know most of them?"

"There is a group I work with on most of our jobs whose labor and bids are always the best. However, tonight there were many I'd never seen before. A job of this magnitude really draws them out."

"Like Salva?" he asked bringing my hand to his heart.

"Yes, like Nick Salva. I've heard the name before. However, tonight is the first time I've met him. Hopefully, it will be the last." Alex looked up at the sky; *maybe I've judged Gary too harshly. When he wasn't coming on like a bull moose, he seemed very nice. I could have handled Nick myself, as they say, the bigger they are the harder they fall. Gary's arrival made it a quieter escape.*

"Here we are," he said, letting my hand go, standing beside the black Corvette.

"Why doesn't that surprise me you drive a vet," I laughed, more at ease this time.

"You don't think it fits me or what?" he asked, jokingly unlocking and opening the door

"Part of you, it fits very well, as the person I know at the office. But the part of you that I've seen tonight a Cadillac would a better fit."

Gary helped me inside the car, walked around the front his eyes still on me. He slid silently inside, started the engine letting it purr a few minutes before he put the top down.

"We shouldn't waste this beautiful night sky. I'll turn the heater on." He pulled out onto the road, after shifting into fourth gear; he laid his hand over mine, again. Neither of us spoke for a while.

"When will the bids start coming in?" Gary asked.

"They'll start next week, depending on the area the contractor is bidding for. The information and deadlines were in their packets they were given, so it will rely on that. The proposals will go faster than the land right-a-ways and the environmental impact studies that have taken two years." I'd forgotten about Gary's hand on mine when we started to talk shop. Most of the time I was all business. Feeling exposed on a night like this, and letting my guarded persona down, was something I didn't like to do. There had been few casual nights out since breaking up with Joe, but even they had been work related.

"Well, Cinderella here you are, home safe."

"Thanks, Gary, no need to get out," I said, sliding out of the car.

"You mean I don't get to come in for a nightcap?"

"Not tonight. I'll see you on Monday." Walking up to the door, the house key slid easily into the lock. Turning around I waved goodbye, and noticed an unfamiliar black truck parked across the street. Opening the door, I went inside closed it, resetting the alarm. Turning on the hall way lamp, I climbed up the stairs fully exhausted. Looking out the hall window, I watched the unrecognizable black truck across the street for several minutes before continuing to my bedroom. Changing into pajamas and then glancing at the diamond-faced watch, fifteen minutes had passed before I heard the engine start, and whoever it was, drove away.

CHAPTER 2

Monday morning, came early. Arriving at work at six thirty I was going over email when Mr. Oshler walked into my office. He was a handsome man in his sixties. Silver hair, deep blue eyes, tan skin and a body you knew worked out. He was happily married to a woman that I adored.

"Hello, Alex. What is your opinion of the banquet?" He asked, sitting down in the chair next to a small round table. Setting in the center of the table was a picture of Alex, Marsh, and Oshler at a groundbreaking ceremony in a gold colored frame.

"I think it was a great success. I saw few empty seats."

"I heard you had a bit of trouble with one of the contractors."

"Really, who did you hear that from?"

"I was talking to Lester Kierbow. You know he is quite fond of you. They don't make them any better than Lester, and he's been great to work with over the years."

"Yes, he has. I stop and visit with him and Ateara whenever I go down that way. I think he's just a protective father figure."

"So, there isn't anything I need to take care of?"

"No, everything is fine. Would you like a cup of coffee?" Picking up the phone, I rang for my secretary to see if she was in yet, and surprised when it only rang twice before Terry picked up.

"Yes, I would. Ask Terry to check if there are donuts left that I brought in this morning."

Five minutes later Terry, a blonde, slender women, not showing her fifty some years, walked in with two cups of coffee and plate hosting three chocolate éclairs. She set the tray on the table next to Mr. Oshler and then left closing the door behind her.

"How do you think Gary is going to do?" He asked.

"I don't know." *Now is not the time to train another assistant, I thought.* "I relied so much on Sharon. She had a sixth sense and had things done before I needed them. I hope he can catch on quickly.

"Sharon was here nine years I believe. She hadn't mentioned looking for anything else, or leaving here?" *Mr. Oshler asked, taking a bite of his éclair.* "You really need to try one Alex. I buy them at that French Pastry Shop on the corner of 59th."

Walking over, I sat down in a chair on the other side of the table. Picking up a éclair, took a bite before answering.

"Yum, these are good. No. I was shocked when Sharon told me about leaving and without any explanation why."

I thought back to the day Sharon had come into the office and gave her week notice. She didn't want to talk about it, and just said Friday would be her last day. It was so unlike her.

"Let me know about Gary, and if you need more help. By the way, you will need background checks on all contractors before the bids are presented for a vote. I know it's extra work Alex, but they are calling for stricter compliance. I'll talk to you later." Oshler picked up the last éclair leaving my office, a bounce to his step probably from the sugar rush.

I rang Terry and asked her to have Gary stop by my office when he came in. I finished eating my éclair and drinking coffee sitting in front of the large window that faced west. Sitting at the window always gave me a sense of calm. Watching the traffic below and outward, you could see for miles especially on a day like this when the sun was bright and not a cloud in the sky. *That's a good omen; I will get more things accomplished than I planned today.* With that thought, I moved back to my desk and sat down to the stack of white envelopes. Some contractors handed them in before leaving Saturday night, which I was grateful for. It was a jump start on processing background checks.

It was nine a.m. when Gary walked into my office.

"Good morning. I stopped by my old office to clean out my desk and get the rest of my things before coming up. It's rewarding having a larger space," Gary said, sitting down in the chair in front of Alex's desk. "Where would you like me to start?"

I was thankful that Gary didn't bring up Saturday's eventful evening. Even seeing another side of him, I still preferred a professional level between them. Nevertheless, I had to admit, there was an attraction. Maybe it was just having someone look after me. Sure, I could take care of myself, spent years refining martial arts, gaining the confidence that added to the outer exterior people saw as a savvy business woman. However, it was nice being looked after. I missed that part of companionship not having Joe around.

"Background checks, have you done them before Gary?"

"I have, but it's been awhile. How about a quick refresher?" he said, leaning on the front of my desk. Walking Gary through the procedures, I caught him staring at me couple of times and decided to let it pass and had continued.

"Okay, how many do we have?" He asked. I lifted the stack of envelopes and laid them back down.

"There'll be more arriving in the mail," I replied.

"Let's do this. You take the top half, and I'll do the bottom half," Gary said, splitting the pile.

"Are background checks always required on contractors?"

"No. Most jobs do not require them. With a job this big there will be more paperwork and more accountability."

"Okay, I'll get started on these, and I'll see you at lunch," he stated, walking toward the door.

"Lunch?"

"Yes. You do eat, don't you?" He asked, half grinning

"Yes, I do eat," I started to laugh. "I'll see you at lunch."

It was 12:30 when Gary knocked on my door and came in as the phone rang.

"Alex Kendall."

"Alex, this is Joe. How are you?"

"Joe...I'm doing all right. Just a minute," I responded as I put my hand over the phone. "Gary, I'm going to be a few minutes. Why don't you go ahead?"

"I'll wait for you in my office," he said, without waiting for her to reply before he walked out and shut the door behind him.

"Joe, this is unexpected. How are you?"

"Doing well, business is good. The reason I called Alex, Lester and Ateara stopped by on their way home to Louisiana and told me what happened between you and Nick Salva. I just wanted to make sure you were all right, and there were not any repercussions."

"Repercussions, why would there be, Joe?" I sat back in my chair and took out the small picture of Joe that was kept in my desk drawer. Looking at the photo gave butterflies flight inside. Joe expressed warmth in his blue eyes even in his picture. His blond hair, straight nose, the small scar on his chin added to his charisma. Standing by the corral in his white tee shirt, jeans and boots he could have very well have been a calendar model.

"I know Nick Salva, and that doesn't sound like him to just walk away. Be careful when you are out and about."

"I'm sure he has returned to Louisiana by now Joe. He's a contractor; he has his business to run."

"Just the same, stay alert. You haven't reconsidered my proposal, have you?"

"Joe," I paused. "I love you, but I'm not ready for marriage and give up everything I've worked so hard for."

"Alex, I wanted to ask you one more time. Since that is still your answer, I will let it go. Take care of yourself."

The receiver went dead. Slowly I hung the phone up, and placed the picture back in the drawer and closed it. Walking out of my office, Gary was standing by his door.

"Five more minutes this train would have left without you. I'm hungry," Gary said, smiling at me. I quickened my step.

"Good afternoon Miss Kendall," was the greeting when they walked into the restaurant. "Follow me, please."

Following the hostess to a corner booth I sat down. Gary sat down across the table.

"You're a regular here I see."

"When you eat at a place two or three times a week over a few years, I guess you could say I'm a regular."

When the waiter came by, we gave him our order.

"We have deadlines. Terry can bring you up to date. How you coming with the background checks? I had a few more come in after you left." I paused, taking a sip from my water glass.

"It's amazing. Are you always all business?

"It depends on where you want to go in life. I want to go to the top, so I guess ninety percent of the time you could say I'm all business."

"What do you do with the other ten percent?" Gary asked, reaching for my hand resting on the table. I retracted my hand before he could hold it. "All right back to work and we'll work on that ten percent later. Question, work related."

I was thinking of the differences between Joe and the man sitting across from me. Both were exceptionally good looking, personalities were a big difference. Joe was serious where...

"Alex, are you listening to me?" He asked, hitting his spoon lightly against his glass.

"I'm sorry, what did you ask me?"

"How thorough are the background checks? Am I looking for anything particular?"

"Yes. Has the contractor had a bid retraction, completion times on other jobs, were they within contractual limits. Are they insured and bonded? Have they had contractual disputes after signing and are they financially stable. Those are the big ones. When we're done those that qualify, they will be sent an invitation to bid on their expertise on the pipeline." I paused again, waving to a couple who sat down at a booth.

"That's why we need to have the background check done by Thursday. Invitations go out on Friday," I said.

Gary asked questions about the different parts of his job. What he needed to learn right away, and what could be put on hold for a while until they had more time. They finished lunch, and Alex asked the waiter to add a large coke to go.

"I'll get this," Gary said, reaching for my bill.

"Thank you for the offer, but I prefer to pay for my own," I said smiling, picking up the bill and the coke.

Returning to the office, I received a surprise. Sitting on my desk were a dozen red roses.

"Wow!" Where did these come from Terry?" I asked her while the appraising the flowers.

"I didn't look at the card. The roses were delivered fifteen minutes ago," Terry replied.

I opened the card. Leaning back on the desk, the smile that had taken residents on my face, made a quick retreat.

"Well, who are the roses from?" Terry asked, curiosity getting the best of her.

"Just an admirer."

"If I could be so lucky, I'm going to lunch. Is there anything you need me to do before I go?"

"No Terry, I'm okay. See you when you get back." Walking around my desk to the black leather chair, I sunk down reading the card again. Till we dance again, Nick.

It was late afternoon when Gary popped back into my office to tell me he was leaving.

"Roses huh, someone beat me to the punch."

"Here's the card, you can read it yourself," I replied, handing it to him.

"I thought he would have taken the hint when you slapped him the other evening. What are you going to do?"

"What can I do? Enjoy the roses I suppose, they are beautiful," I replied, smelling the roses that graced the desk.

"I'm leaving Alex, and looking at your desk, you're working late."

"Yes, that's part of the 90%. Oh, Gary, I have a meeting tomorrow on the other side of town so it might be after lunch when I get back."

"I have enough to keep me busy, tomorrow then."

It was dark when I walked out of the building and across the street to the red BMW car. Opening the door, I picked up the envelope that was in the seat and slid in, and opened it.

"Alex, the distributor cap was off. Don't know how you manage that one. Your spare keys are in the glove box. See you later, Ryan."

Turning on the car, it purred like a kitten. Looking for a different radio station, I glanced up observing a black 4 x 4 truck parked a few spaces behind me. It had the appearance of the vehicle I saw parked on the street the other evening. It couldn't be.

Pulling out onto the road taking the route that led home, I kept an eye on the black truck watching it pull into traffic. It could be anybody. There were a lot of people that drove black 4x4s. The vehicle followed for six blocks before turning on to another street. I sighed with relief. Continuing a few more miles before turning onto Magnolia Street, I drove half a block more, turning into the flower lined driveway, and activated the garage door, pulled in and closed it.

Going straight to my room, I undressed, turned on the water in the shower and then stepped inside. The hot water ran down my back, easing the tension that had accumulated. I let run until all the tension washed away. Stepping out I pulled on a robe, wrapped my hair in a towel, and went back downstairs. Opening the front door, I retrieve the mail and a tall white box leaning against the house. Picking it up, and glancing across the street, was parked the black 4x4 truck. I closed the door and reset the alarm before walking back to the kitchen with the box and the mail.

Inside the box were a dozen long stem red roses. Looking at them, I knew they had not been on the porch very long. Putting them in a vase, and looking for a card, I found it at the bottom. Opening it up, it read, "You're the fire in my heart," Nick. I laid the card down and walked into the living room, looked out the corner of the window, and saw the black 4x4 drive off.

What does he think he's doing? I jumped when the phone rang.

"Alex Kendall."

"You answer the phone at home like you do at the office," Gary laughed.

"Habit I guess," I replied, trying to relax the muscle that was tightening in the back of my neck.

"Wanted to see if you made it home okay?"

"Yes, I did. And guess what, I received another dozen red roses."

"From Nick?"

"Yes, with a note that read "You're the fire in my heart, Nick."

"That guy doesn't know when to give up, but I can't blame him, Alex. You looked exceptionally beautiful Saturday night. You'd make any man's blood run hot."

"It's just that attitude why I dress the way I do at the office. Anyway, I think it will blow over when he doesn't get response. He'll look somewhere else."

"You're probably right. I'll let you go and see you tomorrow."

"Goodnight Gary."

Next day at the office, Gary watched for the mail clerk to come up and then waited half an hour before he stopped at Terry's desk to ask about it.

"Hi Terry, any more contractor envelopes come in?" he asked.

"I have three that came in this morning."

"From whom?"

"One is from Salva Construction, Kierbow Construction, and the Jensen Brothers."

"I'll take the one from Salva and Kierbow, and Alex can check on the Jensen Brothers. Here I'll put it on her desk for you," Gary said, taking the three envelopes from Terry. "Terry when are the bids for the pipe banding and yard clean up going to be awarded?"

"Let me check the schedule, Gary," I said, pulling a chart from her drawer. "In two weeks."

"Thanks, Terry," Gary replied, and walked into Alex's office placing the Jensen Brothers envelope at the bottom of the pile. Taking a smaller white envelope out of his pocket, he placed it on top of the pile and returned to his office.

I returned around two p.m. with Mr. Oshler and went directly to my office. Sitting down at my desk, and putting the stack of contractor's information off to one side, I noticed the small white envelope on top of the pile. Opened it, and found a dinner invitation for Friday night from Gary. Sitting back in chair, I slid my shoes off, and closed my eyes.

Should I go to dinner, or not? I like his company. Office romance never work, and in particular with a person I work with on such a close basis, it could be disastrous. I don't know. I won't need to give him an answer for a couple of days. I need to think about this, I struggled with emotions. Emotions I didn't have room for with things starting to buzz on the pipeline.

It was 4:00 p.m. when Terry buzzed me on the com.

"Yes, Terry."

"Miss Kendall, there is someone here to see you," Terry said.

A stranger, I thought. Terry only calls me Miss Kendall when it is someone she doesn't know. Did I forget an appointment? This wasn't good. The sidetracks of Nick, Gary and the call from Joe had my mind going every which way.

"Give me a couple of minutes and then send them in, Terry."

"Yes, Miss Kendall."

I put my shoes back on, finished a note to remember two scheduled meeting later this week, when I heard, "I hope you enjoyed the roses," said the deep sensual voice belonging to Nick Salva.

My head came up with a jerk.

"Mr. Salva," I said, calmer than what I felt. "Yes, they were beautiful, but you shouldn't have wasted your money on them."

"Anything I spend on you Alex, is not a waste of my money." His voice was husky. "I'm going to be in town for a couple of days and wonder if you'd have dinner with me Friday night."

"I'm sorry, but I already have plans for Friday night," I replied, thinking of Gary's invitation to dinner.

"That's a shame. I was looking forward to your company."

"Mr. Salva,"

"Please call me Nick," he said, moving closer to my desk. My stomach tightened as nervous tension coiled inside.

"Mr. Salva, restrain yourself from sending me roses or anything else, because I have no intention of going out with you now or anytime in the future."

"You never know what the future holds," he said, smiling as he moved around the desk toward me.

"Mr. Salva, that's close enough," I said, standing up. He stood eight inches taller than my five feet seven inches. Looking up at him, his eyes full of lust, the coil in my stomach tighten another knot. "I suggest you don't do what you're thinking of."

Our eyes locked, time seemed to stand still. From what Ateara had told me about Nick, he was used to getting what he wanted. His very presence demanded submission. I held my ground until he backed away.

"I will have you, and you will enjoy it."

"In your dreams Mr. Salva. Now, I have work to do."

"Until our next meeting Alex," he said, smiling at me. He turned and walked to the door opening and then closing it behind him. I sat back down, legs shaking. In all my dealings with men on the job, I'd had never felt more threatened. It was the calm exterior, the silence before the storm.

Ten minutes passed until I'd collected myself, and let out a long sigh. Now *would be a good time for a cup of coffee.* Opening the office door and looking straight ahead, Gary was talking to Salva at the end of the hall next to the elevator. Continuing to the break room, I poured a cup of coffee and started back to my office. Checking to see if the two men were still standing in the hall I ran into Gary, spilling coffee down both of us.

"Oh Gary, I'm so sorry. Did I burn you?" I asked, setting the cup down on Terry's desk.

"No, are you?"

"No. I'm glad it's almost the end of the day. Neither one of us look good with coffee stains on our clothes. In fact, I'm calling it a day," I said sighing, looking at the ugly coffee stain down my pale blue blouse. "I'll see you both tomorrow."

"Alex what about Friday night?" Gary asked.

"What about it?" Alex looked at Gary wondering why he'd been talking to Salva. "What did Salva want? I saw you talking to him at the elevator.

"I told him if he needed information to speak to me. After the other night that would be best. He asked me when the bids would be awarded. I told him in two weeks." Gary shortened the distance between them. "You didn't want to talk to him, did you?"

"No Gary. I don't want to speak to him and if he calls you for information that would be great."

"Friday?" he asked again.

"What time do you want to pick me up?"

"Around seven. If you can wait five minutes, I'll walk you to your car," Gary said, backing up toward his office.

I looked at the elevator and then down to the floor thinking about what Salva had said.

"Okay. Five minutes." Going back to my office I cleared my desk, put things away that were left. *I think I'll call Ateara when I get home,* looking up the number in the Rolodex.

The ride home was uneventful, and I was thankful the street was empty when pulling into my drive. Parking the car in the garage, I waited until the door closed before stepping out. As habits go, I reset the alarm and put my purse in its usual place after I entered the kitchen. Taking a bottle of wine from the fridge, poured a glass, and sat down at the counter to call Ateara. Picking up the phone and dialing the number, it rang five times before I heard a "Hello" on the other end.

"Ateara, this is Alex."

"This is a surprise. Yeah all traveling down this way?"

"No, not yet, I had a couple of question I wanted to ask you."

"Shoot, girl."

"Have you seen Nick down there since you returned?"

"Hell no, Alex. I stay out of that man's way. I thought ya didn't want anything to do with him?"

"I don't. What kind of vehicle does Nick drive?"

"He has a couple. A black and maroon Cadillac and a black 4x4 truck, I think it's a Ford 350," I paused. "Why Alex, what be going on?"

"I've seen a black 4x4 truck parked across the street from my home and the same truck when I left work last night."

"Girl, you be careful. I've never seen Nick go after something and not get it one way or the other."

"How's your dad doing?" I asked to change the subject. I didn't need to worry Ateara about Nick's actions. Tonight, I was doing enough for both of us.

"He be real quiet the last couple of days," Ateara said. I could hear the tightness of real concern in her voice. "When we returned home last Sunday he be in such a great mood talking about this being his last job before retiring. Now, I don't know. Something be bothering him."

"Tell your dad hi for me, and I'll see you in a couple of weeks. I must check on the pipe at Joe's plant, so I thought I'd come visit for a couple of days. It would be great to have your dad cook me catfish he's so famous for."

"Look forward to it. And Alex, like I said, ya be careful."

I said goodbye and went upstairs to shower. The job hadn't even begun and the pressure felt like another twenty pounds had been added to my shoulders. What was happening with Lester?

The water running down my body did little to relax me trying to put Ateara's remark about Salva out of my mind. But the statement Salva made in the office still haunted me. Turning the water off and wrapped in a terry robe, I stopped at the window at the top of the stairs before going down to fix something light to eat. I was relieved that the black truck wasn't parked across the street and the knot started to lessen in my stomach.

This is so silly, letting my imagination run away with me. Eating quickly, I checked the house alarm before going back upstairs to bed.

Friday night I dressed in a pale-yellow spaghetti strap top with a sheer long sleeve olive shirt, olive colored pants with sandals to match. I wore a delicate gold chain holding a Capricorn with matching earrings that both had diamond set eyes. Wearing my hair pulled behind my right ear, it was parted on the side hanging in waves over my left eye. After checking makeup, I started down the stairs when the doorbell rang at 6:55.

Opening the door, was startled to see Nick Salva standing there and parked at the curb, a blue Cadillac convertible.

"What are you doing here?" I asked, not caring that my voice sounded like chipped ice.

"You look beautiful, Alex. I told you I would be in town a few days and wondered if you'd changed your mind about having dinner with me?"

"I told you, Mr. Salva, I have other plans." Just then Gary pulled up in his Corvette. He hurriedly stepped out, and walked expediently up to the porch.

"Everything okay Alex?" He asked, reaching for my hand.

"Yes. Mr. Salva was just leaving, weren't you?"

He smiled at Gary, and then back at me. "Yes, I am going, perhaps another time Alex," he said before turning around and walking back to his car. They watched him get in and drive away.

Well, seeing him in the convertible smashes my idea that's it's him driving the black 4x4.

"Come on in Gary. I'll be just a minute. I forgot my watch, and my purse," I said, starting up the stairs. It took a few minutes to settle my stomach, and find my purse and watch, realizing I had set them on the table in the hall outside my room.

When I came back down Gary was standing by the kitchen counter.

"You ready," he asked, taking my hand.

"I am now," I smiled, although it was shallow.

"Let's go. I've reservation at Cajoles."

"Gary, that's my favorite restaurant. Their pasta is excellent."

"Then I'm starting off on the right foot." We walked down the drive to Gary's car. Helping me in before walking around to slide into the driver's seat.

"How many contractors have you finished?" I asked.

"Oh no, you don't, no business tonight. We're on that ten percent you mentioned," Gary said, taking hold of my hand, and kissing it lightly.

"All right, no business tonight." Gary kissed the back of my hand again which sent shivers down my spine.

Don't get excited Alex. Just because he is the first man, you've dated since Joe. Enjoy the evening; get to know him before you do anything crazy. Just remember one-step at a time.

CHAPTER 3

It was a week after the contractor's banquet in Nebraska when Lester Kierbow had a second visit from Nick Salva.

"Mr. Kierbow, Nick Salva be here to see yah," his secretary said over the intercom.

"Send him in, and dat there letter be finished, ya can be going home."

"Yes'em. See ya tomorrow," was his secretary's reply.

"Nick, sit down," Lester said, leaning back in his chair. A low growl came from over in the corner.

"Roxy settle down girl, guess ya know vermin when ya sees it. What be on your mind, Nick?"

"I think you know what's on my mind Lester," he said lighting up a cigar.

"Did you decide to sell me the patent on the banding? You know since you patented that pipe banding no one can use it without your permission, or owning the patent." Nick leaned forward and blew a puff of smoke into Lester's face. "I'm bidding on that job, and I need it."

"I be bidding on that job, so you'll have to find another method to protect that pipe in shipping if you be the one awarded the contract."

"You best think twice before you decide not to sell me that patent." Nick stood up slowly, took another pull on his cigar. "You can't work that job if you don't have a crew. Besides, Lester, you're getting too old. You should have retired a few years ago."

Lester stood up. "Nick, I have two good crews, dat be with me a lot of years, and I might be old, but I have a few good years left. Don't be making threats to me!"

"Then I guess I'll leave. Be talking to you when you decide to sell." With that, Nick Salva walked out of Kierbow's office shutting the door behind him.

Lester sat back down in his chair, leaned forward on his desk putting his head in his hands. *I won't be giving into him or his threats.* Roxy padded over to Lester and put her head on his leg.

"We gotta few good years left in us don't we girl?" Lester patted the black Coonhound on the head. He'd gone up against Nick Salva in the past, but stakes had never been this high. Money to be made on this job only came around once in a lifetime. This would be his last job and he would never have to worry about Ateara. She be well taken care of. She can set up that little shop she always be talking about.

Lester stood up, walked over to the catfish hat hanger took his hat from its resting place and put it on.

"Come on Roxy, it be time we be going home." They shuffled out the front door, which he locked, then stood back as he did every night and looked at the sign, Lester Kierbow Construction since 1951, Crowley, Louisiana.

"Yes'em, that be me, Roxy," he said, looking down at the long-eared hound. "When I started out, I was a young'n, but I had a dream."

Roxy barked twice as if to say, "That be true" looking up at him with love in those large brown eyes."

"Back then it be tough for a black man to have his own business," he said, walking around the corner to where his truck was parked. "But we didn't give up then, and I be darn we be given up now. Right Roxy?" Opening the truck door, the hound jumped up on the seat and barked again. After starting the truck, Lester backed out onto the street, shifted gears, and drove the familiar ten miles to his home.

Next morning Lester and Roxy walked out the side door to drive to the office and found his front tire flat.

"Roxy, wouldn't you know it, we be in a hurry, and having a flat tire to fix before we can go anywhere."

Twenty minutes later, they were on their way. After stopping for coffee and a donut, they arrived at his office a little after nine. When they walked into the office, he found his secretary in tears blowing her nose into a tissue.

"What be going on here?" He asked. He set a coffee and donut down on his secretary's desk he'd brought her.

"Oh, Mister Kierbow, both crews came in early dis mornin, and they say they be quitting. They say Mr. Salva's men paid them a visit, says terrible things gonna be happening to their families if they don't quit. So, they came in for their pay and they be going to work for him. Your foreman Jasper, refused, and they beat'em up bad. They had to take'em to the hospital," she said sobbing.

"Stop crying. Yeah, go on home now. I be taking care of things here. Go on now," Lester said as he patted her back walking her to the door.

"Yes'em. Sure, ya going to be alright?" She asked, taking a hankie out of her purse to blow her nose again as she stepped through the opened doorway.

"Yes'em, I be just fine. I be seeing ya Monday morning." He closed the door.

Lester looked around the office at the worn brown leather couch, two chairs that had seen better days. His secretary's desk, neat and tidy with a small vase of fresh flowers, and behind it a picture of Martin Luther King. On the other wall an image of the Bayu, and two file cabinets that stood side by side next to the door going into Lester's office. The worn wood floor still mustards a shine on both sides of the worn trail from the front door, to the inner office brought back a flood of memories. Lester felt a nudge against his leg and looked down to see Roxy looking up at him with those big brown eyes.

"Come on Roxy let's go make some phone calls." Shuffling into his office, he sat down in his wooden swivel chair with the cushion that read (sit-in's fine if ya working the mind). He smiled, remembering when Ateara made the cushion for him when she was in Junior High. Seemed like such a long time ago. He picked up the phone and laid it back down in its cradle. Leaned back in his chair and surveyed his office. He smiled when he looked at the seven certificates across his wall from different jobs, different wording, but the same. Thanking him for a job well done. The gold framed article from the newspaper for a businessman of the year 1978. Below them on the long bookshelf, three trophies for catfish cooking, a picture of his wife and daughter a year before his wife passed on, and the recent picture of his daughter and Roxy.

Lester pulled his Rolodex toward him and started thumbing through it when he heard the front door open and close. Looking up he saw Nick Salva walking toward him, and heard Roxy's low growl.

"It be okay, Roxy."

"Heard you had some trouble with your crews, Lester," Nick stated, and sat down in the chair in front of Lester's desk.

"Nothing I can't handle," Lester said soberly.

"Really. I heard both your crews quit. Can't pipeline without your crews," Salva said, leaning back in the chair. "No sense hanging onto that patent now. I pay you a fair price for the rights."

Lester leaned forward. "You think I can't get a crew together that you can't intimidate? They're always good men looking to work da pipeline. Here, in Crowley, and about you might be King Pin, but I ain't afraid of you Nick Salva! I'm putting in my bid when I get the invitation in a couple of days, so you'll have to find another way to protect that there pipe for your submission."

Nick stood up knocking over the chair he was sitting on. Roxy growled louder. Lester reached over and touched her lightly on the back.

"Old man, you listen, you know there isn't a more efficient cost-effective way to protect that pipe. Maybe Miss Kendall won't send you that invitation to submit a bid if it does come..."

"Miss Kendall has nothing to do with us. She just be doing her job. You leave her be Nick."

"You best think twice before submitting that bid if the invitation does come." With that, Nick turned around, and left Lester's office Roxy barking louder at his heels as he went out the door.

"Come here, girl," he said, patting her when she came back. "Maybe we be getting too old for this business," he said, playing with one of her long ears. She barked. "Yes'em, I guess you be right. We're not going to let him bully us. Lester picked up the phone and dialed the number that lay in front of him.

"Galvestone Steel. How may I direct your call?" Answered the voice on the other end of the phone line.

"Mister Joe Larkin, please.

"May I ask who is calling?"

"Lester Kierbow of Kierbow Construction," he replied.

"One moment sir, I'll transfer you."

Lester sat back in his chair and doodled on the pad of paper in front of him.

"Hello Lester, how are you?"

"Hi, Joe. I be doing all right. Yourself?"

"Busy getting ready for that big pipeline job. Glad I still have a supply of your supports here; it will save that coated pipe. Have you been awarded the job yet?"

"No, not yet Joe. How are you and Alex be doing?" There was silence on the line. "Joe, you still there?"

"I'm here Lester. We have not been together for some time now."

"Didn't you call her after I talked to you," Lester asked, hitting the end of the pencil on the pad.

"I did, but you know Alex, Lester. She's as stubborn as a jackass. She didn't seem to be worried about Nick. Why has something happened?"

Lester revealed what had taken place earlier with his crew, and the conversation with Nick.

"Did you call the police?"

"Joe, you know Nick has most of them in his hip pocket. What good it be doing me. Besides, I can always get another crew. That, not what be worrying me. I didn't like the reference to Alex, and I know he be spending time in Nebraska. What be in Nebraska to keep Nick up there after the banquet. I see how he looked at her."

"Well, we know she's safe now with Nick in Crowley. I was going up in a week, but if you hear Nick leaving before then let me know, and I'll go earlier."

"Thanks, Joe." Lester hung up the phone. "I think we be going to see Jasper in the hospital. Then we take the rest of the day off, we be going fishing. What you think Roxy?"

The hound wagged her tail happily. They walked out of the office, locked it up and left for the hospital. After finding a parking spot, Lester turned off the truck and got out. Roxy sat in the driver's seat as if she owned the white pickup truck, and watched Lester enter through the main doors of the hospital.

"Can I help you, sir," asked the friendly voice behind the information desk.

"Yes, ma'am. Could you tell me what room be Jasper Baits?"

After receiving the room number, Lester looked for the closest elevator that would take him to the third floor. Matching the room number with the one on the piece of paper he stood in the doorway, tears filled his eyes when he saw Jasper lying in the bed. His arm was in a cast, his ribs taped, his head bandaged and both eyes were black. Several stitches crossed his right cheek. Lester walked over to the bed, and put his hand on Jasper's shoulder.

"We aren't as tough as we use to be," Jasper muttered, trying to force a smile.

"Jasper, I be sorry, didn't mean this to happen."

"Not your fault. You be a good man and a good friend," he sighed. "Don't ya be given into Salva, and don't blame the guys. They just be protecting their families."

"I don't be blaming them for leaving. Around here, Salva pretty much runs things. At least they still be working," Lester said, placing a chair beside the bed. "You still have a job with me. When you be released from the hospital, just you be lying low. I have another job in Alabama that will be starting in a month. That's if you still want to work for me?"

"Lester, it be taken a lot more of a beating to get me to quit."

"You be a good man Jasper. You just be getting better, and I be talking to ya."

Lester left the hospital. He and Roxy drove to their familiar fishing hole, a favorite place to go when he had a lot on his mind. It seemed he could think clearer sitting on the edge of the river, and of course, Roxy sitting right beside him.

It was close to sunset when Lester gathered the string of catfish, and he and Roxy drove home.

"Where ya been Pa. I be worried?" Ateara asked, walking up to the truck.

"We be fishing." Lester opened the door stepped out Roxy right behind him. "We be having catfish tonight."

"Your secretary called, told me what happened. What ya going do Pa without a crew?"

"Don't be worrying child. It takes more than Salva hiring my team to stop me. There be lots of men following that pipeline looking for work," he said, putting his arm around her shoulders. "How about ya cutting up some spuds to go with these ere fish. I be mighty hungry."

"Dad, maybe I could go talk to Nick."

"No! Yeah stay cling away from tat man. Nick only brings ya trouble. I know he be sweet on you a lot of years and ya been smart staying away from him. No sense getting tangled up with him now. We talk no more of it ta-night.

CHAPTER 4

I arrived earlier than usual at the office Monday morning, going first to the break room to start coffee, only to smell the aroma of fresh brewed. I was not surprised to see the box of donuts on the table with the name of the French pastry shop written across the top, which meant that Mr. Oshler was also in early.

"Coffee should be ready," he said, from the doorway.

"Good morning Sir, I believe it is." I took our cups down from the cupboard, and filled them. "Did you have a nice weekend?" I asked before taking a sip from my cup.

"Yes, and it will be the last for quite some time. Marsh and I will be flying out tonight for Alaska. We will be gone until Friday, and I am leaving you to take care of things here Alex." He paused and opened the pastry box. "I never worry about things when I leave you in charge."

"Are you going to check on schedules or have problems crept in?"

"None yet. Our crews do an excellent job of getting things off to a good start." He took out a éclair and put it on a small plate. "By the way, how is Gary working out?"

"He's catching onto things faster that I thought he would. Time will tell." Picking up my briefcase in one hand and coffee in the other, I walked to the door.

"Alex, before I forget, after the bids have been awarded I want you to go down to Galvestone and check on the pipe coating. I would think by then Gary will be able to handle things why you're gone."

"I was already anticipating that Sir," I said, and walked to my office. I put my briefcase on top of the dark wood desk, before I strolled over to stand in front of the large picture window with my coffee. Most buildings were still in shadow at 6:30 a.m. There were a few clouds but nothing threatening. However, a cloud hovered over my heart at the thoughts of seeing Joe again. Talking to him on the phone was one thing, but seeing him face to face would be another. I still love him. What they each wanted were two different lifestyles.

Why did he have to be so old fashion? Gary, did distract me last week. However, he isn't even close to replacing Joe. I don't think there is a man who could replace him. Both men were the total opposite in many ways. I don't have time to think of relationships right now. Turning around I looked at the stack of envelopes piled on my desk. Next to them a small pile of white invitation that I still insisted on signing myself. I've always said, the personal touch always makes a difference, and over the years, the business relationship with contractors I've worked with, that theme has held true.

It was eight in the morning when I buzzed Gary. "Would you bring me all the contractors' folders that we'll be sending the invitation out to?"

"You don't want me to send them out?" he asked.

"No Gary. That is one part I do myself."

"I'll be in, in a few minutes," was his reply.

"Gary, when you come in, bring Terry in with you."

"Okay, boss."

Ten minutes later Terry and Gary walked into my office. Gary's arms full of folders and Terry was carrying another cup of coffee, which she replaced the empty cup on my desk.

"Thank you, Terry. You can always read my mind," I said pointing to the chair to the right of my desk. Terry sat down knowing the routine.

"Here Gary, let me take a quick look." Gary handed the envelopes to me after he sat on the edge of my desk. I thumbed through them, giving a quick glance at the name on each corner. I was puzzled and looked through them again.

"I don't see Kierbow Construction in here. I know it wasn't in my stack."

"Kierbow, doesn't ring a bell with me, are you sure we have one from them?"

"You had the envelope, Gary," Terry stated. "Last week I gave it to you along with Salva and Jensen Brothers."

"Really. Well, maybe I didn't pick it up with the others. I'll go look." A few minutes later Gary returned carrying a large white envelope with Kierbow Construction typed in the corner.

"You have an excellent memory, Terry. It was on the table, I missed it when I picked up the rest."

"Gary, I want you to go over the number sequencing for the pipe stringers starting at Glasgow, Montana to the pipe storage yard in Watertown, South Dakota storage yard. I know you are familiar with those."

"What time you going to lunch?" he asked, moving toward the door.

"I'm not. I'll order something for Terry and me to be delivered. I want to finish these by tonight."

"Well, if you need any help give me a ring."

"You have your hands full with what you are doing, but thanks for asking." With that said, I took out my favorite pen used to write the invitation, and put pen to paper.

Terry started separating the folders into categories, pie yard clean-up, banding, unloading and stacking, stingers', etc. I started with Kierbow Construction, who would be bidding on the yard clean up and banding.

Dear Mr. Kierbow, it is our pleasure at Oshler & Marsh Construction to invite you to bid on the pipe yard clean up and pipe banding for the Northern Lights Pipeline. All submissions must reach Oshler and Marsh Construction no later than one week from Friday the 25th of this month.

Sincerely,
Alexandra Kendall,
Vice President, Pipe Line Division

Terry had typed the invitations for each category leaving space for me to sign my name. I had always hand written five letters, Lester Kierbow being one of them.

"Here are the other five for pipe banding and yard clean up." I took them from Terry and laid them on my lap. Looking at the name on the top, Salva Construction, I'll do it first and get it out of the way. Taking a pre-typed invitation, I signed my name, handing it back to Terry so quickly you'd thought it burnt my fingertips as Terry missed it, and it fell to the floor.

"This must be Mr. Red Roses?" She asked as she bent down to retrieve the fallen invitation.

"I'm sorry Terry. You're right, and not one of my favorite people. We'll finish my stack and order lunch. I want to check some of the ones Gary did. I'm sure they are all right, but..."

"Checking things twice and being conscientious is part of the reason you're where you are in this company Alex."

"I'm really surprised you didn't put in for my assistant. You know as much as Sharon working with us over the years."

"I did. I filled out the application. I asked about it a few days after it closed and personnel told me they hadn't received it."

"Terry, why didn't you say something to me?"

"You were so busy getting ready for the banquet, so I just let it go. It looks like Gary is working out and he does put a smile on your face."

I started to laugh. "You have got to be joking?"

"No, I'm not. You were blah after you and Joe broke up. Everyone noticed it."

"I didn't know it was so obvious." *Had it been that obvious? I'd had my heart torn into. Joe wanted a family and I wanted a career. The career straw had been pulled out. I rubbed my chest as though I could still feel the terrible pain when we split. I'd made the right decision, hadn't I?*

I finished signing my name to the last invitation in the stack. "I'm hungry. What should we order?"

They decided what to order and called it in. Half an hour later, it was delivered.

"I know you like Gary, but I also know you still have a lot of feelings for Joe, or you wouldn't keep his picture in your desk."

"You've been in my desk?"

"Yes. You forgot to give me your stamp to sign the contracts you ask me to take care of. Remember, last week when you spilled coffee down your blouse. Don't worry your secret is safe with me."

They finished eating lunch when Gary poked his head in the door.

"How are things going in here?"

"Great. We have the first batch of invitation to mail."

"I can take them down for you. I'm going to lunch."

"Thanks, but no thanks. I'll take them down. I have some other things to take with them."

"I can wait."

"Gary, go to lunch. I've got it handled," Terry said as she walked past him.

Gary nodded his head. "All right, see you later." Terry picked up twenty of the signed invitation and the other mail on her desk she was taking down to the mail-room when the phone rang.

Terry had looked at the code on the phone before she picked it up. "Yes Mr. Oshler, what can I do for you?"

"Terry, I have some letters that need to go out in the afternoon mail. Can you take them down?"

"I'll be right in, Sir." Terry set her bundle on her desktop, and scurried back to his office. Returning to her desk, she saw Gary walking toward the elevator.

"I thought you already left for lunch," she said.

"Forgot something in my office, I'm going now. See you later," Gary said, stepping into the elevator.

Terry picked up the bundle of mail from her desk and noticed an envelope on the floor. It was addressed to Kierbow Construction. *How did you get down there? I was sure I had a rubber band around all the envelopes.* She picked it up sliding it between the others before continuing to the mail-room.

It was two hours past dinner time when I finished signing the last invitation. The ones Gary had done, were all in good order which I was thankful for. Cleaning off my desk, and putting the rest of the letters in the wire basket for the outgoing mail, I called it a night.

"Miss Kendall, I was asked to give this to you on your way out."

"Thank you, Martin," I replied, accepting the white envelope from him.

Putting my briefcase in the back seat of the BMW, I stood for a moment enjoying the warmth of the sun on my face. It felt so good. Winter had been cold one this last year.

I looked at the envelope in my hand. *What could this be,* opening the envelope? 'Come to Cajoles and give me the pleasure of your company.' It wasn't signed. Gary said nothing about going to Cajoles.

After sliding into my car, I turned the ignition and listened to the car purr before looking for a break in traffic. *It wouldn't hurt to drive by Cajoles.*

Coming from the office, I was on the back side of the restaurant. Looking at the parking lot, I saw the black 4x4 truck with Louisiana plates. *I don't think so, Mr. Salva.* Making a U-turn, I drove home.

Doesn't he know when to give up? Concern was turning into anger overriding the fear that had taken hold of me the last time she'd seen Nick in my office. *I've never had anyone be so persistent after I've told them I'm not interested,* the thoughts raged in my mind.

Arriving home, I waited for the garage door to open, driving in before the door reached the top. Letting out a long sigh, I closed the garage door, and waited until it was completely closed before stepping out and going inside the house. Entering the kitchen, I stopped dead in my tracks. On the kitchen counter, a vase of red roses set in their glory, their fragrance spread throughout the room.

"He's been in my house!" I hissed. Walking up to the counter and picking up the card lying beside the vase.

"Alex, only you can put out this fire," Nick. I laid the card down. Picking up the heavy flashlight as a weapon, I looked around cautiously going from room to room downstairs. Relieved I found nothing, the tension eased from my shoulders until standing at the bottom of the stairs. My heart pounded, threatening to come out of my chest. Twisting to one side, my back against the wall, I crept up the stairs. Hands were clammy, especially the one holding the flashlight. Letting out a long sigh, not realizing I'd been holding my breath. I stopped at the first bedroom door and peered in.

Everything looked the same as when I had left this morning. Standing straighter inching across the floor, entering the bathroom, nothing.

I'm sure if I were to find Nick it would have been in my room. Gathering my courage, I quickly checked out the other three rooms on the second floor. I was alone. The grip relaxed on the flashlight as I made my way back to the kitchen. I had no qualms facing someone head-on. However, the unknown in my house had me rattled. Picking up the phone I called Gary.

"Hello."

"Hi, it's Alex."

"This is a pleasant surprise."

"Gary, he's been in my house!" I blurted out, going over to stand in front of the roses.

"Who, Nick?"

"Yes, Nick."

"How do you know?" Gary asked, hearing my voice strung tight as a violin string.

"There's a vase of red roses sitting on my counter and a card he signed," I breathed in deep sitting up on the barstool.

"Are you going to call the police?"

"Sure Gary. When they ask me if anything was stolen, I can tell them no, but someone left me a dozen red roses."

"I'll be over in a minute." I started to protest when the line went dead. Fifteen minutes later I heard the doorbell chime.

After seeing who was standing on the porch, I opened the door, "You didn't need to come over," I said, stepping back allowing him to enter.

"Yes, I did. Are you, all right?" He asked, putting his arms around me.

"I'm okay, just rattled." Not resisting being held in his arms, but to tell the truth, right now the delivery boy could have giving me a hug and I'd have felt better.

"Do you know how he entered?"

"I have no idea," I replied.

"Okay, let's check the windows and doors. Finding nothing downstairs, they went up to the second level.

"Really Gary, it would be hard for anyone to get in on this floor. Gary looked at the lock on the French doors leading out to the balcony.

"You're probably right." Walking over to where I stood, he pulled me in close and kissed me. His lips were soft and I gave in to the kiss wrapping my arms around his neck. I realized then, that Gary had lifted me up and placed me on the bed. His hands pushed up my blouse and under my bra cupping my breast. The cold reality hit me. I didn't want this. This wasn't Joe.

"Please Gary, stop," I whispered pushing his hand away.

"Alex, you know you want me." His hand moved down between my legs. I felt the swell of his manhood against my hip. Taking my hand, he placed it on his harden flesh. Undoing the button, his hand searched for my zipper to pull it down.

"No Gary!" Stop. I'm sorry I can't do this," I cried pushing him away harder this time.

"Alex, I want to make love to you," his voice husky with desire.

"I'm sorry, I shouldn't have let it go this far. I need more time." Gary rolled over and let me up.

I buttoned my pants before walking out of the room and downstairs. Opening the fridge, I took out a bottled water and sat down at the bar. My eyes glared at the roses. I wondered, *which one was more dangerous. The man sending me roses or the one I'd left in my room.* I shook my head to clear off the various emotion invading my mind. *The roses? How did he get in? I'm sure I locked the door and set the alarm when I left this morning.*

"Alex, are you okay? I didn't come over with the intention of making love to you. Honest."

"Let's just forget it. Right now, I'm more concerned how Salva entered my house. I took another swallow of water pushing the fear of the unknown back down, breaking it into pieces I could handle.

"Alex, I didn't see where any of the locks had been forced. Are you sure you locked up when you left this morning?"

"I'm sure I did. Living alone, that's just something I do automatic, the same with my car."

"Do you want me to stay the night? I can sleep on the couch."

"No. That won't be necessary. I'm going to change the security code. But thank you for the offer, and thanks for coming over."

I walked Gary to the door and let him kiss me before he stepped into the soft glow of the night.

The amber glow of streetlights revealed nothing out of the ordinary parked on the street. Alex closed the door and changed the code to the alarm. Making a sweep through the house once more I checked the doors and windows to the satisfaction that I was secure within the walls of my home. I put water on to boil for a cup of tea before taking a turkey sandwich out of the fridge.

Don't you dare be afraid of Salva. You've faced down more belligerent men than him. You've trained to defend yourself. The tea kettle whistled bringing me out of my thoughts. Filling my cup with hot water, I placed a tea bag inside and let it steep. Sitting up at the counter I jumped when the phone rang.

What's wrong with you? Calm down. Letting the phone ring two more times before reaching for it, taking a deep breath, I picked it up.

"Hello," I answered, putting more confidence in my voice.

"Hi Alex, this is Ateara. How ya doing?"

"Ateara. This is an unexpected pleasure. I'm fine and you?" *I always enjoyed spending time with my friend. At first, there had been cautionary fear knowing Ateara dabble in Voodoo. Later, awed of the things I had seen Ateara do. It had only been white magic, but I knew my friend could conjure black magic no doubt in my mind.*

"I be all right, it's Pa I be worried about."

"What's wrong?" Alex asked setting the teacup on the counter. Ateara related the story about what had happened with her father's crews and Nick Salva.

"Did he go to the police?"

"Around here that do no good. Nick has most of dem in his pocket, and da men are scared to go against Nick."

"Ateara, would Lester fill out a complaint if I sent him one?"

"Alex, you know he not be doing dat. He be doing things on his terms. He be refusing to give into Nick. Is there anything you could do?"

"My hands are tied unless he'd fill out a complaint. I did send out his invitation to send in his bid. He should have it in a couple of days."

"One more thing Alex, Dad said Nick brought up your name. Have ya seen him?"

I drank from my tea cup contemplating to say anything about the roses before forging ahead.

"Not in person, but when I arrived home tonight, I had a dozen red roses and a note from Nick sitting on my kitchen counter. I don't know how he entered."

"Alex, he been in your house! What you be doing about it?"

"Nothing now. I did change my security code and checked all the doors and windows. I don't think Nick will try anything. It sounds like he wants this job anyway he can get it. If he did anything to me, he wouldn't have a chance at it. Right now, all he is guilty of is sending me roses, and since I'm not the one who decides on the bids, I couldn't even accuse him of bribery."

"What about breaking and entering?"

"I couldn't find anywhere that would indicate he broke in. At this point, I'm worried about Lester after what you've **told me. Ateara, keep me posted if anything else happens.**"

"*I will, and yeah be careful Alex.*"

&&&&&

The next day at the office neither I nor Gary brought up last evening's events. He was busy working on his assignment from yesterday and from the looks of it would take him into next week. I was in meetings most of the day with Oshler and Marsh, and it wasn't until seven pm I walked back to my office. Terry and Gary had both left for the day. Things were starting to roll, and I had to keep my mind on this job.

Picking up my purse from under the desk, I turned off the lights and left. Walking out on the street and to my car, nothing was out of the ordinary. The night air was warm for a spring evening, and I would be home before dark. Letting the top down on the car, the fresh air would feel nice against my skin.

Stopping at my favorite deli for a sandwich, bought it to go. Laying it in the passenger seat, I smiled. *I really didn't want to cook tonight.* Ten minutes later pulling into my garage, the door closing before I stepped out of the car. Punching in the new code, entered the kitchen placing my purse and sandwich on the counter.

I'm taking a shower before I eat. Perhaps that will leech the stress from my shoulders. I started up the stairs to the bed room, when a hand covered my mouth, and an arm reached around my waist.

"*It's alri...*" I didn't wait to listen to the intruder. Instinct took over. My elbow struck my assailant in the ribs, freeing my hand, I brought it up to backhand him in the face. Both of us fell backward onto the floor, and I sprang to my feet in a defensive stance and heard...

"Dammit Alex, did you have to hit me in the face?" Joe asked, feeling his nose for breakage.

"Joe, I'm..., I paused, stunned, then collecting my senses, "Did you have to scare me to death? What are you doing here anyway? And how did you get in? Reaching out my hand to helped Joe off the floor, I said "Come in the kitchen and I'll get ice for your face."

Joe could feel his nose bleeding and pulled his handkerchief out of his back pocket.

"I come up to make sure you were okay. Lester called me, and told me Nick had left for Nebraska, and shortly after Ateara called telling me Nick had been inside your place." He took the ice pack Alex handed him, putting it on the left side of his face.

"I took a taxi from the airport. You didn't give me a chance to say it was me."

"You could have said hello when I walked in the back door." Again, I asked, "How did you get in?"

"I used a key, and I figured you would have changed your code to the alternate, and I was right, thank goodness. I don't know what I'd have told the police had it gone off." He sat down on the bar stool and put the ice pack on the counter. His nose had stopped bleeding, but the side of his face hurt like hell.

"We need to check your system because when I pushed the code in, it should have gone green; it switched to amber and stayed." Joe went into the laundry room and opened the control panel for the "security system.

"Alex, how long has this light stayed amber?" He asked, looking at the wires.

"I really don't know, I hadn't noticed."

"You have a wire off. Anyone could have come in, and the alarm wouldn't have gone off.""

"How did that happen?" I asked, standing next to Joe to look at the security panel.

"I don't know. These don't slide off easily."

"That explains how Salva got in without tripping the alarm." Standing next to Joe, sparks of electricity raced through my blood stream. *How can Joe still do that to me?* I watched him secure the wire; shut the panel, and turning Joe stepped into me.

"I'm sorry. I didn't realize you were so close." Standing with only inches between them I could smell the scent of his aftershave. Breathing him in my body trembled. Joe put his hands on my arms for a moment. My heart fluttered, standing mesmerized by his touch they gazed into each other's eyes. Joe dropped his hands to his sides walking around me.

I felt like I'd been hit with a cold rag when he dropped his hands walking back into the kitchen. Knowing it was my own fault. When I told him no the last time he asked me to marry him, I knew there would be no more lovemaking between us. He had bent his rules for me the past three years, now it was all or nothing.

"Would you like some coffee?" I asked, following him in.

"Coffee would be great. Will it take long?" he asked, sliding onto the barstool. "I need to call a taxi and get a hotel room."

"Joe, you don't need to go to a hotel, you can stay in the spare bedroom." Filling the coffee part with water and the filter with coffee I turned it on to brew. "Have you eaten?"

"No. I didn't have time before I left. I didn't even pack a bag."

"There is an excellent Chinese restaurant a few blocks away that delivers. I'll order something." Taking the number off the side of the fridge, I called the ordered in. My usual for two, and put the sandwich back in the refrigerator.

"I see you order from there often," he said, his focus on me full lips.

"Why would you think that?" I replied, pouring us both a cup of coffee.

"The only magnets you keep on the fridge are the ones you use all the time," he said, his lips moving into a slight crescent.

I started to laugh. "Yes, you're right, and yes I do. I don't like cooking for one." I moved the roses to the table and sat down at the counter. Taking a sip of coffee before speaking. "Joe, you still have some things here. I put them in the spare bedroom. You could use them since you didn't bring anything with you."

Joe studied her face, Alex was such a beautiful, sophisticated woman, and he missed her. Then reminded himself why he was here.

"Alex what is going on between you and Salva?"

"Roses and a black 4x4 truck." Relating everything that had happened to date looking at the roses sitting on the table. Picking up the note, I gave it to Joe. Then the doorbell rang.

"Great, food. I'm starving." Opening my purse...

"Here Alex, I'll pay for dinner." Taking the money, I went to the front door and opened it, only to find Gary standing there.

"You're going to pay me first that might not be enough for my services," he said, looking at the twenty in my hand and smiled.

"This isn't for you, it's for him." I stated, smiling at the boy walking up the driveway. "What are you doing here?"

"I just come by to see if everything was all right."

"Is that enough money, Alex," Joe asked, walking up behind me.

"I didn't know you had company Alex, or I wouldn't' have stopped," Gary said, his voice tight.

I paid the delivery boy and opened the door wider. "Come on in Gary. I guess this is as good of time as any for the two of you to meet."

Gary walked in, and both men sized the other one up.

"Joe, this is my assistant, Gary Spindle, Gary this is Joe Larkin. He owns Galvestone Steel. I'm sure there will be times you will be talking to Joe on different jobs. Galvestone is our largest supplier of pipe." They shook hands, and Joe walked back into the kitchen.

"What happened to your face, Joe? Hate to see what the other guy looks like." Gary chuckled.

"The lights were off, and I walked into a door," he said, giving me a sharp look.

"Have you eaten Gary?" I asked, motioning him to the kitchen.

"Yes, I have Alex. But I will have a cup of the coffee I smell."

"I didn't know you had a new assistant. What happened to Sharon?"

"To be honest Joe, I don't know. I came in one day gave me a week notice, no explanation why. She worked the week, and I haven't heard from her since."

"That's strange. You and Sharon were so close."

"That just goes to show you, you never know people like you think you do," Gary said, taking the cup of coffee.

Joe and I ate, and the three of us talked about the pipeline and the millions of dollars that would be spent on the project."

I don't know about you two, but I have work to do in the morning so I'm going to turn in," Joe said, getting up. He walked over to me and kissed me on the cheek and shook Gary's hand before leaving the room.

Gary watched Joe go upstairs. "I... I guess I'd best be leaving Alex." They went to the front door, and Gary opened it, but before walking out, he kissed Alex on the cheek. "Good night."

Alex shut the door and leaned against it. *Wouldn't you know it, dry as the Sahara for months, could have rained tonight and all I got were two sprinkles. I really need to re-evaluate my personal life. However, in a week-n-half I'll be on the road, I won't have time to think about either one of them in that light.*

After cleaning the kitchen, checking the doors making sure they were locked, and the alarm was on I turned off the lights. Starting up the stairs, stopping at the landing to look out the window out of habit, I saw the black 4x4 was parked across the street.

"Joe! Joe!"

Joe walked out of the spare bedroom wearing only his pajama bottoms. "What's the matter, Alex?"

"The black truck, it's parked across the street again."

Joe was down the stairs and out the front door running across the lawn when whoever was in the black truck turned on the lights and sped away.

"Windows were tinted. I couldn't see who it was." We walked back inside the house, closed the door and locked it.

"Alex, I'm going to be here for the next four days. I'll stay here, and I'll work something else out when I leave."

"You don't need to do that, but thank you."

"I can't shake the feeling that something else is going on here. I know Salva, and this isn't his style. If his sole purpose were to have you, he would have done it by now. There's more to it Alex. Anyway, whoever it was, he's gone for the night." We walked up the stairs stopping at my bedroom door. "When are you coming to Galveston for the inspection?"

"In a week and a half I'll be flying to Houston," I answered, my hand on his bare chest.

Joe felt a surge of electricity run through his body from her mere touch. He steeled himself remembering the vow he made and planned to keep.

"When are they awarding the bids?"

"One week from tomorrow. All bids have to be in my office by Tuesday and Thursday they'll go to the table."

"Have you known Gary for a long time?" Joe asked, considering his vow as he considered her sea green eyes.

"Gary, why?"

"Just curious. Never mind. I'll talk to you tomorrow. Good night Alex," he said, turning away.

"Joe, you don't need to call a taxi in the morning. The keys to the Ford are hanging where they always were."

"Thanks, Alex. Goodnight."

I watched him disappear into the spare bedroom, letting out a heavy sigh, I entered my own room.

When I woke the next morning, I'd overslept. Showering and dressing was done in quick order. Entering the kitchen to start coffee I saw that Joe had already left, leaving a note on the counter.

Alex, I'm not sure what time I'll be back, but it won't be late. Stay alert, Joe.

Taking down my shopping list to add things to it, knowing I was having company for the weekend. Putting it in my purse, I would be stopping at the store after work.

CHAPTER 5

Lester was sliding his bid into a large envelope when Roxy growled, and the front door of the office opened.

"Roxy, that be enough, lay down," he said, reaching down to pat her on the head. "Good morning, Nick. What can I be helping you with today?"

"You know what I want Lester," Nick Salva said, pulling the chair back, and sitting down. "That wouldn't be your bid you just put in that envelope?" Salva watched Lester touch his tongue to the glue edge and then seal it.

"It sure is, and there be nothing you can say to change my mind."

"You're a stubborn old fool," he expressed in a vicious undertone. Roxy growled as Nick stood up when the front door opened.

"Good morning, Mr. Kierbow, sorry I be late. Can I be getting ya anything?" his secretary asked.

"In fact, there be something ye can do. Would you take this here envelope around the corner to the post office?" He asked, smiling at Nick, giving it to her to deliver.

"Yes'em, I do it right now." Neither man said anything until they heard the door close. "I do know ye don't own the post office, Nick. I be hoping you found a suitable method for your pipe banding."

"You bit off more than you can chew old man. You had your chance," he glared at Lester, then turned around and left with Roxy barking at his heels all the way to the door. "Get away from me, you old hound." He kicked at her before he went out.

"Roxy come here," when he saw Nick kick at her. "You don't wanna be biting him. It be like biting an old polecat." He said, watching Nick hurry across the street. Lester went back to work, and Roxy settled in her usual corner in his office. It was three o'clock when Lester finished the work on his desk.

"Ye know Roxy. I think we go catch some catfish for supper. That sounds appetizing, what ye think?" Roxy jumped up, her tail wagging, and excitedly hurried to the front door.

When Ateara arrived home, she could smell catfish cooking and sweet potato pie.

"That be done soon, Pa?"

"Should be ready in about fifteen minutes. You be in a hurry?"

"There's a dance down at the church tonight. Why don't you come with me?"

"No. I be thinking I just sit and listen to the bullfrogs with Roxy for a while before turning in early."

They ate, Ateara did the dishes before she left for the dance. She left Lester and Roxy sitting out on the back porch listening to the night orchestra of nocturnal creatures.

"What you smelling out there girl, you mighty restless? Ateara probably has some creature out there in a cage gonna use for a spell for somebody. Ya come on over here, and lay down." Lester patted her, before sitting back in his chair listening to it creak as he rocked.

"Guess I be letting you out, then we be going to bed." Opening the screen door, Roxy ran out into the backyard. "Don't you be going far, I be right back." He stepped inside the house when he heard the phone ring. Strolling to the stand where the phone set, he picked it up. "Hello, hello, anybody there." *Must be a wrong number.* In his smooth stride humming a tune through the kitchen, he opened the screen door.

"Roxy," Lester called. Again, "Roxy." He stood silent until he heard a whimper. "Roxy, where ya be girl. Too late to be playing games. Stepping down the five steps to the lawn he found Roxy with a knife in her side, and blood running through her shiny coat.

"Roxy, Roxy." Tears started running down his cheeks, gently he picked her up. He wiped his eyes looking around the yard as far as he could see in the dark but saw nothing. The bullfrogs and crickets were silent so he knew someone was still in the shadows. He wanted to go after them. However, the blood running over his arms quickened his decision to go inside the house.

"Roxy, don't you be dying on me," he cried, carrying her into the kitchen. He laid her on the table, pulled the knife out, before placing a towel around her to stop the bleeding.

She looked up at him with pain filled eyes, blinked once and was still.

"No, no, no, Roxy," he cried picking her up in his arms. "You can't be dead, you can't be dead," he sobbed, struggling to reach his rocking chair, the tears blinding his vision. Holding her, blood dripping to the floor, he held her close to his face. "What I be doing without ya, Roxy girl. You my best friend. You can't be leaving me now. Oh, Roxy."

Lester was still sitting in the rocking chair holding Roxy, blood covered his lap and the floor beneath him when Ateara arrived home.

"I thought you be turning in early Pop." The eerie silence gave her goosebumps. "Pop," she said, seeing the pool of blood beneath the rocker. "Pop." Walking around to stand in front of him, her heart nearly stopped.

"He killed Roxy. He killed my Roxy," he started sobbing again.

"Pa, who killed her, what you be talking about. What happened?"

"Nick Salva or one of his thugs." Tears a steady stream down his face now.

"Pop, why do you think it was Nick?" She asked, trying to take Roxy from him.

"I should have sold him that patent and my Roxy would still be alive. I shouldn't have been so stubborn. No, you be getting blood on your dress." His sobs had quieted, and he pushed her hands away. "I be going to bury her out back." The rocker creaked as he stood up and he looked as ten years had been added to his frame as he slowly made his way outside carrying his beloved Roxy.

Ateara left in her car and drove to Nick Salva's home. There was light on in the house, and her stomach knotted as she drove through the open iron gate up the long drive stopping at the top of the circle. The large plantation style home had two large weeping willows, one on each side of the house. The pond in the middle of the circle drive was surrounded by red roses. A stone alligator lay between each of the fifteen rose bushes, and in the center of the pond was an alabaster statue of a maiden holding a basket. The sculpture was so real that the tears looked like they would spill into the water that surrounded her.

Looking at the statue, something inside Ateara told her to leave, but she couldn't without an answer. Walking up to the door she steeled herself as she raised her hand to the alligator door knocker. Hitting the plate beneath it three times she waited. Only moments had passed before the door opened.

"My, my, you surprise me, Ateara. Please come in." Nick opened the door wider, but just enough that she had to brush against him to enter. He was dressed only in a pair of silk shorts.

As angry as she was when she turned around to face him she felt butterflies in her stomach. His muscled body rippled with power. Dark hair curled around his ears, not combed back tight to his head as he wore it in public. His full lips were slightly parted and those sexy charcoal gray eyes met hers and held them daring her to look away. Her feelings coming to the surface that she had kept hidden all these years were about to betray her. Still, she was afraid, she couldn't let him know that. Watching him smile at her she felt like a hen in a hen house with only the Fox, and in fact, she was.

Thinking of her Pa and Roxy, her resolve returned, tucking her fear and feelings back down where they belonged.

"Why ye do it, Nick?"

"Why did I do what?" He asked innocently his smile slacking only slightly.

"Ye know what. I be talking about Pa's dog. Why ya have to kill her, Nick?"

Nick walked out of the foyer into the living room and over to the well-stocked bar. The candles flickered on the mantle.

"Can I fix you something?" He asked, pouring himself a drink.

"No Nick! I just be wanting an answer."

"Is that all you want?" His eyes taking possession of the only woman he had ever loved. Now, here she was in his home standing before him. His eyes undressed her, his desire growing.

"Nick please, why ye have to be so mean?"

He ignored the question leaning against the bar he took another swallow of the golden liquid. "Do you know how long I've waited to have you here with me? All this could be yours. It took killing that damn hound to get you here. If I'd known it would take something like that, I'd have done it years ago."

"I'm not here about us Nick," she said, adamantly crossing her arms across her chest. "It's about the patent isn't it, and that pipeline job." Ateara jumped when the tree branch hit the window and lighting flashed.

"Little jumpy aren't we."

Ignoring his question, she continued. "Nick this would have been Pa's last job. It's not that you need the money."

"There are too many things in motion that can't be stopped, Ateara," he uttered licking his bottom lip.

"Ye have everything," she stated.

"Not everything," he said, setting the glass down before strolling toward her. Thunder rattled the windows, flashes of lightning lit up the room, and it started to rain.

"I gotta be going," she said, wondering if she could make it to the door taking one step and then another.

"I was hoping to persuade you to change your mind and stay, but I can see it's too late for that." Nick grabbed her arm swinging her around.

She felt his arms around her holding their bodies so close she could feel his hard erection against her belly. His mouth claimed hers, tongue demanding entrance. The kiss was passionate, and her body wanted to respond, for a moment, she relaxed into him.

"I love you Ateara. I've always loved you," he breathed out slowly as he released her mouth. One hand cupped her breast, the other her bottom as his lips followed the curve of her neck.

"Stop! Nick, stop!" Pushing away she freed one hand and slapped him across the face. The softness left, his eyes harden.

"I was hoping this would be mutual, but you're not leaving until I have you." Nick picked her up carrying her into his bedroom, throwing her on his bed. She tried to get up. He pushed her back. She struck out at him, scratching his face drawing blood. Straddling her, he took her left arm stretching it above her head. She felt something cold close around her wrist. He smiled when he saw the fear in her eyes. Pulling her right arm, he did the same making sure it clicked.

"Nick, don't do this. Please," she begged, her heart rate accelerated, tears started to fill her eyes. "I'll scream."

"Who do you think will hear you in this storm, this far from the road?" Pushing her hair from her face, he kissed above each eye, down her cheek taking her mouth, his passion growing more aggressive. Getting off her, he caught her leg bringing it to the bottom of the bed, the steel cuff clicking loudly as it secured her ankle.

Kicking at him didn't last long when he took hold of her other leg pulling it to the other side securing it. Sitting next to her he slowly unbuttoned her dress. Taking the scissors from the nightstand, he cut the straps. Pulling the dress from her, she was naked except for her lacy panties. His hand ran over the lace capturing her sex in his hand as tears ran down the sides of her face. He cut the lace away placing them and the scissors back in the drawer. His eyes studied every inch of her as a man would at a banquet table, starving, yet not knowing where to begin.

Placing his hand on her full rounded breast, he teased her nipple. A smile crested his lips as they budded. Leaning over his tongue licked and sucked the pink harden buds.

"Your body wants me, wants this." He sucked hard, his hand tracing the lines of her body. Fingers reaching down the folds of her lips he found her wet. He moaned changing to the other breast relishing the smell of her body, jasmine. Bringing his fingers to his mouth, he sucked off the nectar.

"You say you don't want me, but your body betrays you," he said taking off his shorts, his manhood long and thick. He climbed on top of Ateara, relishing in the feel of her beneath him, struggling. He kissed her again more forcefully driving his tongue deep into her mouth exploring.

Ateara forced her head to the side, feeling his lips kissing down her neck down to her breast again. He suckled each one a moment more before kissing down her stomach and between her thighs. The more she struggled, the higher his passion rose. His tongue slipped inside her and then pulled out playing with her clitoris. His hands wrapped around her bottom pulling her closer. He fed on her juices and sucked her clitoris, feeling her body tremble, knowing she was close to a climax he sucked harder until he took her over the edge.

Her body rippled with pleasure betraying her again.

She watched him rise to his knees, his hand sliding up and down his hard cock.

"Please, please don't do this, Nick," she begged again. The anger rising inside her for her bodies betrayal and the deep satisfaction on Nick's face. He may have said he loved her, but she knew he would add her to his list of conquest. This wasn't the Nick she had fallen in love with in high school. She'd lost him a long time ago.

"The best is yet to come," he said drawing his tongue up her body to claim her mouth. She bit him drawing blood. His eyes went wild, and he gripped her flesh and surged inside surprised when he felt the resistant inside her tight sheath. His eyes widened pulling out slowly, more blood raced to his penis enhancing his size realizing she was a virgin. He surged his engorged cock fast and hard breaking through the hot resistant flesh that cocooned him.

Relax, Ateara, relax. Stop struggling. Don't give him the satisfaction. Your struggling only excites him more. She centered her mind, letting her body go limp, letting any fight dissolve putting her in a trance.

He looked at her and kissed her deeply while driving his cock deeper and harder into her. When he seen, nor felt any response, his passion again turned into anger. Placing his hands on her shoulders, his head on her breast sucking, he surged again and again until he cried out his release. He sank down onto the rag doll that lay beneath him. Turning her face, he kissed her gently running his fingers through her hair, but there was no expression in her eyes. He moved off her, standing beside the bed.

"I know you wanted me. You love me. Your body didn't lie. Using your witching ways to remove your passion is no consequence to me. You'll remember this night, and you'll remember your mine" Walking over to the dresser, he picked up an ivory handle knife.

"Anyone you're with in the future will know you belong to me, and I was your first," he said arrogantly. With the tip of the knife, Nick sliced an N into her left breast.

Ateara in her trace showed no emotion while her flesh was cut deep enough to leave a lasting scar, her breathing almost nonexistent. Nick placed a towel to her breast to absorb the blood before releasing her hands and feet. Bending over her he kissed her gently on the forehead. Putting his shorts back on, he walked out of the room closing the door behind him.

The wind howled as the rain drove against the roof, the sound a steady beat in her head. Her breathing returned to normal. She placed her hand on the towel over her breast as she moved to the edge of the bed, then to the bathroom. Looking at the sliced flesh, she knew it would leave a scar. The feelings she did have for Nick died like ashes doused with ice water. Now rage built, filling her body. She put her dress on buttoning the buttons leaving the rest of her things to lie. Glancing at the blood-stained knife she picked it up. She took three quick steps toward the door.

Nooo, nooo, Nick. Your death will be painful. I be making sure of that. She put the knife back down before going to Nick's closet. Taking one of his ties, she put it inside her dress. When she walked out of the bedroom, seeing no sign of Nick she rushed out the door into the storm.

CHAPTER 6

Alex left work early to shop and had dinner fixed before Joe arrived back. I had made his favorite, ribs, mashed potatoes with parsley and onions, French green beans. Garlic bread was ready to go into the oven and a Dutch apple pie. I started a fresh brew of coffee and put place settings at the bar. It was eight pm when Alex heard the truck pull into the garage. I sat at the bar waiting for Joe to come in. Her heart beats quickened.

"Something sure smells good. You mean you cooked? What's the occasion?"

"My way of saying thank you, for coming up even though you didn't need to."

"I almost stopped and picked up something to eat. I'm glad I changed my mind. How was your day?"

"Busy. You know how it is getting things ready for the field. Still have bids coming in," I stated, pausing to put the garlic bread in the oven. "How was yours?"

"Great. Even saw your boss on short notice."

"I didn't know you were going to the office. Who did you see, Marsh or Oshler?"

"Oshler. In fact, I went to lunch with Dave. We had a nice chat. Things seem to be going pretty much on schedule according to him, and not surprisingly he gives you most the credit."

"I'm surprised. I don't feel that efficient. I realize how much Sharon did for me. Lots of little things that I overlook, she always just picked up. It will take Gary a long time to get to that point if he ever does."

The buzzer on the oven dinged.

"This is done, sit down." I fixed our plates and opened a bottle of Soft Red, part of the Chateau Series. Joe poured the wine into the goblets. I sat down beside him.

"Have you heard anything from Sharon since she left?" Joe asked.

I haven't in fact, I drove over to her place, and the house was vacated. Her landlord didn't have a forwarding address. She had no family here, a sister in Ohio I think. It's so strange."

The phone rang while I was doing the dishes. "Hello."

"Alex, it's Gary. Missed seeing you today at the office, and wondered how everything was going?"

"Going great, how's the stringing project coming?"

"I should be done in a couple of days. Terri showed me the sites for the pipe storage yards."

"I'll talk to you in the morning Gary. Joe, please hand me my wine glass."

"Joe's still there?" Gary's voice tightened.

"Yes, he'll be here until Saturday."

"Oh."

I heard the undertone of a growl.

"I'll let you go then. See you in the morning."

"Goodnight," I said, hanging up the phone, and started back on the dishes. "Do you want coffee and pie now?" I asked watching him.

"I'm full," he rose his half glass of wine to me. "That was great. Here let me dry those for you," he said, coming over to stand beside me.

"I'm going to rinse them off and put them in the dishwasher. The pans I've already done.

"Alex would you like more wine?" he asked, filling his own glass.

"Please, just half a glass, thank you." Alex took the glass before walking out onto the terrace. "The night is beautiful, isn't it," I commented, sitting down on the swing.

"That it is," he replied, sitting down next to me.

I felt deliciously serene sitting next to Joe. Thinking back how it once was between them. How I wished, it still was. Resting my hand on his thigh, the feel of him sent waves of rapture through my body, until I felt his muscle tighten.

"I'd best turn in. I have a lot to do tomorrow." *I want to hold you in my arms, Alex, kiss you, make love to you. But I've made my decision. I want you for my wife, and I'll settle for nothing less.* Joe let out a long sigh feeling his pants tighten in the crotch when Alex had laid her hand on his leg.

"All right, I didn't realize it was so late. Good night Joe." I watched him go into the house while emptiness filled me. *I'd made the right choice. I'd worked hard to get to where I was in the company with my career. Then why am I crying? Stop it right now;* I scolded wiping the tears from puffy eyes. Walking back into the house I locked the doors behind me and went up to bed.

Friday morning, I was working out when the aroma of coffee made its way down to the workout room. *Joe must be up.* I cut the session short and hurried up the stairs. I slowed my pace entering the kitchen.

"Good morning. You're up earlier than I thought you would be."

"Well, I wanted to get an early start. I'm meeting a rancher this morning in Fremont. I'm looking at a couple of studs to use for breeding," he said, handing me a cup.

"So, you're not here just for business, as far as the pipeline goes?"

"No. I try to mix the two whenever I can," Joe said, sipping his coffee. He wasn't going to let Alex know he'd made a special trip up to make sure I was all right. Luckily, he had been able to do some of the business he'd planned to do later.

"Your face looks better. It was a good thing we iced it."

The four days Joe stayed at Alex's home, they had not seen the black 4x4, nor had I received more roses.

Sunday, Joe's last day Alex woke to not only coffee but bacon cooking.

I hurried with my shower, dressed in jeans and a tee shirt paying attention to my hair and makeup. Opening the French doors of the room I could see the sun was up, not a cloud in the sky. *What a beautiful spring day.* Sitting on a chair on the balcony tying my tennis shoes, and after closed the doors, locked them, before proceeding down the stairs.

"This is a pleasant surprise," I said, taking a stool at the counter.

"I thought turnabout was fair play," he said, taking the eggs out of the fridge. "How would you like your eggs?"

"Scrambled please," I said, pouring a cup of coffee. Hearing the timer go off I took the biscuits out of the oven. "I have plum jelly if you'd like some on your biscuits."

"I've not had Plum Jelly since..." Joe pretended to cough and went on, "Your eggs are done, and I'll let you get what bacon and hash browns you want."

As I watched Joe in the kitchen, a warm glow spread through me. Today I could spend the day with him without work being the topic, and it was a beautiful day for a ride. They sat down to eat when the doorbell rang.

"Who'd be calling on a Sunday morning?"

Opening the door, Gary was standing on the front porch. "Gary this is a surprise. What's up?" I asked, opening the door wider to let him in.

"Stopped by to see if you wanted to go to breakfast?" he asked, moving closer to me.

"Joe and I were just sitting down to breakfast. Would you care to join us? I can whip something up for you."

"I would enjoy coffee and toast, which would be enough right now."

"Sure, come on back." *There went the day alone with Joe.* The thought coursed its way through my mind leading Gary back to the kitchen.

"Hi, Joe. I thought you left yesterday?"
Alex heard the small dig in Gary's voice.

"I was going to but had some last-minute business," he said, smiling at me.

I knew by the smile the implication was Gary. "Would you like some coffee?"

"I'll get it, Joe," I said, taking a cup off the cup tree. "Gary, you want toast or biscuits" There are biscuits in the warmer, but if you want toast I can put bread in the toaster."

"Biscuits are great. I can get them, Alex, eat before it gets cold," Gary said, taking two biscuits from the warmer and applying butter to each one. "Get all your business taken care of Joe?"

"For this trip. Alex told me you're working on the stringing?"

"All right, enough talk about work," I projected. "It's Sunday. What do you do on your days off, Gary?"

"Anyone need more coffee before I sit down?" Gary asked, holding up the coffee pot. He refreshed their cups and sat down. "I ski, and when I get a chance, I hand glide."

"Joe skydives, that gives the two of you something in common. You both like that adrenaline rush."

"You mean Joe hasn't taken you skydiving?" Gary mused.

"Yes, I have in fact taken her, however, one time was enough she told me."

"Really Alex? You didn't love the adrenal rush?" Gary smiled. "I'll take you hand-gliding. You know you can stay up longer and have more control."

"Good luck with that. It took me almost a year to get Alex to agree to go up with me, but you probably don't know that she is afraid of heights," Joe stated, spreading plum jelly on another biscuit.

"I didn't think that Alex feared anything," Gary replied.

"I'll tell you both right now. I won't be doing anything recreational that takes my feet off the ground. There are too many things one can enjoy without taking flight with the birds. You both would know the old saying if God wanted us to fly he'd given us wings."

"He did give us wings Alex. They're just attached to planes," Joe replied, and chuckled.

"Very amusing, all right you got me. If you finish your breakfast, I'll get this cleaned up. However, I'm telling you both I'm not hand gliding or parachute jumping. Subject closed.

I sat between Joe and Gary most of the afternoon watching my favorite baseball team get beat. Feeling completely deflated after wanting to spend the day with Joe alone. My team had lost, and with the subtle undercurrent rivalry between Joe and Gary, I was almost relieved when Joe asked me to take him to the airport. Gary left. I'd have an hour to spend with Joe.

The drive to the airport had been a quiet one, almost unbearable. It wasn't how I wanted to spend the last hour with him.

"When are you coming down for the inspection?" he asked rolling the window down.

"In a week I told you, remember. I'm going to take a couple of days and drive down to Lester's. Ateara has been worried about him. I'm not sure that I'm the only one Salva has been irritating."

"Nick always had a way of doing that when he wanted something. I'm surprised he gave up on you so quickly. However, that may have been because I've been here. You watch yourself, Alex.

Alex drove to the private hanger where Joe kept his plane when he flew up. I pulled in front and stopped.

"Till next week," Joe said getting out of the car.

Alex watched him until he disappeared into the hanger before turning around. I took one more glance in the rear-view mirror letting out an exhausted sigh, fighting back the tears that threatened to roll down my cheeks. *That's enough,* I scolded. *You don't have time for this. Just let it go.*

CHAPTER 7

Thursday morning, I arrived an hour earlier at the office. They had received the bids back for the pipe banding and yard clean up. The board would meet this morning to decide on the winners. I'd order donuts and juice from the French Pastry Shop on 59th that Mr. Oshler was so fond of. The coffee would be ready when the group met.

Looking out the large window of the conference room, clouds were gathering, thunderstorms had been predicted for the morning hours. *A bad omen,* I thought. Then laugh out loud. *I'm thinking like Ateara, and it's silly to believe in superstitions. Things would go just fine. Lester would get the bid, and that would be the end of Nick Salva.* That was all he had bid on.

"Oh, there you are Alex," Terry stated, closing the door behind her. "This came for you last night, and they just brought it up. I think it's important."

I took the overnight envelope and opened it.

Dear Miss Alexandra, I've changed my mind about entering my bid and wish to withdraw it from consideration. Thank you. Lester Kierbow.

"Are you all right Alex?" Terry questioned, walking over to where I stood by the window once more.

"It's Lester. He's withdrawing his bid." *I guess those thunder clouds were bad omens.*

"I'm sorry; I didn't hear that last part."

"Nothing Terry, just talking to myself. Terry will you make my plane reservation for tomorrow morning instead of Monday. I'll also need a rental car for four days."

"You want to come back on Tuesday night or early Wednesday morning?" I asked.

"Make it the redeye on Tuesday night, if they have one. Oh, and Terry, don't say anything to Gary. Take Lester's bid and put it in my desk drawer, and bring the others in here."

"Yes, Alex. I think the coffee is ready. I also started a smaller pot so you'd have some this morning. Which I'm sure is ready." Terry left the room closing the door behind her.

I stood in front of the window and watched the splatters of rain hit the pane. Lightning flashed to the West. *I can't believe that Lester has withdrawn. I have a gut feeling Nick Salva had something to do with it. If only Lester had filed a complaint, I could have done something. I will find out soon enough why.*

The pastry table was arranged, when Gary poked his head in the door.

"Is there anything you need me to do? he asked, strolling over to me.

"Yes. You can bring the coffee in. The others will be arriving shortly. I want everything set up before they arrive."

Terry brought in the bids setting them on the table in front of Mr. Oshler's chair. Without saying anything else I left.

"I see only five bids for the banding and cleanup. I thought we had six," Gary asked, lifting the white, nameless sealed envelopes.

"Maybe you miss counted." Ice hung on my words.

"Are you, all right? That was a frosty reply." He set the envelopes down and walked around the table coming to stand behind me.

"I asked you to bring the coffee in," my tone unchanging.

The doors opened, and the first board members walked in. I turned abruptly knocking Gary off balance walking past him without saying a word.

Good morning," I spoke with a tight cheerful voice. "We have pastries, juice, and coffee for your pleasure. The others will be here shortly. If you have any question or need anything, I'll be in my office."

"Thank you, Miss Kendall," was the reply. I walked out into the hallway and continued to Terry's desk before Gary caught up with me.

"What was that all about," he asked assertively.

"What's what about," I replied not looking at him, but looking through the mail on Terry's desk. Seeing in my peripheral vision, Terry was wheeling the coffee cart toward the conference room.

"You all most knock me over in front of the board members, and then acted as if I wasn't even there. No, excuse me, Gary," he whined. "No, I'm sorry Gary, before you walked out. What's got your panties in a wad?" his hands fisted, his face reddened.

I turned slowly looking at Gary. Waited a moment before I spoke.

"Gary, please go to my office, and I'll be there in just a minute."

Gary glared at me before walking down the hall to my office. Taking a deep breath, set the mail back down on Terry's desk. Terry came out of the kitchen and handed me a cup of coffee.

"What was that all about? It sounded like Mr. Charm has another side." Terry sat down at her desk knowing I was contemplating what I was going to say to Gary. Never had anyone talk to me that way, at least in this setting.

"Alex, your plane leaves at seven in the morning. I called Joe and told him you would be at the plant around eleven."

"Thanks, Terry, and thanks for the coffee." I was surprised at Gary's remark. *This is the reason people shouldn't get involved at work.* I thought walking to my office. *No one talks to me that way in front of another employee. Who does he think he is?*

Opening the door to my office, I walked straight the oak desk and sat down. Gary was standing by the bay window.

"Alex," Gary started.

I held up my hand looking at him. "Gary, I'm going to let the remark slide. However, don't speak to me like that again. I want stringing reports on my desk by Wednesday morning, the names of the managers of the pipe storage yards also. Terry can supply names, besides contact information for you to sort. I'll be leaving early today, so unless there is anything else work related you have a question on, ask them now, or before I leave." I waited a moment before turning back to work.

"No, no questions Alex." Hearing the door close I sat back in the chair. *I have far more important matters to worry about right now,* dismissing Gary from my thoughts.

It was eleven thirty when Mr. Oshler called me for lunch to be brought in.

"Did you have something in mind?" I asked, tapping a pencil on a yellow pad.

"Yes, sandwiches from the deli, now that all twelve of us are here."

"Yes Sir," I said, putting the pencil down. "Terry come in please," speaking into the intercom. *Well, that took care of that decision quite nicely.* Sipping my last swallow of coffee, and pushing the intercom on, I relaxed back into the chair.

"Terry will you call the deli, and order a dozen sandwiches besides our usual order. I have some things to go over with you before I leave. Having lunch here will save us time."

It was three o'clock when Terry and I finished the project. I was clearing my desk when Mr. Oshler walked in.

"Well, how did it go?" I asked, shutting the drawer.

"We made our decision on the string and yard clean up. I didn't see a bid from Kierbow. He was so excited about this job when I talked to him at the banquet."

"I know Sir. I received a request from him this morning to withdraw his bid."

"That's a shame. I liked working with Lester. Always did an excellent job. The contract went to Nick Salva." He started toward the door and turned back. "Alex why don't you leave a day early, and check on Lester why you're down that way."

"I was thinking of doing that Sir."

"Have a safe trip and say hi to Joe for me. I really like that young man." He closed the door behind him. Under my breath, I said, "So do I."

CHAPTER 8

"Joe, I'm at the airport in Houston and should be at the plant in forty-five minutes," I said, my heart fluttering at the thought of seeing him again.

"Alex have you had lunch?" Joe asked.

"No, not yet."

"Why don't you meet me at Christi's in Seabrook? Do you remember where it's at?"

"Yes. It hasn't been that long since I was there." I smiled bringing the memories to surface of one particular night at Christi's Texas Sea Food. I'd opened a large oyster shell to find a diamond ring inside. That was the night Joe had proposed.

"I'll see you there in twenty minutes," was his reply.

After getting into the white convertible, taking a scarf from my purse, tied it around my hair, adjusted the mirrors and laid my purse on the floor. Turning the ignition, listening to the station playing, I drove out of the rental area enjoying the beat of the music, fingers tapping on the stirring wheel while easing into the flow of traffic.

While looking for the sign to Seabrook the car traveled in the full stream of traffic. A few minutes later seeing the turnoff my concentration went from the road to Joe. Anticipation at seeing him again surprised me with intensity, feeling like a teenager on my first date. Turning into the gates of Christi's, I spotted Joe's Jaguar, parking beside it. Releasing my bound hair, and running a brush through the silky stands before checking my makeup smiling in approval. Stepping out of the car my pants eased down over the alligator boots, tucking in the royal blue shirt I adjusted the ruffles down the front.

Walking up to the glass door of Christi's, I saw Joe talking to the owner in the lobby which separated the lounge from the restaurant. My stomach felt nervous, twisted and uneasy.

That's enough already. You don't have time for a romantic escape. This is work. Let's keep it in perspective.

Putting on the aura of a business woman I had modeled myself after, confidence grew, until Joe saw me coming and released that sexy smile. My resolve melted like marshmallows.

"Ren, you remember Alex?" Joe asked.

"Yes, Joe. How could I forget anyone so beautiful? I've never seen anyone enjoy oysters as much as you, my dear," Ren said, taking my hand bringing it to his lips.

"Thank you, Ren. You do have exceptional oysters here," I replied, giving him a bigger smile.

"It was nice seeing you again, Joe, Alex. The hostess will seat you. Enjoy your lunch."

The hostess placed them at a window table that overlooked the fountain and gardens. Sighing with relief for this location, and not at the table where Joe had purposed.

"How's the pipe production coming?" I asked, trying to contain the leg bouncing out of control under the table and thankful for long tablecloths. Placing one hand on my leg to stop it, while the other one picked up the water glass.

"We're on schedule. Has the committee awarded Lester the contract yet? I'd like to start the banding process?" Joe asked looking at the menu.

"Lester didn't get the contract. He withdrew his bid." The language of work brought Alex back in control.

"What! Are you jesting? He was so excited about this job."

"Nick Salva was awarded the contract, Joe. I don't know why Lester withdrew. I've called. However, neither Lester nor Ateara has answered the phone. In fact, after the inspection, I'm driving down to see him." Opening the menu, my mind not on the food, but the man sitting across from her. "What do you suggest?"

Before Joe gave me an answer, he said, "Maybe he has decided the years are catching up. Tracking up and down that line can take a lot out of a man."

I raised an eyebrow before the smile left my face. Thinking a moment before getting angry at Joe, he had a right to his own opinion. Pipe-lining wasn't a soft job and even thought Lester was close to seventy-five you'd never guess to look at him.

"You don't really believe that do you, Joe?"

"No, I don't Alex. When it comes right down to it, I think Nick has something to do with Lester pulling his bid. I have a gut feeling, something else is going on. Besides harassing you, Nick has threatened Lester. He wanted that patent on the banding method Lester has, and..."

"Are you ready to order?" The waitress asked.

"Did you decide Alex?"

"I'll have what you're having," I said, not wanting to take more time looking at the menu. Not listening to Joe give our order, but glanced around the restaurant waiting for him to finished what he was going to say, my mind raced. *If only Lester had filed a complaint. No, Lester wouldn't do that to his worst enemy, and Nick was his worst enemy.*

"In fact, Alex, it sounded like Nick was putting some heavy pressure on Lester to sell him that patent when he called me. Knowing Lester, something big had to have happened for him to withdraw his bid."

"I'm worried about him Joe," I said. My chin sat on my hands my elbows on the edge of the table. My emotions mixed, worry about Lester and the emerging feelings for Joe. I felt like a checkerboard one thought counteracting the next.

"After the inspection, if you don't mind I'll fly you down."

"You don't need to do that. However, it would save time. Thanks."

We talked about when the first load of pipe would arrive at the Watertown pipe storage yard. The forty-two-diameter pipe would travel by rail, unloaded by cranes at the site and stockpiled.

"The contractors will be selected this week while I'm gone. I feel comfortable with Terry tying up any loose ends. I also left Gary enough to do until I arrived back next Wednesday," I paused to enjoy a bite of Shrimp Scampi. *Seafood always tasted better down here.*

"I didn't leave Gary my entire itinerary. I left Terry instruction to give him enough information to keep him satisfied without divulging where I was going after my visit to your plant."

"I bet he's not going to like that, not knowing your every move," Joe said, a smile crossed his lips. His smile gave him a younger look, but nothing was boyish about my former lover.

Joe had his secretary call ahead to have a rental car waiting for us when we arrived in Crowley around seven pm. It was after five when we arrived at the private airfield where Joe kept his plane. He filed a flight plan with aviation personnel before Joe taxied onto the tarmac. I parked the Jaguar in the hanger and closed the large door.

I always enjoyed flying with Joe and today was no exception. I always sat in the aisle seat flying commercial, so this was always a treat.

"See that cargo ship, its bringing additional material to the plant," he said.

Our conversation was business. However the closer we were to Crowley the less conversation we had. Both of us I believe, wondering what we would find when we reached our destination.

After we had landed, Joe tried to call Lester, and there was still no answer. When Joe went to secure the rental, I attempted to call Ateara, and she didn't answer either. I tried to think of reasons neither answered their phones that weren't on the dark side. With the possibility, Nick was involved it didn't make it easy. Waiting outside the hanger seemed like forever waiting for Joe to pick me up. By the time he picked me up, I'd tried both Lester and Ateara twice more.

"No answer, Joe. I hope he decided to go on a fishing trip, and all this worry is for nothing." I couldn't shake the feeling that wasn't the case. We drove through Crowley and past Lester's office, knowing it was late for him to be there. There were no lights and like most small towns business closed early, other than three restaurants and two gas stations. Both of which would be closed for the night in a couple more hours.

We turned off the main road heading north to Lester's. When we pulled up the drive, we saw amber lights on in the house. Lester's white truck was parked in the front of one of the double garage doors. I took a deep breath as Joe parked behind the truck. Waiting for Joe to open my door I sent up a quick prayer.

He took my hand to help me out. Then led the way up the walkway to the five steps, stopping in front of the door. I turned to look at Joe finding courage in his blue eyes and the gentle squeeze of my hand. I was glad he'd come with me.

When I rang the doorbell, we waited for a minute, nothing and I rang it again.

"That's strange. Roxy comes barking at the sound of those door chimes," I murmured.

"Maybe they're out back. It is a lovely evening," Joe said putting his hand on my waist. "Come on, let's go check it out. They turned around and started down the stairs when a car pulled up in front of the other garage door. Ateara stepped out of her car and stood to look at us like she didn't know what to say. I picked up on her demeanor right away. I left Joe's side and walked to the car she stood by.

"Ateara I've been trying to call you and your father. What's going on?"

Ateara stood still a moment longer before she burst into tears. It was the first time she had cried since everything happened. Seeing Alex released the flood banks.

I walked around the car and put my arms around her. She sobbed another minute, and the tears stopped as though that had an on and off switch.

"Dad didn't answer the door?"

"No. We were going to go around back thinking Lester might be outside," I said, shutting Ateara's car door.

"Dad hasn't been out of the house since it happened," Ateara murmured.

"Since what happened Ateara?" Joe asked.

"Let's go inside. I don't know he be talking to you or not." Ateara led the way to the side door, and they went inside. The house was quite as a tomb, and it might have been except for the sound of their shoes on the tile floor. The air felt tight, hot like a hot air balloon was being pumped up to take off. Perspiration prickled on my face, and Joe took out his handkerchief to wipe his forehead.

"I'll turn de fan on and open de windows in here. That will help stir the air."

"Where's Roxy? She is usually the first one to greet me." I didn't wait for an answer. "Where's Lester?"

"I know where he be. You best sit down and let me be telling you what be happening down here."

We sat down around the dining room table, and Ateara brought Joe, and I a glass of ice water before she started.

"Nick went to Pa and be trying to get him to sell him that patent for that pipeline job of yours Alex. But Pa be stubborn and he not be selling. That night Nik sent one of his thugs to do a terrible thing," she paused a moment gaining her composure. "I'd left Pa and Roxy out on de porch because I be going to a dance. Pa let Roxy out to do her nightly biz and the phone rang. He came in to answer it, but nobody on the line. When he be going out to get her, he found her a ways from the back step, a knife embedded in her side. Wassa nothing he could do to save her. When I come home, he be sitting in the rocker holding her in his arms. Rocking and talking to Roxy. He finally dun buried her in de back yard. Pa be on the back porch sitting in his rocker."

Joe looked at Alex and then at Ateara. "I'm going to go talk to him."

I nodded, clasped my hands on the table watching Joe leave the room. "When did all this happen, Ateara?"

"Monday night," Ateara answered.

"Did you call the police?" I asked looking at her intently, knowing that Ateara was never short on words, but right now she seemed lost, and it was like pulling teeth to get an answer out of her.

"No Alex. We didn't have no proof who done it, and they do nothing anyway. Nick wanting that patent, he be good at making things happen where it wouldn't lead back to him."

We sat in silence for a while. I wiped my face again with a tissue. The fan and the opened windows did help with circulating the air. However, it didn't cut the sorrow I felt in the dining room.

"Why didn't you call me, or at least answer my phone calls? I was worried and...."

Joe walked back into the room with the devil's fury.

"Did you tell Alex the rest or do I have to Ateara?"

"Tell me what? What else happened?" I tried to stay calm. Ateara said nothing for a moment. She just stood looking at us.

"There ain't anything to tell, and there be nothing anybody can do about it anyhow," Ateara said flatly.

"All right then. Alex, Ateara went over to Nick's after they killed Roxy. Nick raped her and branded her with a knife."

"What!" I yelled. "What were you thinking? You must call the police. He can't get away with this." I stood up and made fast tracks to Ateara's side. "Where and how badly did he cut you?" I asked still in shock that someone could be so cruel.

Ateara pulled her blouse aside to let me see. I felt the rage inside my belly boil to the point I thought I might be sick.

"That son-of-bitch. You have to call the police," I shouted.

"I be calling no police. I be taking care of Nick myself and anyone else who be in my way." Ateara looked at both of us. All I could see were vengeance in her expression. Her lips curled, her eyes cold as ice, and for a moment, I didn't know her. The fun-loving person I'd know disappeared. Hate and rage consumed her. I didn't doubt for a minute that whatever Ateara had in store for Nick, he'd suffer more than I could imagine.

"You can't take the law into your own hands, Ateara," Joe responded.

"Nick should have thought of that before he killed Roxy and forced himself on me," she said angrily.

Joe moved toward her.

"Joe, don't?" Ateara said adamantly.

"Ateara, listen to Joe this isn't going to help you or Lester. We can go to the police outside of Crowley. Nick has to be brought in." I took a step closer to Ateara and Ateara backed to the end of the table.

"Stay there Alex. It be too late for that now. I've started the spell." She looked past both Joe and me as Lester walked into the room.

"I love ya Pa. I'll always love ya," were the last words Ateara spoke before she ran out the side door. Lester started to collapse, and both Joe and I rushed to his aid.

"I shouldn't be so stubborn," he said between sobs. They helped him to a chair and heard Ateara's car race down the drive.

"Lester, you couldn't foresee this, and you can't blame yourself," I said, patting his wrinkled hand.

"I've lost Roxy, and now I've lost my little girl. See what an old man's pride has done." Tears ran down his cheeks in an uncontrollable stream.

My tears mixed with his falling into his lap as I knelt in front of him holding both his hands.

Joe stood behind me. his mind racing, what to do, what to say, so many thoughts trying to process all at once. Stopping Ateara was lost now. His heart ached for both Lester and Alex. Alex, who was always in control, keeping her emotion bottled up. There was nothing he could do for either one at this point, other than standing there until the rivers ran dry.

CHAPTER 9

It was ten o'clock when Joe and Lester both looked at Alex as her stomach growled.

"I be sorry Miss Alex. I not be a very good host. I need to fix you both something to eat," Lester said getting up from the rocking chair.

"Why don't I drive into town and pick something up?" Joe offered.

"Heaven's no. I have plenty here to eat. Besides everything closed up for the night Joe."

"When was the last time you ate, Lester?" I asked walking into the warm colored kitchen.

"I don't reckon I remember. Time just seemed to run away, and I didn't rightly care to keep track." Lester strolled over to the refrigerator and opened the freezer part. "It won't take long to thaw out catfish Miss Alex. You can peel these here spuds. Also, Joe, there be some greens for salad in the bin in there." We all pitched in and it wasn't long before they were sitting down at the dining table to eat.

"Lester has Nick been by?" I asked. *Questions needed answering and time was of the essences. The pain had to be set aside. The pipeline was starting and not knowing what Ateara had planned, they had to act.*

Lester continued eating for a moment and then laid his fork down.

"Mr. Oshler awarded him the contract," I cited. "Did you sell him the patent?" Tension hung in the air like the humidity that clung to their skin even with the swap cooler humming in the background.

"Nick sent one of his thugs over with a contract and a check. Asked if I be ready to sign it now, it be laying on my desk." Lester picked up his fork taking another bite of catfish before he continued. "Yes'em I did. I don't think he be using it long." He continued to eat.

"Why's that Lester?" Joe asked, setting his own fork down.

"My Alisha, my wife, her spells, people de come from all around for her to do. She be good with Voodoo magic and other things that folk don't talk about. Things supernatural, she done taught Ateara all tats she knows. Ateara better than her ma. If she has her mind set on killing Nick, he won't be around long. It might be tomorrow or next month, but he's a dead man just de same."

"Lester, we can't let her do that. Nick needs to be brought to justice for what he's done, but through the courts!" I sat back in my chair horrified what Ateara might do. "Lester, you and Ateara need to file a complaint and get a warrant for his arrest."

"No. I be signing no complaint, Miss Alex. I got no proof who killed my Roxy. They just be laughing at this old man." Lester continued to eat his supper for a few more moments.   "As for Ateara she won't be signing no complaint either. I already be talking to her about tat and there ain't no way."

"Lester, do you have an idea where she's gone so we can talk to her?" Joe asked.

"I'd say her be gone into the swamp for a while until she be dun casting her spell. She be full of hate that Nick would dare to carve her up. It be bad enough what he dun to Roxy, but to cut my baby like a piece of wood and take her soul he..." Lester's eyes watered again, and tears spilled out.

"I'm so sorry Lester. You were worried about me, and the devil was at your door," I said, choking up again.

"Don't ya all be worrying about me, Miss Alex. You have enough to worry about with this job be ready to start.

"Lester, what are you going to do now?" Joe asked.

"Joe, I be having other jobs I've bid on and have people depending on me. Not all my workers got scared off by Nick's boys." Lester picked up his plate and set it in the sink. "I be glad ya all came down, and brought me back to my senses, or I might still be sitting out on that porch, and that not be helping anybody. It be late, and I be tired. I'll clean this up in de morning. Miss Alex, you can sleep in Ateara's room and Joe the spare bedroom is at the end of tat there hall."

"Maybe we should be going, Lester?" I asked questioningly.

"I won't be hearing that. You be staying here tonight, and we be talking in the morning when we have clearer heads." With that said Lester walked down the hall to his room and shut the door behind him.

"Alex, do you think Ateara will try and kill Nick?" Joe asked taking hold of my arms.

"I've seen Ateara place Voodoo magic on someone who did something just a fraction of what Nick has done. It was not a pretty sight. I just hope if she does it's here."

"Maybe Nick has already left Crowley, and if he's on the pipeline, that's a long way from here. Perhaps it will give Ateara time to cool down, and we can talk some sense into her later," Joe said, escorting me to Ateara's room.

"Yes, we can hope for that. Good night, Joe." I opened the door turned on the light and walked in taking in the room around me. The primary color was a soft rose, the accents done in pinks and purples. Pictures adorned her dresser of her family. A small photo of a dark-haired young man who looked in his late teens. I guess it was an image of Nick before he focused on greed and power. Beads of an array of colors hang over the mirror on one side. Numerous dolls of different sizes lounged on a hope chest under a window.

Not bothering to take off my clothes, I slipped off my shoes and laid down on the white ruffled bed covering adjusting the pillow. Sleep rushed in to retrieve me only to carry me away into nightmares of swamps, hanging vines and alligators.

The smell of coffee woke me. Looking at my watch, it was seven am. Getting up, I walked to Ateara's bathroom. Washed my face before reapplying makeup and brushed my hair into a ponytail. I looked around the room again seeing things I'd missed last night, being so tired.

There was nothing in the room that indicated Ateara was into witchcraft. A large jewelry box sat on another dresser, a photo album stood against the cedar chest. I was surprised at the picture of me and Ateara at the house on one of her visits. The picture that caught my eye, was one of Ateara and Nick in High School, and love showed in her eyes. *What webs we weave.* I closed the album when there was a knock at the door.

"Alex, are you dressed?" asked Joe standing on the other side.

"I'll be right out," I replied. I straighten the bed and put my things back in my purse before I left the room. "You two are early risers. Who made the coffee I've smelled?" I asked with a wild excitement to have a cup. "There is nothing like a great cup of coffee in the morning."

"That be me Miss Alex. How ya like French toast and sausage this morning?"

"That sounds scrumptious, if I can help," I replied.

"I not stop ya from helping, Miss Alex. Ya all can get the eggs out of the fridge. I already started the sausage."

"You need more coffee, Joe?" I asked, walking back with the eggs.

"Yes, I could use a warm-up."

I sat the eggs down and procured the coffee pot. After filling Joe's cup, I looked through the French doors to the sun porch. The rocker was in the same place as last time I was here, beyond that was the pool and a quarter acre of flower gardens. Just beyond the gardens was a fresh mound of dirt, which I suspected where Lester laid Roxy to rest.

"Lester, what are your plans now?" Joe asked before sipping his coffee.

"Like I was telling ya all last night, I have two jobs in Alabama and another one in two months upstate. I have plenty of work Joe."

Separating the silverware, I set the table glancing up at Lester. "I could use a good supervisor to overlook the unloading of that forty-two-inch pipe, Lester."

"That be mighty kind of you Joe, but that would have me crossing paths with Nick. I don't know if I could stop myself from not killing dat man. Besides, Miss Alex has enough to worry about with all she be doing along dat line. However, Joe, I appreciate the offer." Lester turned back to his cooking, and it wasn't long before they sat down to breakfast. The conversation was on everything but the pipeline, Nick, and Ateara. It was late morning when Joe and I were ready to leave.

"Lester, you'll call me if you hear from Ateara, won't you?" I asked, putting my arms around my friend and giving him a hug.

"Yes, Miss Alex I be calling. Joe ya be taking good care of her. I keep in touch."

We drove down the drive, heading back toward the small airport.

"Do you think he'll be alright, Joe?"

"If he doesn't see Nick Salva, Ateara is the one I worry about. You know her better than I do. Do you really think she will use that voodoo to snuff out Nick?"

"Yes, I do. I've never seen such a wild look in Ateara's eyes. It's not a matter of will she, but a matter of when." I sighed placing my hand on Joe's arm. "How are you going to handle it when Nick comes to the plant, and he will now he's been awarded that contract?"

"I think I'll be like Lester. Let my foreman handle it. If I saw him, I'd beat the crap out of him. I doubt I could talk business with him knowing what I know. I could ask you the same question. You'll be interacting with him through most this contract."

"I'm not sure how I will react. My primary concern is this job. That we meet the deadlines, and everyone works safely. This is the longest job we've had, and I'm not excited about living out of a suitcase. I have to put my personal feelings on the back burner."

"You're good at that," Joe remarked. I looked at Joe then looked away. I wasn't going there. With this job, I had Nick, Ateara, and Gary back at the office to worry about. My plate was full. Someday I will have a personal life, and hoped Joe would still be there. For now, again, I had no time.

The plane ride back to Houston was a quiet one as we mulled over our concerns with this job. I suspected Joe was more concerned about me, more than ever after seeing what Nick had done to Ateara. I'd been around pipeline workers a long time on my own. If Joe had thought Nick Salva was dangerous before, he knew nothing would stand in his way if he wanted something now. Perhaps Joe was hoping I was just a passing whim, and Nick would leave me alone.

After landing in Houston, we drove back to my rental car at Christi's. I called the airport to change my flight, however, I couldn't get a flight out that afternoon.

"That's great," Joe grinned

"That's great? I don't think so. I have a lot to do."

"I can take you out to the ranch, and you can see the changes I've made."

"I don't know, Joe," I said, thinking of the memories I'd tucked away of times on his ranch. Being with him the last two days had feeling stirring inside me I'd tried seven months to extinguish.

"Nothing to know, you're my captive until tomorrow morning." Joe put my bag in the Jaguar and helped me in. "I'll be right back." He went into the restaurant and was back in five minutes. "I wanted to make sure your rental would be alright to leave until tomorrow," he said, after getting in the car.

We talked about the stallion Joe had bought on his last visit. He had a black and white paint he wanted to breed and was excited for me to see it. We drove up the quarter-mile driveway to the ranch house. I loved the trees that stood along the drive like sentries. The white fence that pastured the many horses Joe raised were well cared for. Running to the car to meet us was Andre and Wesley, Joe's great Danes. He stopped in the front of the Spanish, ranch style ranch home which gave him sixty-five hundred square feet of luxury living space. I didn't wait for Joe to open the door, but got out to hug the matching duo.

"Hi, boys, how you been?" I gave them each a big hug, and they about knocked me over with their enthusiasm. Joe grabbed my bag out of the car and started making his way to the house. I was met in the entryway with a hug.

"Miss Alex, I'm so happy to see you again," cried Maria, Joe's housekeeper.

"Good to see you also, Maria. How have you been?"

"Me doing very well, thank you."

"Maria put Miss Alex's bag in the guest bedroom, please."

"Si, Mr. Joe." She picked up the bag and hurried down the hallway.

"Come see the new addition to the barn. I put in a small vet hospital so when Chad comes he has what he needs." They had taken an hour tour before they returned to the house.

"Miss Alex, I fix your favorites tonight," Maria giggled, quickly leaving for the kitchen.

"Would you like a Margarita?" Joe asked, before going back into the house.

"Yes, I would, thank you." I looked out over the pool to the hills beyond. *Joe and I had spent many mornings riding over hills to the river. This was such a different lifestyle than living in Nebraska. I have a big beautiful home and pool, however, I spent at least half the year away from it. My biological clock was ticking, a few more years. Then again, that's what I always said, a few more years.*

We had several drinks. Maria had outdone herself with the cheese enchiladas, tamales, and Spanish rice and I ate more than usual.

"Look at the time. I have an early flight. I'm going to turn in," I said, getting up from my chair. "Thank you for going with me today, Joe. You made it easier to face the situation in Cowley." I leaned over him and kissed him on the cheek.

"You're welcome Alex. Do you know what you are going to do now?"

"Wait and see what happens, I guess. There's not much more I can do. Good night." I walked down the hall and saw Maria and one of the hands at the kitchen table eating ice cream.

"Thank you, Maria, for the scrumptious meal. It was kind of you to fix my favorites."

"I hope to see you again soon Miss Alex. Mr. Joe isn't quite the same when you're not here,"

I smiled, but didn't say anything and went to my room.

At eleven p.m. I was still awake. I heard Joe go into his room and close the door. I could picture him shedding his clothes. First his boots, placing them in the closet side by side, next his shirt which would go in the hamper inside his large walk-in closet. My mind conjured up memories that warmed my body. How he would walk around the bedroom, his buttons on his jeans undone. I remembered the dark blonde trail that disappeared down the V of his stomach. Trying to close my mind to the memories faltered as the ache grew stronger between my legs and my nipples harden.

It was eleven fifteen, and the house was silent. Pushing the covers aside, I put on my robe and walked to the door and opened it. The lights were out. Stepping past the threshold, I closed the door behind me walking to Joe's room. Taking a deep breath, I opened the door and walked in. Hearing the water running in the bathroom I stood still my heart beating wildly while I waited. Letting my robe fall to the floor when Joe walked out of the bathroom I moved toward the bed.

Joe was about to send her away, but the sight of her standing there her full breast, the small waist, the line of her thigh sent his blood racing. His need for her becoming unbearable, *maybe this would be my last chance to change her mind.*

When Joe didn't protest, I made my way to him. My hand traced along the side of his face the other through the downy hair on his chest. His hands slid up my arms, and his lips kissed me lightly on my eyes, down the side of my face, the tip of my nose and feathered across my mouth. I felt his heart beat accelerate matching my own. His hands slid the tiny straps of my gown over my shoulders letting it go landing in a heap at my feet. Fingers followed the curve of my body, and I caught my breath as his hand moved slowly over my sex. I was wet, so wet.

The tender kiss deepened as his tongue slipped past my lips and tangled with my own. It felt like the first time, and I was hungry for him. Joe backed me up against the wall still kissing me. His hand followed the curve of my body down to my bottom pulling me closer before traveling back up to my breast. Kisses sprinkled down my neck until his mouth covered one hard pink nipple. A quick intake of breath as that one act had electricity shooting through my veins.

He raised up, his thumb brushed over my lower lip. "I've missed you so much."

Before a word could leave my mouth, he took it again and our tongues tangled in a sweet dance. My hands ran through his hair down his neck. Pushing my body tighter against him. Slipping a leg over his, feeling his hardness against my stomach, I gasped.

Pressing me harder into the wall, he slowed his seduction. His hands less demanding as if they were memorizing the feel of me all over again. Pushing away gently my thumbs slipped beneath his silk boxers taking them down as I went to my knees. Joe stepped out of them, and Alex tossed them to the side. Sliding hands slowly up his thighs, nails pressed just hard enough to make his cock jerked.

His raspy voice spoke my name, his hand's tight knots in the dark strands of my hair. My tongue flipped over his crown taking the first moisture, licking over and under until taking him into my hot moist mouth. The fire building inside as I relaxed my throat taking him in completely. His groans of pleasure driving me into a frenzy as I sucked harder and stroked faster.

"Alex, don't," he cried, taking hold of my arms, pulling me up his body. He swept me into his arms taking the few steps to the bed, he laid me down legs hanging over the edge. He took a step back his eyes devouring every inch of my body, taunt red nipples, the rosy flush of my skin.

His fingertips traced the line down my throat past the valley of my breast to my flat stomach. Kneeling down he spread my thighs giving him access to the treasure he sought.

Joe's arms wrapped around my legs, as he licked what he called sweet nectar.

I cried out his name as want and need so long held back, escaped. Raising my hips to his mouth, his teeth nipped my clit until desire ripped through me with the first orgasm that raced through my body. I loved seeing the desire in his eyes as he took the last lick before he pulled me further onto the bed beneath him. Opening my legs wider an invitation as I felt the head of his member inch inside of me.

His gazed locked with hers, flames burning in his belly, tightening his groin, hardening every muscle in his body. His mouth closed over her breast, and she cried out again. Once deep inside her, he stopped looked down at her waiting for a signal to continue. Feeling the rise of her hips was all he needed.

Wanting him more than ever before I felt him filling me up, his weight settled on me, his hands on my hips. Invading, claiming, taking me to heights I'd never known possible. His rhythm picked up, driving hard and fast needing to empty himself. Thrusting hard as to reach my very soul, pleasure turned to ecstasy, a dazzling fire I knew was consuming both of us.

Joe collapsed onto me, and I held him tightly. He gently kissed my lips whispering my name.

"Feeling your body under mine was pure joy. I need you, I love you, and holding you close is a waking dream. Oh Alex."

It was in the early morning hours when we finished our lovemaking. I snuggled up against Joe, closing my eyes and slept peacefully in his arms for the short period that was left.

CHAPTER 10

Monday morning, I arrived at work at six thirty, put the coffee on and went to my office. There was a stack of white envelopes on the desk which had been separated by a gold piece of paper. Looking over them Terry had separated the bids for different areas of the pipeline. Putting my purse in the drawer I sat down when my office door opened.

"I thought that might be you in here. You're back early, everything all right down there, I take it?" Terry asked, walking over to the chair next to my desk and sat down.

"Yes, Joe's plant is on schedule and should start shipping by the end of the week. And how have things been here?"

"Great, other than your assistant." Terry frowned.

"I didn't leave him enough to do?"

"Apparently not, because he had time to give me the third degree two or three times on Friday. Where'd you go? Who were you seeing? Where were you staying, when were you coming back?"

I gave a light chuckle.

"I finally told him if you had wanted him to know you would have told him. And I said, "Gary, I know Alex left you a lot to do, will you have it done before she gets back. I really don't know what he accomplished because Mr. Oshler gave me to take the rest of the day off. I was out of here, and I didn't bother telling Gary I was leaving," she took a breath. "How was Joe?" she asked, smiling at me.

"I think the coffee should be ready, and I would love a cup," I said, ignoring the question.

"Well," Terry persisted.

I knew I wouldn't put Terry off long before I would have to answer. However, I would prolong it as long as possible.

"Alex you're back," Mr. Oshler greeted me in the hall. "How was everything down south? Joe ready? And how was Lester?" The questions continued.

"Joe is excellent, and they will start shipping pipe on Friday. Lester is busy, he has two other jobs starting in Alabama that collided with this one. He said, to tell you hello and thank you for the invitation to bid. Next time around maybe." I didn't like lying, it left a nasty taste in my mouth, but I couldn't tell Mr. Oshler the truth either. They all walked into the kitchen area. The coffee was ready and on the table was a box of pastries from the French bakery.

"You do realize Mr. Oshler, buying eclairs, we are all going to have to go on a diet," I said, taking one out of the box. We all chuckled, especially Mr. Oshler who'd never had an extra pound on his body as long as I had known him.

"Oh before I forget I have a meeting in my office at ten this morning. I'd like you at that meeting, Alex. I'm really glad you were able to make it back early."

"Anyone I know?" I asked.

"Nick Salva," he returned.

My stomach knotted hearing the name.

"We'll be going over the contract, and I want you there. I'm sure you will see Nick out on the line, and I want the parameters set. It seems when they know there will be someone checking on them things flow easier. I've not worked with him before so let's say it's a safety precaution. Anyway, I'll see you then."

I leaned back against the cupboard and took a sip of coffee. I was trying to control the anger growing in my gut.

"Ok, what's going on Alex? You look hot enough to melt butter when the boss mentioned Salva's name."

"Something I don't want you involved in Terry. The less you know, the better off you'll be. Please let's just drop it." I threw the éclair in the trash, picked up the coffee cup and hurried back to my office.

I walked over and stood in front of the large window in my office and took in a deep breath. At least I was given a warning, and time to collect my thoughts before seeing Salva again face to face. How bad I wanted to hurt him, that I hadn't noticed my fists were so tight that my nails drew blood.

"Alex, what are you doing?" Terry said aghast. I hurried over to the desk laying the armful of folders down and grabbed a tissue before rushing over to me.

"Thanks, Terry. I didn't realize I did that."

"I won't ask, but something is going on with this guy to have you so upset. Do you want me to make an excuse for you for the meeting at ten?"

"No. I'll be seeing him on the line, so I'd rather get this over with while I'm here, and have to show some self-control. Thanks for the tissue, Terry."

I walked back over to my desk and sat down. The anger was turning into pure hate. I had never loathed anyone as I did Nick Salva.

"Alex when you're ready to go over these submissions, buzz me. Oh, I just saw Gary in the hall, and I'm sure he will be in here shortly. Do you want me to tell him you're on a conference call?"

"Oh, yes, please. One problem at a time. Thanks, Terry." Terry rushed out of my office and turned the lock shutting the door behind her.

I knew office romances can kick you in the butt and still I broke one of my iron-clad rules I'd held tight to all these years. Romance in the office was always messy. Going through the envelopes wasn't helping and placed them on the table. The board would meet Wednesday and Thursday to approve the final bids. Most names I recognized having worked with them before. For the most part, things would get off to a great start.

When I stood up feeling more in control, I left for the meeting.

It was nine forty-five when I knocked on Mr. Oshler 's door and walked in.

"Ah Miss Kendall, I do believe you have met Nick Salva?" he asked, standing up along with the corporate lawyers.

"Yes, I have." I stretched out my hand to shake Nick's.

"Miss Kendall it's such a pleasure to see you again so soon," he took my hand raising it to his lips. "It looks like you've drawn blood," he said, kissing my hand lightly.

I withdrew my hand, trying to control anger boiling inside. I looked at the side of his face.

"Looks like you have also had blood drawn." Our eyes locked. My glare as cold as his was hot.

"Yes, a frightened kitten," he answered, feeling the scratch marks on his cheek. "Some have sharper claws than others."

"Shall we sit down and go over the contract." I motioned to his chair. I sat down and let the corporate lawyers go over the contract. Feeling Nick's leg brush against my own, the urge to hit him was almost uncontrollable. I watched his face and knew now he was playing a game. As I pushed back the chair I was sitting on, and stood up, the phone rang which gave me an excuse to walk over to Mr. Oshler desk and answer. When I came back to the table, I pulled the chair to one side and sat down.

It was after twelve when we finished. I started walking down the hall when Nick caught up with me.

"Miss Kendall, can I take you to lunch?" Salva asked, smiling.

I turned around and smiled as the lawyers walked past. And in a quiet voice, I said, "I'll see you in hell first." Our eyes met and mine didn't look away first. He reached up taking hold of my arm rubbing his thumb against my skin.

"Not before I have you."

"Is that a threat?" I asked. "You just signed a contract, and you're threatening a corporate officer?" I reached up and removed his hand from my arm.

"It's not a threat Alex. It's a promise," he said, looking at me for a few seconds more before he walked away.

I went to the ladies room in the opposite direction. Pushing the door hard rushing in. Reaching the sink I walloped my fists against the porcelain sink.

"I hate that man," I cried aloud. The fear of Salva I had inside was running sidekick to my anger. *That man has no soul. Whatever Ateara has in store for him, won't be enough for all the pain he has caused.* Whoosh, I released a breath I'd been holding. Pacing back and forth for a few minutes trying to get my composure back. *Oh, I shouldn't say that. If I could only get Ateara to testify against him. Putting him away for a long time would be more painful I would think. At the moment, there is nothing I can do and next Monday I'll be on the road. Focus, focus on your job and we'll see how things unfold.* After walking back to my office I'd just sat down when Gary walked in.

"Well hi stranger, how was the trip?"

"It was good," I lied thinking of Lester and Ateara. "Things are ready to roll. The first rail cars will leave on Friday. I suspect they should roll into Watertown Monday or Tuesday."

"Great. Where would you like to go to dinner?" He asked.

"Not tonight Gary, I have work to catch up on, and I've asked Terry to order us something in," I lied again.

"You know, I would think Terry is your assistant," he said, sitting on the edge of my desk.

"Why would you think that?" I asked, leaning back in my chair.

"You stick me on projects that keep me in my office. I feel out of the circle. I should be doing more with you," Gary said, flicking the top of his pen.

"Gary, this was a bad time for me to lose Sharon and I don't have the time to get you up to speed. Terry's been with me almost long as Sharon. It's easier letting her do the things that she knows needs to be done until I can spend more time with you."

"I see, second string," he said, standing up and walking back to the door. "Well, I guess I'll see you in the morning."

"Gary, we have a conference at ten tomorrow. I'd like you to be there. It will give you a broader view of what's going on in the field. If I remember right, you've never worked out on the pipeline." I sat forward and reached for my phone and continued.

"Knowing what's going on out there will help you when I call in."

"You're going out in the field?" he asked surprised.

"Yes, I am Gary. That's part of my job."

"When are you leaving or is Terry the only one supposed to know?"

"Gary, I'm tired. I have a lot of work to do, and I don't have time for this conversation. You'll find out what you want to know tomorrow at the meeting."

Gary's dark expression passed in two seconds. But not fast enough that I didn't notice the change.

"Okay then, I'll see you in the morning." He opened the door and left.

I buzzed Terry and received a quick response. A minute later Terry strolled into my office.

"What's going on? Gary walked by and told me to have a nice dinner. Does he know something I don't?" she asked, sitting down in the chair in front of the big desk.

"I told him we were working late and going to order in. He wanted me to go to dinner." I leaned back in the chair far enough to open the middle drawer giving me a view of Joe's picture. "Can you stay late tonight?"

"Sure. Do you want me to order lunch in?"

"No, Terry. I think we'll go out, my treat." I closed the drawer and sighed. "I need some fresh air."

"I never turn down a free meal. I go clean my desk off, and we can go." Gracefully Terry slipped out of the chair and left me alone.

I picked up the phone "Mr. Oshler I'm going to lunch. Would you like me to bring you something back?"

"No thank you, Alex. Mr. Salva has invited me to lunch, and I'm taking Gary? Gary mentioned you'd rather him be the liaison with Mr. Salva. This will be an excellent opportunity for Gary." There was silence for a moment. "Oh, Alex, I won't be back after lunch. I have a meeting with Crossland, so I'll see you in the morning."

"Yes, Sir. Enjoy your lunch." I waited until the phone went silent, before putting the phone in its cradle harder than necessary. My angry racing alongside my fear I had for Salva.

Fifteen minutes later Terry re-entered my office.

"Are you ready?" she asked. "Are you, all right? Your face is flushed, how's your blood pressure?"

"Right now, it's boiling. I think we will take an extended lunch. Let's go to Sebastian's to eat." We walked to the elevator, rode down to the main entrance, and two blocks to the restaurant before I said a word.

"I'm sorry Terry," I confessed, pushing through the brass doors.

"Alex, I've seen many jobs come and go. However, I've never seen you stressed as you are now." Terry stopped turning to face me. "Is it this job or the people you'll be working with that's the cause of your distress?"

Before I could answer, the hostess greeted us with a smile.

"Good afternoon Miss Kendall, Miss Rogers, do you want to sit with your friends or at a different table?" she asked.

"My friends?" I asked puzzled.

"Don't look now Alex, but here comes Gary," Terry whispered.

I turned to the left, and saw Gary walking in our direction and in the background Mr. Oshler waved us over. *So much for a stress-free lunch. I'd best put on my Rhino armor. I'm entering hell.*

"I guess it will be with my friends. Thank you," I said politely. We followed Gary back to the table. Watching the swagger in Gary's walk, his suit looked tailor made, the way it fit his body. I hadn't paid attention to his suits before or the rich material they were made from.

When they reached the table, Nick pulled out a chair next to him. I motion for Terry to sit down and took the seat next to Gary.

"Alex, I should have asked you where you were going," Mr. Oshler said apologetically.

"It was a last minute decision. Since we're working late tonight, I decided we would take a longer lunch," I said, studying the other two men at their table.

"Would you like something from the bar?" The cocktail waitress asked her eyes on Nick as she licked her top lip. His gaze was on me devoid of any desire to reciprocate her flirty attention.

"Would you like something, Miss Kendall?" Nick asked, his eyes on my mouth. A pregnant moment went by. I was going to decline and changed my mind. A mixed drink would relax the tension I had building inside. I wasn't about to let Nick know how much he unnerved me.

"Rum and coke, thank you."

"And you Miss Rogers," he asked, briefly taking his eyes from me.

"Make mine a Margarita, please."

The waitress took the rest of the orders and left. I looked again at the other two men, Matt, who was over Human Resources, and Grant one of the corporate attorneys.

"Matt surprised to see you here," I said smiling. He was another admirer who's attention I had deflected.

"I just happened to be at the right place at the right time when Mr. Salva put out his invitation for lunch.

"How convenient," I said keeping my voice neutral. "Grant what time will you start tomorrow going over the last bids?" If I could control the conversation to business I might make it through lunch.

"Can we start around nine in the morning? Mr. Oshler mentioned you have six other divisions ready. An Early start would be convenient for us."

I nodded, smiling inward. Their early, was my mid-morning.

"Alex, haven't you heard all work makes for a dull girl?" Nick asked with a devilish smile.

"Alex has been a workaholic for as long as I've known her." Mr. Oshler smiled at her. "I'd put her up against any man that works for me. She has earned ever promotion she has received through hard work."

"Alright enough about me. Gary, how is your stringing project coming? Are you down through the Dakotas?"

"I'm getting close. I'll have it finished by Friday." Gary said, resting his hand on mine that was in my lap. The cocktail waitress sat their drinks down, and it gave me an excuse to move my hand from under Gary's to pick up my drink.

"Mr.Salva, you're fortunate that the former contractor left the excess banding at the steel plant, and the rail cars can leave on schedule. It would have been unfortunate to have a penalty coming right out of the gate," I said, and then took a sip of my drink.

"Alex, Nick assured us the pipe would leave on time, and sounds like you have confirmed that," Mr. Oshler stated.

"What's good here Miss Kendall. I believe this is one of your favorite places to eat?" Nick asked looking at his menu.

How does he know this is one of my favorite places? I only bring Terry here for lunch. Keeping my composure even though it felt like Nick was probing trying to get a rise out of me.

"Mr. Salva..." I was cut off.

"Miss Kendall since we will be working together, please call me Nick. May I call you Alex?"

I felt everyone at the table look at me. "Of course Nick. I'm usually on a first name basis with the contractors I work with. And to answer your first question anything on the menu is excellent. I've never been disappointed."

"Nor I doubt that I will be," Nick said. The look he gave me I knew he was not talking about the food on the menu, and let it slide.

The conversation went smooth during their meal and the second rum and coke.

"Gentlemen, we need to leave now. We have a long afternoon ahead of us. Thank you for lunch." I stood as did Terry.

"Alex, I'll go with you. I have plenty to do also," Gary said and quickly stood up.

"I look forward to our next meeting, Alex," Nick said, winking at me. I nodded and started to maneuver around the tables feeling Gary's hand on the small of my back as we walked out of the restaurant. Terry was talking enough for the three of them and I listened to only part of what she was saying, so absorbed in my own thoughts. Gary seemed to agree with everything Terry said, finely noticing that I was really out of the loop of conversation.

Arriving back at the office, Gary went straight to his office, which I was most grateful. Terry and I stopped by the kitchen and put on a pot of coffee.

"Alex, I think it was my fault that we meant them at Sebastian," Terry said, putting the coffee filters away.

"Why do you say it's your fault, Terry?"

"This morning Gary stopped by to chit chat, and he asked me where you went if you were stressed during the day. I told him Sebastian's. I'm sorry Alex. I didn't think anything of it."

"Don't worry about it Terry. Let's get started on this so we can walk out of here before midnight." My mind was racing , and taking a few deep breaths seemed to chase all the thoughts to the back of my mind and the door closed. There would be plenty of time on Friday on the drive to the Dakotas to rummage through thoughts.

CHAPTER 11

Early Thursday morning I was in the kitchen fixing breakfast when the phone rang.

"Hello."

"Good morning. I see you're still an early riser."

"Some things never change. How are you, Joe?" I asked, smiling while flipping my eggs over.

"Busy as hell. Tuesday morning some of Nick's men brought enough of those rubber bandings to last the next month," he exclaimed.

"Where did he get that many so soon?"

"I think, Nick had them made long before Lester agreed to sign that contract. So he was getting desperate when Lester wouldn't sell. Have you heard from Ateara?"

"No Joe, not a word. I haven't called Lester either. I've been so busy this week. I'll make it a point to call him tomorrow before I leave," I assured him.

"Alex you're leaving tomorrow? Where's your first stop going to be?"

"Watertown. I'll call when I stop for the night. Joe, Nick was in the office Monday. He came in to sign his contract. Ateara left him with three long scratches down his left cheek. It took everything I had not to yell at him."

"Did he say anything to you?" Joe asked, trying to control the anger in his voice.

"Nothing worth mentioning," I said, looking at the snagged fingernail.

"How's your new assistant working out?" The tone in his voice going from anger to something I couldn't put my finger on.

"Gary, fine," I smirked. "He thinks we should have a closer relationship."

"Yeah, I bet he does. He's not going on the road with you is he?" Joe hissed, then worked at steadying his voice. "I know you use to take Sharon with you."

"No, he doesn't know enough yet. I'll have to play that one by ear." I smiled hearing the jealousy in Joe's tone.

"The first rail cars leave in the morning. You should see them in Watertown on Friday. I've got to run. I'll talk to you Friday night then?" Joe asked.

"Okay, Joe."

"You be careful."

"I will, good-by." I hung up the phone, and grinned feeling a warm glow spread through my body thinking of the night before I left Texas.

I decided to go to work for half a day, and finish compiling the paperwork needed, and the directory of the managers who'd be overseeing the line and the pipe yards. That would give me plenty of time to pack the fifth wheeler, gas the truck and be ready to leave early Friday morning.

It was eight a.m. when I arrived at the office. Terry was watching the coffee pot fill up, and Gary was sitting at a table eating a donut when I walked in.

"Well, good morning. Nothing exciting happening here I see," I said, setting my briefcase on a chair.

"Indulging in a sugar high to start the day and waiting for a cup of coffee to wash it down. You know these really can get addicting." Gary laughed. "You look perky today after lunch with Salva. By the way, you handled the whole thing admirably. I was waiting for you to take off his head."

I made no remark to Gary's comment. "I came in today to finish getting things lined up for you. Things you'll need to keep on top of while I'm gone. Go over a few things with Terry, pick up my papers and I'll be leaving. That should take me until noon." I took a cup down from the cupboard and set it on the counter.

"If that coffee is ready Terry that you've been watching over, I'll have a cup."

Terry filled my coffee cup and two more before she and Gary followed me to my office. Gary opening the door before I had to stop.

"Thanks," I said stiffly. Looking at my desk, coming to a dead stop three steps inside.

"They came last night after you left Alex. Martin brought them up and set them on the reception desk. I didn't open the card." Terry said, moving around me taking the coffee from out of my hand and setting it on a coaster.

I set my briefcase on the floor letting it lean against the desk. If the room temperature had been checked when they entered, now it would be twenty degrees hotter as I walked forward to stand in front of the beautiful rose arrangement. Taking the card from its place I opened it up and read. "Have a safe trip. Love Joe. The room temperature went back to normal, and I sighed with relief. Slipping the card back inside the envelope before placing it in my purse.

"Wait a minute," Gary protested. "You're not going to tell us…" he stopped in mid-sentence. "If there not from Salva, Joe must have sent them. Am I right?"

Terry sat back and watched the sparks fly from Gary and realized he had a full-scale crush on Alex. Another in a long line of hopefuls.

"Yes Gary, they are from Joe," I agreed picking up a pen.

"Does that mean you're back with Joe?" He walked around my desk putting his hand on the back of my chair.

"It means Gary, that Joe sent me roses wishing me a safe trip. Now can we get down to work?"

"Sure," he said, tongue in cheek.

I moved them to the round table where everything was laid out I wanted to go over. It was eleven forty-five when I looked at my watch, the same time the phone rang. Terry walked over to the desk and answered.

"Alex Kendall's office. There was a pause. "Yes Sir, she is right here. One moment, please. Alex, it's Mr. Oshler."

I quickened my step over to my desk and took the phone from Terry. "Hello, Sir," I answered. "Yes, I'll be right there." Turning to Terry and Gary I told them, If you have any questions for me, write them down and I'll be back in a few minutes.

I knocked on the door before walking into Mr. Oshler office.

"Are you ready to leave," he asked, still sitting at his desk.

"Just about, I want to leave early in the morning."

"Alex, sit down. I'm worried about you. There seems to be a lot of tension between you and Nick Salva."

"Really Sir, what makes you think that?" I asked sitting in the chair in front of his desk trying to put on the calmer exterior. I had perfected this obeisance when inside I was in turmoil wanting to keep control of outside factors.

"Alex, you've worked for more than ten years and in that amount of time, I think I've grown to know you pretty well. I know when you're on an even keel and when you're not. I know Nick Salva seems to be an irritation. After you left Sebastian's yesterday, he casually asked questions about you. Questions I deemed irrelevant to a working relationship, which in turn I didn't answer. I..."Before he could finish the sentence, I interjected.

"Sir, traveling the pipeline I have met a lot of characters and I've taking care of myself just fine. Most of the bosses I know if I needed any help I can always request it. I'm hoping my contact with him will be brief, and there will not be an issue."

"I'm still thinking of sending Gary with you," he said, leaning forward on his desk. His intense blue eyes holding mines.

"Sir," I said, not breaking eye contact. "Gary is not ready for the field. He'd be more hindrance than help at this point. Maybe in six months. If I was to take anyone it would be Terry. I see no evidence at this point the need to take someone with me. I want to get a feel for what's happening or not happening first. This is a bigger job more territory, and I promise if I need help you will be the first one I call."

"Okay, Alex you win. Did you get your CB fixed?" He asked, sitting back in his chair.

His dark brown hair was laced with silver on the sides. I hadn't noticed that or the smile lines around his eyes that had appeared at sometime, going unnoticed over the years. His sky blue eyes had never lost their twinkle. Perhaps that is why I had never noticed the other until now.

"Yes, I did. Turned out to be a couple of loose wires. It's ready to go. I'll be calling in every other day giving you progress reports. I'll make them as close to three p.m. as I can. Now, is there anything else."

"No. I'll look forward to your call on Monday. Be safe and be careful." I stood up and walked to the door, turning to look at him and smiled. He was still watching her. On the way back to my own office, I tried to consider what kind of questions Nick would have asked. What was he looking for? This was one job I wished I had a dog. I wonder if they have rent a dog for a day, a week a month, laughing to myself. Well, it was a thought.

I entered my office and by the tone of conversation Gary's mood had improved.

"Okay, do you have any question?" I asked clearing the top of the desk, and putting papers I needed in my briefcase.

"No I'm good," Gary responded.

"I'm good also," Terry replied.

"I'll be calling in every day around three, starting Monday Terry. My first stop will be Watertown. You can leave a message there if something comes up before I get there. The truckers are usually great at getting to me on the CB. You have my handle. Okay, I'll talk to both of you on Monday." I took one red rose out of the vase and then sat the vase on Terry's desk on my way out. "Enjoy these."

It took the rest of the afternoon to stock the fifth wheeler, gas my red Ford 350 and reach the Jackson's across the road who would kept a watch on the house while I'd be gone. That evening I ordered dinner from Chung's. Too tired to fix anything, wanting to just relax. Seven thirty the doorbell rang which was a good thing because I was starving. I hadn't eaten anything since that morning.

"Good evening Miss Kendall."

"Hello, Sue Lin." I took the sack and gave Sue Lin what I owed plus a generous tip.

"Thank you," the young girl said, nodding her head.

I remembered the mail before going back inside. I pulled it out of the box and looked around, nothing out of place on the road. I locked the door and reset the alarm.

I put the letters on the bar and decided to eat before looking at them. After turning on the stereo to my favorite station, I poured a glass of wine. I ate and filled the glass again, after which I sat down in the rocker working on clearing my mind when I remembered the mail. There were six or seven envelopes, mostly junk. One had no return address, but the handwriting looked familiar. Tossing the others, I sat back down and opened it up.

"Dear Alex, I'm sorry I left the way I did, but was too scared to say anything. I won't tell you where I'm at in case this doesn't reach you. Just watch your back."
Sharon.

I read it several times. What's going on? Looking at the postmark, Santa Clara, California. Reaching for the phone I called Joe. There was no answer. However, I did leave a message in hope he would listen to it and call me back before I left in the morning.

Maybe I should call Terry, no that wouldn't be wise. Until I know what and where the danger is I don't want Terry in harms way. If she didn't know anything, she wouldn't have to lie. I wonder, thinking back when I asked Terry, why she hadn't put in an application for my assistant; she said she did. She said she did...and was told they hadn't received it. I know Terry would have hand delivered the papers to personnel. So who received it or tampered with it?

I stood up and put the letter in my purse. My muscles tightened. Raising my arms above my head trying to stretch out the tension, I wished I'd not drained the hot tub. Rolling my head in one direction, and back the other way hoping the pressure would subside, which it didn't. Turning the stereo and the lights off, I started up the stairs stopping at the landing to look out the window. The street was still clear. I think it's time for a hot bath, it would have to do, and besides it will be awhile before I am able to do that again.

CHAPTER 12

I was up at three a.m. and on the road at four. I'd checked for messages, and there had not been one from Joe. I suspected he'd been at the plant late. The first shipment of the forty-two-inch pipe would leave today. As I reached the freeway, turned on the CB to listen to the truckers chatter. It would be about a five-hour drive with stops, and that would help the time go faster or so it seemed.

Thinking about Sharon's letter, and what would have frightened her so much that she wouldn't say anything even as close as we were. *Why do I need to watch my back?* If this job wasn't stressing enough, I now had Nick, Ateara, and some phantom to look out for. Reaching under the seat I felt the holster that cradled my gun. I was an expert marksman, but was thankful I'd never had a reason to bring it out other than target practice. Still it gave me comfort knowing it was there if I needed it.

I pulled off the freeway into the truck stop at Sioux Falls and decided to fill gas first before going inside to eat.

After I had ordered breakfast I told the waitress, I was going to use the phone. I called Joe's office, and his secretary told me he hadn't arrived yet. I didn't leave a message. However, I would try again when arriving in Watertown. I sat down just as the waitress brought my order when someone came up to my table and started to speak.

"Howdy stranger, I thought you would shot gun this job."

"Aren't you a sight for sore eyes Andy. How you been? Come join me." I offered.

"You headed up to Watertown?" He asked, sitting down across from me.

"That's my first stop, Andy. Then Aberdeen, Wishek, Dickenson and Williston for starters," I said before taking a bite of my toast.

"I heard old Lester was outbid on this job."

"Would you like to order now Sir?" Andy gave her his order and continued. "Can't imagine who'd outbid Lester. He was a good old boy."

"Whom did you hear that from?" I asked.

"My foremen on my unloading crew stopped at Watertown a couple of days ago. He said there was a guy he met who'd be working with the cleanup crew. I think he said it was Salva Construction. The name didn't sound familiar. Anyway, he was telling him that his boss had underbid Lester. My man thought he was part of Lester's crew. Said he seemed like a nice guy."

"Lester withdrew his bid. Said he had too much on his plate." I paused then changed the subject. "So, you should have pipe on Monday, Andy."

"We'll be ready. Glad to know the pipe is on schedule. Some storage yard's offices aren't even set up yet."

"Andy, things just get more exciting. I'd better make a note of that so I can call when I get into Watertown."

"Is Sharon coming up to work with you again?"

"No, Sharon left the company."

"You're going to need help, Alex. Some of these office managers don't know their ass from a whole in the ground. You're telling me they are new to this."

Andy just smiled. They finished their breakfast and then headed out.

When I reached Watertown, first thing I did was locate the closest KOA to the pipe storage yard. I unloaded the fifth wheel then went straight to the yard. I was stopped by a security guard and asked to show my badge before he agreed to let me in. *At least they have security set up here. That's a good sign.* Walking into the trailer office, I was greeted by many familiar faces. It was always great to work with the people you had a track record. I knew they were responsible, and they had a remarkable work ethic. Some sites you didn't find that, and you spent more time babysitting till you could attract replacements. They made me a place to work, and have use of a phone.

"We're going to lunch. Do you want to join us?"

"No thanks, I just ate a couple of hours ago. Besides, I have plenty of work to do. See you later." I was thankful to be left alone in the trailer. I'll try Joe again, and dialed his number. The phone rang twice and was picked up.

"Joe Larkin."

"Joe, it's Alex. How are things going?" I was happy to hear his voice.

"Smooth, so far. Sorry, I didn't get back to you last night. I didn't see you'd called until this morning."

"Joe, I received a letter from Sharon yesterday."

"From Sharon! Where is she?"

"She didn't say, but it was postmarked Santa Clara, California. I'm going to read it to you. Dear Alex, I'm sorry I left the way I did. I was too scared to say anything. I won't tell you where I'm at in case this doesn't reach you. Just watch your back. Sharon."

"My hell, Alex, what's going on? That's a mysterious letter. Any idea what she is talking about?"

"No. I don't have a clue,"

"Have you heard or seen anything of Nick or Ateara?"

"No, Joe. I haven't either one. I wouldn't be surprised to see Nick on Monday when they start unloading pipe. I'm thinking of having Terry come up and help me."

"What about your assistant, what's his name?" Joe tried to keep his voice level.

"You mean Gary? He's not ready for the field, I told you that." I smiled at the touch of jealousy in his voice.

"Alex, I'll be up in two weeks. We have train cars leaving every day. I want to see how the binding holds up, especially on that coated pipe which starts leaving the plant next week. You call me if anything out of the ordinary happens. Be careful Alex."

"I will Joe. Goodbye." I hung up the receiver, sat back in the chair tapping my fingers on the desk. *This might be a good time to call Lester*, I thought and dialed his number.

"Kierbow Construction, how I be helping you?" The receptionist answered.

"Is Mr. Kierbow in?" I asked.

"Yes'em he is. Can I tell him who be calling?" She asked.

"Alex Kendall," I said, and waited patiently for Lester to pick up.

"Miss Alexandra, how you be?" he asked, trying to sound cheerful.

"The question Lester, is how are you?" I asked, hearing the sadness in his voice.

"I be jut fine," he replied.

"Okay Lester, now tell me the truth. I can hear it in your voice you're not fine."

"Oh Miss Alex, I can't hide anything from ya girl." He said, the forced cheerfulness fading from his voice.

"Lester, have you heard from Ateara?" I asked, crossing my fingers in hope.

"No. Not since that night yeah all were here. I don't know where that child be. I've asked around, but nobody seen her for a while." He scribbled his daughter's name on a pad of paper.

I'm glad you're back in the office. I have had some of your old pipeline friends ask about you."

"That be mighty kind of them to inquire. Has Nick, he be bothering you Miss Alex?"

"No Lester. I've not heard or seen him since last Monday when he was in to see Mr. Oshler."

"That be good. He be an evil man, Miss Alex. Ya see him coming, ya run the other way."

"Lester, I'll watch for him. I'll keep in touch every couple of days. You need to get in touch with me call Joe. You take care now."

I put the phone down and pulled out the papers I needed to work on, besides the list of numbers of the other storage facilities. Calling the managers at the storage yards hoping they were further along setting everything up.

The more I thought about bringing Terry up, the more I liked the idea. Having a person here at Watertown at the base of operation that knew corporate procedures would be a big help. That would give me freedom to move up and down the line. I had to swallow my pride and admit Alex Kendall needed help.

It was five o clock when I called the corporate office hoping Terry was still there.

"Good afternoon, Oshler and Marsh Construction. This is Terry, how can I help you?"

"Hi, Terry. I was hoping you were still there. How's it going?" I asked tapping my fingers on the desk again.

"Busy as always. They sent Alva up to help me for a while. They're bidding on the southern leg of the line. It won't start until next summer," she said.

"How's Gary doing?

"He's busy trying to keep up with all you gave him to do. He has asked me every hour on the hour I think If I'd heard from you. He left about fifteen minutes ago believing you wouldn't call until Monday. I didn't say anything to change that idea. I knew I would hear from you this afternoon that is why I stayed. So, how is it going?" She finally asked wanting to hear everything that was happening.

"Some of the offices aren't set up yet, and they'll be receiving pipe on Monday. I need you here at the base office. I've already asked Mr. Oshler. That's why he sent Alva up to help you. She's very knowledgeable and will be able to keep up with what you do. And, she will keep Gary busy," I laughed. "There's a nice motel not too far from here. I'll reserve you a room."

"I'd be happy to. What day do you want me there?"

"Plan on being here next Friday. That will also give you a couple more days to go over things with Alva. Terry, there is so much money that could walk away. It's going to be hard to keep it under control. It bothers me that the security guards haven't been hired for a few of the storage yards. Oh, and Terry, you need not say anything to Gary until you leave. I'll talk to you on Monday. Have a great weekend."

I was impressed with how well this office was running. I made arrangements for a desk to be set up for Terry, with a separate phone line. Once the pipe started arriving it would be harder to reach me. I'd heard the phone for the Wishek storage yard was in an office in town two miles away. I'd defintely look into that next week.

Monday morning the first train load of pipe rolled into the yard. I was there early in anticipation, and greeted Andy, who owned the company that would be unloading the pipe from the rail cars and stacking it in the yard. The crane was in place ready to go.

"That's some big pipe," he said looking at the long line of train cars with the secured forty-two-inch pipe.

"Yes, it is, Andy." I agreed to watch the conductor uncouple the first car attached to the engine. Twenty rail cars were now ready to be unloaded.

"Good morning," Nick greeted them. This is exciting seeing the first cars arrive isn't it."

"I better go start up the crane. Talk to you later Alex," Andy said, leaving me standing alone next to Nick Salva.

"Yes, it is exciting Mr. Salva," I said, trying to keep the distaste from sounding in my voice.

"Alex, I thought we had settled that we were on first name basis," he said, smiling at me.

"Mr. Salva, I agreed in front of Mr. Oshler because I didn't want to cause a scene. Knowing what I know I will keep you as impersonal as possible." I turned away from him, but not missing the dark expression cross his face. I walked back and stepping into the trailer closing the door behind me without looking back.

I saw Nick a few times that day with his men. A couple of them looked more like bodyguards than pipeline workers. The office manager showed Nick where to pile the discarded pipe banding until the final disposition at the end of the job. Looking at my watch, it was almost three p.m. time to call Mr. Oshler with my first report, and Terry coming up on Friday.

"Alex things are going well here, and I've decided to send Terry on Wednesday instead of Friday. I assume you have accommodation secured for her?" he asked.

"Yes Sir, I have," I told him and then gave the report on the amount of pipe unloaded for the day and other general information. "I will look for Terry Wednesday night then Sir. Thank you." I called Terry next and gave her a list of things I needed from the office to bring up with her.

"Alex I will call before I leave in case you think of something else you need. Thought you would like to know Gary was miserable that Mr. Oshler was sending me up instead of him. Just a heads up when you call in. Not sure what kind of reception you'll receive," Terry said.

"You don't always get what you want, and that is something Gary will have to learn if he wants to continue to be my assistant. If he'd had more experience in the field, I would have brought him with me. I don't have time to do on the job training. This contract is too big. I'll talk to you later."

Everything was going well in the yard and decided to take a ride up the line. I was about ten miles out when something ran in front of the truck. Whatever is was I thought for sure I'd hit it. Stopping, I turned the truck off and stepped out hearing a small wine. Looking under the truck, I couldn't see anything. Tracking around the truck, down the grassy slope where I thought the sound was coming from.

"Oh dear," I cried looking at the small black shaggy dog laying at the bottom of the ditch licking its back leg.

"Little fella, what are you doing all the way out here?" I asked, moving down the slope. "It's okay, I'm not going to hurt you. I hope your leg isn't broken." Keeping my voice low and calm I knelt down beside the dog. Putting my arms around the small dog, I lifted it up and made my way back up to the track road. I was happy the dog didn't try to bite, setting down the black curly bundle on the passenger side of the truck.

"Let's see if we can find a vet to look at your leg. Hopefully, the wheel dumped you out of the way as it didn't feel like I ran over anything. Do you belong to someone?" I asked as if I would receive an answer back. There was no collar around the dog's neck. However, I had seen pipe-liners's that had dogs that wore no identification.

"I bet as cute as you are someone is looking for you." I drove back to town and stopped at the café, writing down the instruction where to find the vets.

Pulling up in front of Watertown Veterinarian, I saw a man locking the door.

"Oh please, before you leave could you look at the dog's leg? I hit him driving out on the pipeline. I didn't see him, and I don't know the extent of his injuries," I pleaded picking up the small dog.

"Okay bring him in. That's saying something about you if you stopped and picked him up." The Vet took him from me and put him on the stainless steel table.

"Little one, it will be all right. He's not going to hurt you," I cooed.

"The bone isn't broken. I think it's bruised, and it will be sore for a few days," he said. "Oh, your he is a female."

"I didn't know, thanks. Can I leave her here?" I asked, thinking now wasn't the time to take care of a dog.

"That I can't accommodate. I have a full kennel," he said, giving the dog back to me.

"What do I owe you?" I asked thankfully he'd taken the time to look at the ball of curly black hair.

"Don't worry about it. Most people would have left her along the side of the road."

"Thank you," I said, walking out the door. "I guess little one, you are stuck with me, or I'm stuck with you depending how you want to look at it. Maybe tomorrow we'll find out who you belong to. I'm sure they're missing you." I put her in the back in the truck. "I wonder what they call you? Guess until we find out, but until then I'll call you Sadie. Don't ask me why, it was the first thing that popped into my head. Are you okay with that?" I asked, not expecting an answer. However, I did get a bark back, which I smiled at.

"I don't know about you, but I'm hungry, Sadie." I drove back to the KOA and parked the truck for the night. After fixing both of them something to eat, making Sadie a bed on the floor, it was eight-thirty by the time both of them were asleep.

I jumped at the banging on the trailer door. "Just a minute, who is it?" I yelled pulling on my jeans.

"It's Hansen Riddle, the security guard," came the reply.

I pulled a tee-shirt down over my head and answered the door.

"Miss Kendall you're supposed to call Mr. Oshler. He said it was an emergency and to call him at this number." I took the paper handed me.

"Thanks, I'll be to the office in just a few minutes. Thanks again."

The security guard left, and I put on socks and shoes. "Well Sadie, should I brave it and leave you here or take you with me?" Sadie tilted her head to the side like she was trying to understand what I was talking about. "Okay, you're coming with me."

My mind was racing. Had something happened to Joe, what else could be wrong? We drove to the office which was only a ten-minute drive. The other security guard let me in. I parked, picked up Sadie, and went inside the trailer to call. The phone had rung four times before someone picked it up.

"Hello." I heard on the other end of the line.

"This is Alex Kendall. I was given this number to call."

"Alex, this is Dave Oshler."

"I didn't recognize your voice, Sir. What's going on?" I asked hurriedly.

"Alex, there's been a terrible accident. Someone ran into Terry's car in the middle of an intersection. The other vehicle left the scene of the crash. They must have been driving a truck to be able to leave the scene, looking at Terry's car."

I sat down with trembling hands. "How's Terry?" Her heart felt like it was in a vise.

"She's in a coma right now. Broken leg and arm multiple cuts and bruises," he sighed.

"What's the prognosis?" I asked.

"She has a steady heartbeat. The doctor believes she'll be okay. Said he'd know more in a couple of days. They were worried about internal bleeding but ruled that out...just a minute Alex." There was silence for a moment. "Alex, Terry's parents are here now so I'm going to go home. Her room number is twenty-six eighteen."

"Thank you, Mr. Oshler for calling me. I'll talk to you tomorrow. Good night." I pushed the receiver down but kept hold of the phone. Without even thinking I called Joe. The phone rung six times before it was picked up.

"Hello, this better be..."

"Joe, it's Alex," my voice quivering and I was just holding it together.

"Are you all right?" His voice alert now.

"Yes, Joe. Terry was in a hit and run tonight. She's in a coma." I started to cry unable to hold back the tears.

"Is she going to be all right? What are the doctors saying?"

I repeated what Mr. Oshler had told me. "Joe, I was bringing her up here to help me. It's my fault," I sobbed.

"Alex it's not your fault. I'm sure they'll locate the driver and find out he was drunk. Alex... I want you to go back to the fifth wheel, take a couple of Tylenol and try to get some sleep. There's nothing you can do right now, honey. Alex," Joe said again more sternly.

"I hear you. Okay. I'll talk to you tomorrow. Good night." I put the phone in the cradle and picked up Sadie. I couldn't remember driving back to the KOA.

But here we were. Going inside I locked the door and took off my boots. Lying down on the bed with Sadie cuddled beside me, I fell asleep.

CHAPTER 13

I woke the next morning to a tongue bath. "Okay, Sadie. I'll get up. You must have to go outside. That's a good sign, your house-broke." I let her out and sat down on the step of the fifth wheeler, and tried to schedule the day in my head. However, thoughts were on Terry, and my mind wouldn't let me focus. Sadie finished her morning ritual and padded back to where I was sitting.

"You're not limping little one, you must be healing quickly. I hope Terry heals as fast as you. Come on, let's fix breakfast. We need to get on the road." Finding Sadie's owner was put on the back burner, besides word would travel fast if someone had lost a small black dog. My eyes wandered over the little dog with pointy ears and dark eyes that seemed to be studying me right back.

"I don't know what you are used to eating, so you'll have to have what I eat until I can make it to a store and pick you up dog food. Do you have anything to say?" I received one bark.

It was ten o'clock when I pulled into the pipe storage yard with my rig. Stepping out of the truck, I marveled at the crane picking up a length of forty-two-inch pipe, and set it down for the front loader to pick up and stack in a designated pile.

"Good morning, Alex. Looks like your ready to move up the line?"

"Yes, Jake. You and your people have done a great job setting up this yard. There isn't a reason to keep me here longer. I'll remain in touch once a week, however, if you need anything, don't hesitate to get in touch with me."

"Alex, sorry to hear about Terry. The guard told us this morning," Jake said, taking off his hat and then placed it back on.

"Thanks," I replied.

"Will they be sending anyone else up?"

"I'm not sure. I'll know in a couple of days. Here's my call name. You can send a message up the line, which works well."

"Really," he said with a grin.

"Something wrong with that?"

"Oh no. I just thought it would be something more feminine."

Of course, you would, I thought. *I'm dressed in boots, jeans, tee shirt and baseball cap, and it still doesn't change.* "That's exactly why I chose that handle," I laughed. "Tell the crew they're doing a great job. Oh, and if anyone is missing this cute little mutt, let them know I have her. Talk to you next week. Come on Sadie we have miles to cover."

The two-hour drive to Aberdeen gave me plenty of thinking time. It was a puzzle I was trying to arrange in my head. Sharon leaving without an exclamation, and then the strange note. Telling Terry, they didn't receive her request for an interview. Why would someone want to stop her from being my assistant? Why would they prevent her from coming up? Was it someone at the home office, or more of Nick's forceful tactics like he'd made to make sure he received the contract. That doesn't make sense after what happened with Lester and Ateara. There was no one else in his way. Two many missing pieces. I was going to have to pull in favors for information. Who could I trust now at the home office that wouldn't put them in harms way gathering information? I wasn't sure of anyone. The information would have to come from an outside source.

The routine started. Finding the closest KOA on the map to the pipe yard. Set up the fifth wheel for a couple of days and find a place to eat. In fact, finding a place to eat was a priority. I had to admit my healthy eating habits did suffer when I was on the road.

"I guess it's people food again for you, Sadie. Then I'll find a grocery store. That looks like an easy access, in and out." I laughed. "Me with a dog, guess you do give me someone to talk to. You stay put, and I'll be right back." I rolled the windows down three-quarters and left the truck. Looking back before going inside, and wasn't surprised to see Sadie with her paws on the window watching me.

Well, you're either really smart and realize you've got it made, or really hungry. And you'll wait around until you find something better, either way, I guess we'll be together for a while.

When I walked back out with the large white sack, the first thing I did from habit more than anything else was scope out my surroundings. That's when I saw the black truck a half block back. A twinge hit my stomach. *Come on Alex, this is farming country, now pipeline country, everyone drives a truck,* I told myself climbing back inside the truck. Putting Sadies lunch on top of the white sack on the floor, and let her have at it. I felt more like eating when the black truck turned at the light and vanished down the road.

"I've got to stop being so jumpy, Sadie." Sadie just looked at me and then at her burger. "No, you had yours this is mine." *You might be a smart dog,* I thought, watching Sadie lay back down on the floor of the truck.

When they pulled into the Aberdeen's pipe storage yard, it wasn't as well organized as Watertown. I could tell at first glance I'd be here for a week. The pipe was being unloaded from the train cars, and left where they were laid. The stacking sights weren't ready yet, there wasn't security at the gate, so anyone could drive in. I watched people come in and out of the office trailer and only recognized one person. That one person was the one person I didn't want to see. Nick saw my truck and walked over. I got out and left Sadie inside.

"Looks like you have your work cut out for you here, Alex," Nick said, leaning against his truck.

I heard Sadie growl.

"Some yards get off to a better start than others, and that's why I'm here," I said, not wanting to get into a conversation with him.

"I see you picked up a stray?" he grinned.

"What makes you think that?"

"It wasn't with you when you left Omaha," he replied.

"How do you know that?" I glared at him, now wondering what else he knew.

"I know things that are important to me, and Alex that mutt won't protect you," he chuckled.

"I can take care of myself. You may be the one who needs protecting."

He laughed louder. "You think so," he said, his fingers caressing the outside of my arm. Sadie growled again.

"One thing about strays, you never know when they'll leave again, or end up dead." With that, Nick turned around and walked back to his men. I walked back to my own truck and patted Sadie.

"You are smart Sadie, you can smell scum." I picked Sadie up and carried her into the office trailer.

"Who's the office manager here?" I asked putting Sadie down.

"Now little lady, it depends on who wants to know?" There were a few chuckles from the other men. They checked her out from her cowboy boots all the way up to the baseball cap that had Northern Lights Pipeline stitched across the front. I took off the sunglasses and gave the small group a quick glance.

"The little lady who can get your ass fired if you really want to know." I looked at each one of them again. I'd learned early on in my career that you didn't get respect being a lady on the pipeline. I'd learned to speak their language to a point, just enough to get their respect. For the most part, I'd accomplished just that.

"Oh shit, that's Alex Kendall." I heard one of them whisper in the back.

"That's exactly who I am, and you have thirty seconds to get a pad and pencil and sit your butts in a chair. Now, I'll ask again who is the office manager?"

"I'm the office manager." A tall shaggy haired man stood up. I knew the moment he opened his mouth he was a Southern boy.

"Rod Perry, mam," he said, taking off his hat.

"Mr. Perry, this meeting will last approximately two hours. After that, you have one hour to have security guards at the gate and arrange twenty-four-hour surveillance," I said sternly.

"Yes Mam, I'll take care of it." He sat back down.

"Okay gentlemen, let's get down to business," I said a little softer.

After the meeting, everyone except Mr. Perry did a walk about with me in the yard. I told them the trash would be picked up daily, and they could start now. Walking back to the trailer and before going inside, I turned around and wasn't surprised to see they were all watching me, including Nick.

"Do you have any question?" I directed at the group of six.

"No Mam," they replied in unison.

"Then let's get started." I turned and went inside shaking my head. Men, it never changes, they all think between their legs.

Walking to the far end of the trailer where Sadie claimed a spot to lie down, I sat at one of the desks. Picking up the phone and dialed home office directly to Mr. Oshler. I gave my report and asked about Terry.

"Terry is doing better. She opened her eyes this morning but is still in intensive care. I would say, Alex, day after tomorrow you may be able to talk to her," he said, concern still laced his voice.

"I was hoping for news like that," I said leaning back in the chair more relaxed.

"By the way, Alex, I'm sending Gary up to help you. He assures me he'll be able to handle the workload up there. He's leaving in the morning."

"Tell him there's a motel in Watertown being held for him at Saw's Landing Motel in Watertown. It's under Terry's name. I've arranged for a phone to be put in the office at the storage yard for his use. I'll keep him based there to coordinate with me," I told him not happy that Gary was coming up. At least he wouldn't be under foot in Watertown.

"That sounds good, Alex. I'll talk to you in a couple of days for an update." I hung up the phone and picked it up again dialing Lester's number. The phone picked up.

"Hello."

I was surprised he picked up the phone and not his secretary. "Lester, it's Alex. How are you doing?"

"I be doing better than yesterday Miss Alexandar," he answered, and by the sound of his voice that was true.

"Lester, I was wondering if you could help me with something?"

"All you need to do is ask. If I can, I will."

"Do you still have that friend that does background checks and a bit more?" I asked, looking out the window.

"I do. Whom ya be wanting to be investigated?"

I gave him the two names.

"Miss Alexandra when I talked to ya last, that night I be noticing Ateara's bedroom doors be partly opened, and I went in to see. Some of her clothes be gone from her closet with her suitcase." He sighed heavily.

"I'm sorry Lester that means she is on the move."

"Yes'm that's what I be thinking. She has left Louisana."

"Thank you, Lester, for your help. I'll call in a couple of days."

Rod Perry came back into the trailer and walked over to where I was sitting.

"Miss Kendall, I have two security guards on their way here. I'll have a third guard here tomorrow. I'll be putting them on eight-hour shifts."

"Good work Rod. I noticed you have two inspectors in here today. They should be out inspecting that pipe coming off those rail cars. Is this your first manager job?" I asked standing up.

"Yes, Mam it is," he replied, holding his hat in front of him.

"Let me give you some advice. You are the manager of this yard, and everyone answers to you. You run a tight ship from the beginning you won't have trouble later on. The inspectors will run you over if leadership isn't established. I'm going to stay a few days to help with that. This yard needs to be up to speed with Watertown by the end of the week. After I leave and you have trouble, call me. If you're doing what is expected, I'll stand behind you hundred percent."

"Thank you, Miss Kendall. I appreciate that," he said sincerely.

"Okay. I'm going to show you how to get your stack sites ready for the loader to stack that large pipe. I'm sure it won't be long until Andy's crew is here to take care of it.

The next couple of hours they spent staking out the ten sites and hammering in the stakes that would secure the forty-two-inch pipe from rolling. Late afternoon when I was ready to leave, I looked over the yard. A considerable change had taken place. Even Salva's men worked at removing the rubber banding from the pipe and had selected a place at the end of the yard to pile the banding.

"Come on Sadie, it's time to get food in our stomachs. Mr. Perry," I yelled walking up to the trailer.

"Yes Mam," he said, making his way out of the trailer.

"Where's there a good place to eat in this town?"

"The best place I've found so far is Molly Brown's if you are looking for home cooking." Giving me directions, he however, declined the offer to join me.

"I will meet you for breakfast there in the morning around seven," he said, and then added. "Thanks for the help and the advice."

I nodded and left.

The directions I was given were right on the money. Pulling up front, I parked and rolled down the windows for Sadie before going inside. The atmosphere was warm, the interior clean and smelled like baking bread. *A mom and pops place*, I thought. Sitting up to the counter, a friendly waitress brought me a glass of water and the menu. After a quick look, I gave the waitress my order and asked for a coke.

I was so deep in thought and didn't notice who sat down beside me.

"They say the food here is excellent," he said casually.

"Most mom and pops do serve great food or are you just following me Nick?"

"I asked one of the guys where a good place to eat was, and he told me to follow that red truck. It would lead me to the best place in town," he said, leaning his leg into mine's.

"How convenient," I answered sarcastically and moved my leg away from his.

"How long are you going to keep running from me, Alex? It's only a matter of time."

I lowered my voice, "Mr. Salva, we are not in Louisana. You may have walked away with what you did to Lester and Ateara. But don't think for a minute I wouldn't have your ass hauled to jail for a very long time." I watched his expression darken, however before he said anything else the waitress brought my order. Paying for the food I left.

Sadie was waiting patiently sitting with her paws on the door, moving to the far side when I stepped inside the truck. The little dog watched me and didn't even sniff the sack. Driving back to the KOA park I was still fuming. My fear of Nick Salva had turned to anger. Thinking back how he had cut Ateara, I recognized it was pure hate I felt for him. Pulling alongside the fifth wheeler, I turned the engine off.

"Are you hungry Sadie," I asked, stroking along the dog's back.

"Wuff."

"Me too, guess you get people food again tonight." Picking up Sadie and our supper, before I reached the door, I saw the note attached with tape.

"Would you look at this Sadie, we've already had a visitor." Unlocking the door and taking the note, we went inside. Taking the contents out of the sack, I sat it on the table, putting Sadie's on a paper plate on the floor. Taking a bite of my burger before reading the note.

Miss Kendall, your assistant called said he was in Watertown and would call you in the morning. Just wanted you to know he'd arrived. Rod Perry.

"Well, Sadie, should we give Gary the benefit of the doubt. I guess we should give him a chance. He can't get into much trouble at home base, and hopefully he will keep his mind on business and off me."

Stretching out on the bed going over what I had wanted to accomplish that day, Sadie scratched at the door. Getting up I let her out and left the door open and waited for her to return. Shutting the door, I picked up the dog and laid back down pulling the covers back over me.

"I think Rod Perry with some help will do a good job," I said to Sadie scratching her behind the ears. "What do you think Sadie?" Looking over at the clock, it was five thirty. "I guess we better get up, no sleeping in for us." Tossing the sheet back and throwing my legs over the edge of the bed I looked at the kitchen floor and the muddy paw prints I hadn't notice when letting Sadie back in from doing her business.

"How did those get there?" I asked. "I didn't see mud on your paws when we came in last night or just now." I looked at the sheets Sadie was lying on. "Maybe I was too tired to notice, and it's a good thing there isn't mud on my sheets," I told Sadie shaking a finger at her and smiling at the same time. *Well, I better get it cleaned up before I shower,* I thought looking at the dry mud on the floor.

Seven o'clock I met Rod Perry at Molly Brown's for breakfast. They had finished eating and were enjoying another cup of coffee.

"Miss Kendall, I want to thank you for yesterday, being my first job as a yard manager I think I was a little intimated by the two inspectors that arrived the day before," he said.

"They have a way of doing that, Rod. You lay down the law, in the beginning, they'll do their job and let you do yours. I'll help you set up your files this morning, and then we'll see how the rest of the day goes. Also, we'll go over what the other three guys here are supposed to be doing," I said pushing my coffee cup away. "There are more than a few first-time managers on this job. It will be a good learning experience and help for you in the future. Just remember to stand your ground, complete your paperwork and you'll be fine." I paid the bill, and we left.

When I pulled into the yard, there was a police car and an ambulance. I hurried and parked the truck and told Sadie to stay in the cab. Rod Perry and I quickly made our way into the office to hear what had happened.

"Excuse me, officer. I'm Alex Kendall, Vice President of Logistics on this project. What has happened?" I asked, looking at the grim officer.

"Miss Kendall, there was a man found dead this morning by the security guard," said the officer.

"Where, how, do we know who he was?" I asked and held back the many more question I wanted to ask.

"What I've gathered so far, the security guard let in a couple of men that said they were with the cleanup crew. He watched them walk back picking up banding as they went to the growing pile at the end of the yard. A half hour later he heard a scream and a man running toward them yelling that he needed a gun. The guard told him he didn't have a weapon but took out his billy club and raced back to the pile of banding, the other man on his heels," said the officer looking away from me, his tanned skin paled. He swallowed and continued.

"We found him on the far side of the pile. He had numerous bite marks on him. By the time we were called and the ambulance arrived the poor fellow's skin had turned black, and his body swelled twice its size."

"Have they called Nick Salva?" I asked, trying to stay calm. "He's the boss over that crew."

"I believe they have called him. However, I haven't seen him. Excuse me Mam, looks like they're bringing the body up now," the taller officer said, reaching for the door knob. The officers stepped out of the trailer.

"Can I see the body?" I asked, not really wanting to, but knowing I had to.

"I hope you have a strong stomach, Miss Kendall. This isn't something we see every day, thank God," the older officer said, stepping down the last step from the trailer.

"I need to see it," I exclaimed.

When the paramedics reached the ambulance, the officer asked them to wait before they put the body inside. I walked up to the stretcher. A stench was already being expelled that made her gag. The attendant pulled back the body cover. The man's face were distorted in terrorr and pain, eyes bulging, blood mixed with a yellow mucus oozed from his nose, mouth and the puncture marks around his neck. The skin had blackened and stretched until it looked like it would explode if touched. I felt my stomach churning, and felt light-headed. I turned feeling arms close around me and relaxed into the body that supported me. I tried to gain composure and looked up into the eyes of Nick Salva. Adrenaline rushed through my veins as I forced myself to push away from him.

Rod Perry standing close, took my arm. "Miss Kendall let me help you into the office." I walked with him without saying a word. Something brush against my leg and looked down at Sadie, who had jumped out of the cab of the truck. They went into the office and sat down. Rod bought her a glass of water. Sadie placed her head against my leg and was surprised at the comfort the small dog gave me.

"Thank you, Rod. Would you find me the other worker, I would like to talk to him." I picked up Sadie and rubbed her behind the ears. Hearing the ambulance leave the yard, and it wasn't until the police had finished questioning the other man that he walked into the trailer with Rod and Salva.

"Please sit down," I offered. I could see the worker was still frightened. His face lacked color, his hands shook slightly. "I know you have told the police what happened, but could you please tell me?" I asked. Salva gave him a nod. He swallowed hard collecting the memory she was sure he wanted to forget.

"The guard let us in so we could start to work. We walked down to where we had begun the pile of banding, picking up a few on the way we had missed yesterday. I had tossed mine onto the stack. My friend who had one in his hand started to throw it, and it came alive. It turned into a snake." The man began to tremble, and tears flowed from his eyes. "It coiled around his arm, hissing, and that's when I ran for help."

His sorrow ripped through me, and I nodded to Rod there was nothing else I wanted to ask. One of the police officer's came in.

"Son, if you want, I can drive you home," the officer said.

"No thank you," he managed. "Mr. Salva I won't be

back for a couple of days," he said, before leaving wiping the tears from his face.

Salva nodded and waved him on.

"Young man in the next day or two will you stop by the police station and give your statement so we have it on record?" The officer asked.

"Yes, Sir," he said, leaving the trailer.

"Nick Salva is it?" The young officer asked.

"Yes. I'm the contractor for the banding and clean up crew," Nick answered.

"How long have the men worked for you that were involved today?"

"I met all the men working for me at this yard a week ago. I only bring my foremen from home. There are always men looking for a job in the local towns. It's easier to hire close to the project," Salva stated.

"Miss Kendall, I'm sorry, but we will need to shut the yard down for a while we do our investigation. Did you know either of these men?"

"No. The first time I saw them was yesterday talking to Mr. Salva," I said taking another sip of water. "I deal more with the contractors and managers setting up the storage yards. You will let me know what you find, won't you?' I asked, worry covered me, wondering if this was the beginning.

"Yes, but I'm not sure what we'll find. His story is kind of hard to swallow. We'll know more after the autopsy. You'll be here for a few more days?"

"Yes, and if I can help in any way, please let me know, officer." I moved to the back desk so I could use the phone. Sadie followed me. I could feel Nick watching her.

"I'm sorry about your worker, Mr. Salva. If you'll excuse me, I have calls to make," I said, not looking up at him.

"Alex," he said, taking a step toward her. Sadie growled. "Perhaps this isn't the right time to talk to you." Stopping where he was, he shot a disgusted look at Sadie.

"Mr. Salva unless it's about work related matters, you have nothing to say that I would be interested to hear. Now if you'll excuse me, I do have those calls to make." I felt undressed the way Nick was looking at me. My confidence dipped a bit. However, Nick turned and walked out of the door, and I called Mr. Oshler.

"Alex, how are things going?" He asked, his mood cheerful.

"The pipe is being delivered on time, and they will start stringing the end of next week in Watertown."

"That sounds great, Alex. Getting off to a good start."

"Sir, we had someone killed today in the Aberdeen yard," I stated. The sight of the body flashed across my mind.

"What happened?" he asked concerned.

"One of Salva's men was bitten by a snake. It was not a pretty sight. I've never seen anything like it, Sir."

"Rattlesnakes usually warn you, did he walk into a nest?" Oshler asked.

"Sir, I don't think it was a rattlesnake. The police are out investigating as we speak."

"You will let me know as soon as you hear something more."

"Yes Sir, I will. How's Terry doing?"

"They'll be moving her out of the ICU in the morning into a private room. I would think you should be able to call her tomorrow afternoon, Alex. She's at Saint Ann's Hospital," said Mr. Oshler.

"Have they found the hit and run driver yet?"

"No, they haven't, but the police have assured me they are still looking for a brown truck. That was the color of paint left smeared on Terry's car. Did I tell you Terry's car was a total loss? She is lucky to be alive."

"I'll call you when I find out something," I said hanging up the phone.

rang the Watertown office. It was now nine thirty.

"Hello, Northern Lights Pipeline."

I heard on the other end. "Can I talk to Gary Spindle, please?" I asked not looking forward to talking to him.

"Hello, this is Gary Spindle."

"Gary, this is Alex," before I could say another word, Gary was asking questions.

"Alex what happened up there? We heard someone was killed!" He exclaimed. "Is it true?"

"I forgot how fast news travels on the pipeline," I said, and paused for a moment. "Yes, someone did. We don't know the cause until after they do the autopsy. We were told it was a snake bite from the eye witness. He was one of Nick Salva's men," I stated, sitting back in the chair.

"Do you want me to come up?" he asked.

"No. I need you there. Have you met Brittan yet?"

"He's a tall redheaded Texan," I said a small curve of my lips lifted thinking of the Texan.

"Oh, he must be the one everyone calls Brit. Okay, I've met him."

"You and Brittan will be coordinating information. The information I send you has to be broken down and put on the forms he gives you. If you have trouble with them, I believe there are a couple of people in that office who have done the paperwork before. You found Saw's Landing I take it? Did you have trouble getting a key?"

"No. Everything is fine on this end. I heard you picked up a traveling companion. I wasn't good enough huh?" He chuckled. "Just kidding Alex."

"Yes, I did. So far she keeps all the scum away, don't you Sadie?" I smiled and patted Sadie's back.

"I can't believe you replaced me with a K-9 Alex."

"I didn't replace you, Gary, you still have the same status you've always had," I said.

"We'll have to talk about that when I see you, Alex," he said, sounding hopeful.

"Gary, I will call you at eight thirty every morning to give you the new figures. If you need anything, call me."

"You can count on it, Alex."

I decided to wait and call Joe when I had more information. There was a meeting at two that afternoon with the stringing contractor, and I was hoping they wouldn't keep the yard down to long. They needed to unload the train cars and keep them moving, hoping to start stringing pipe Friday morning.

My thoughts went to Ateara and wondered if she had anything to do with the death. Just considering it gave me goose bumps.

CHAPTER 14

Riding up the line to see how far the ditch had been dug, I was feeling good about the progress even with the morning's dismal start. Stopping to chat with some of the workers from previous jobs, and confirmed what they had heard through the pipeline gossip, I didn't have any additional news than what they'd heard.

It was around six o'clock when we headed back to Aberdeen. We passed fields, farmers were planting wheat, another feeding cattle with the largest hay bales I'd ever seen. It never ceases to amaze me how miles of sunflowers raised their heads in the morning to greet the sun, follow the blazing chariot across the heavens and say goodnight as it disappeared into the west. I was so enthralled with the vastness of the fields, that I didn't notice the flashing lights behind me until I heard the siren. Pulling over to a stop, and automatically reached in the glove box for the trucks registration.

"Good evening Miss Kendall," the officer greeted me.

It took me a moment and then recognized him as the police office from this morning.

"These rolling hills do have some beauty to them," he commented.

"Yes, they do. I was just admiring them. I hope you weren't following me for too long?" I asked, giving him a gracious smile.

"Only about a mile Mam. I wanted to talk to you about this morning. I'd like to do it someplace more comfortable. If you don't mind following me to Molly Brown's, it is getting to be around supper time," he suggested.

"That would be fine. I was going there myself officer," I responded. "Well Sadie, it looks like this Molly Brown's is the hip place in this town. Do you think it has anything to do with the great home cooking?" I looked at Sadie and laughed. "You seemed to enjoy it last night." Sadie barked laying back down on the seat.

Parking the truck in front of the café where I could keep an eye on my shaggy black dog. I met the officer at the front door, which he opened and motioned me in. There was a table in front of the window and I moved toward it and then sat down. The small red-headed waitress immediately came over with glasses of water and menus. Taking their drink order she left, returning shortly with two cokes. She smiled generously at the officer before asking me what I would like.

"Miss Kendall," he started cautiously.

"You can call me Alex."

"Alex then, did you know anything about the two young men this morning?"

"As I told you earlier, the first time I saw either of the young men was the evening before with Mr. Salva at the yard," I said before sipping my Coke. "A lot of the contractors hire local workers in the communities for manual labor."

"Neither of the young men were from Aberdeen. One was from Texas. He told us he met the victim a few days after arriving here at a bar in town where he had been doing magic tricks. Said one of the tricks he used was with a snake," the officer paused a moment taking a swallow of his Coke. "I don't know a thing about magic. However, the coroner said the kid had enough venom in him to kill ten people. Had to call the Vet to help him isolate what kind of poison. Come to find out the snake that secretes that venom isn't found in the United States. Looks like his magic turned fatal. The detectives couldn't find any sign of a snake while searching the pipe yard."

"Really," I commented a little to enthusiastic. "Then the yard is up and running?"

"Yes. Since about two." He looked at me curiously.

"Don't think I'm callous. I'm deeply sorry about the young man, but I have a billion-dollar pipeline to keep on schedule. I've know men have been killed in accidents in the field, however, never in this manner," I said, glancing out the window at a man standing by my truck.

"Excuse me for just a minute." I stood to step quickly out of the café. "Hey, can I help you with something," I yelled listening to Sadie growl at the black haired stranger.

"No. Cute dog you have. Looks like the one I lost," he said.

"Really. I don't see her licking you in a joyful reunion," I answered, still walking toward him.

"Like I said, she looks like the one I lost. I gotta be going," he said, walking away in a hurry. Stepping up into a blue truck that was waiting for him, he didn't look back.

I walked around to the passenger side. Picking up a piece of meat lying on the ground I put it the truck bed.

"You okay, Sadie?" Sadie licked my face while I rubbed behind her ears. "I won't be too much longer." I walked back into Molly Brown's and strode to the women's restroom, washed my hands before returning to the table where my order was waiting. I needed to stop at a vets.

"Everything all right?" The officer asked.

"Yes. Everything is fine. Where's the Vet's office from here? Sadie had an injury on her back leg. I need to have it checked again."

The officer gave me direction, and we chit-chatted about the pipeline until I was ready to go.

I followed the officer's instructions to the Veterinarians. Pulling up in front, I waited for a car to pull out and then pulled in. Watching a large black poodle come out the office door on a red leash, its handler quickened her step to keep up, and I had to smile. That was a dog that owned its handler.

Stepping down from the truck as Sadie right behind me jumped down. She followed me to the back of the truck sat down while I picked up the wrapped meat.

"Hi, how can we help you today?" Was the greeting when we entered the office.

"I was wondering if you could tell me if there is poison on this piece of meat. Someone was trying to give it to my dog, Sadie," I said, holding up the package.

"Have a seat. It will take a few minutes," she said, and walked back into the other room. She returned with a stainless steel bowl. I laid the package inside.

"This will take a few minutes. Have a seat." The young woman left the room. Half an hour the veterinarian came into the waiting room.

"You're the one who brought in the piece of meat?" He asked, kneeling down to scratch Sadie behind her ears. "The meat was poisoned. Do you know who tried to give it to the dog? I can't believe someone would try to get rid of you girl." He looked up at Me.

"Sadie. Her name is Sadie. No, I'd never seen him before, and I didn't think to write down the license plate number," I replied, I was to upset and foolish not to do that.

"This has been a week for poisons," he remarked.

"Yes, I know," I answered. I'm Alex Kendall from Northern Lights pipeline."

"Oh yes, the strangest thing I've seen. Someone have it out for you or the pipeline?" he said with a slight smile. "I'm just kidding. Is there anything else I can do for you, Miss Kendall?"

"No. Thank you for checking the meat," I said, picking up Sadie. "Well, Sadie, guess we'll be eating meals at the fifth wheeler for the next couple of days until we head up to Wishek. That means my friend, we need to go to the store. But before we do that, I need to call Joe. Everyone should be gone from the yard now." Looking at my watch, it was near seven o'clock. When we arrived at the yard, only the security guard was there. He opened the gate for me and locked it after I drove through and parked parallel to the trailer. Sadie and I climbed down from the truck and went inside to call. I rang Joe at the ranch and Maria picked up.

"Maria, this is Alex. Is Joe home yet?" I asked, clicking my nails on the desk.

"Yes, Miss Alex. He out in the barn. I'll ring you out there," Marie said.

"Alex, I've been worried about you. I'm glad you called. How are things up there?" He asked worry covered his words.

"Oh, Joe. Where to start."

"First, how is Terry?" He asked.

I gave him the update on Terry, the young man who had died, finding Sadie, and how things were going on the pipeline.

"I'm leaving for Wishek on Friday. What I've heard things up there are worst than they were here in Aberdeen. I'm sure this is the first managers job for whoever is up there." I sighed, wishing Joe was with me.

"I've been checking, Alex. There is a small airport in Wishek. I'm flying up on Monday. They should be receiving the coated pipe, and I want to check the banding. I don't think the landing field is too far from the storage yard," Joe said.

"That sounds great, Joe. Things going smooth at the plant?" I asked rubbing the small dog curled on my lap.

"Here things are ahead of schedule," Joe said in his business voice and then remarked with humor. "Alex, I'm glad you have a dog with you. How long have I been asking you to get one? It sounds like she found you, but whatever works," Joe laughed, stirring butterflies in my stomach. "Can't what to meet the mutt."

"Are you a mutt, Sadie?" I grinned down at her. "She didn't deny it, so maybe you are right. Okay,

Joe, I'll see you Monday." I hung up the phone. "Miss Sadie we need to go to the grocery store."

They arrived at Piggy Wiggly, and I rolled the windows up, but for a quarter inch.

"I won't be long Sadie."

I picked up the things we needed for a few days, also two bowls for Sadie, dog food, and treats. We arrived back at the fifth wheeler around nine p.m., not realizing how tired I was until putting everything away.

"You need to go out before we go to sleep?" Sadie went and stood by the door. I let her out and decided to take my gun out of the truck. With everything that had happened, I thought better safe than sorry. Locking back up the truck they both went in. I undressed down to my underwear and climbed into bed, Sadie curled against me.

Thursday was uneventful in the yard. Things were going smooth. Rod Perry was handling his job proficiently as his files were set up and coded. The stacks of pipe looked like a child's playground, thank goodness for the fence. Stringers would be in tomorrow to start hauling pipe out. The crew had gone to lunch, and I thought it would be a good time to call Terry and Lester. Hopefully, both would have news for me.

"Kierbow Construction."

"Hello, is Mr. Kierbow in?" I asked, picking up a pencil and doodling on a pad of paper

"May I asked who be calling?"

"Alex Kendall."

"One moment please, I am transferring you," his secretary said as sweet as honeyed bread.

"Miss Alexandra good news. I have information I think you be looking for," he said, his voice lighter than I'd heard for a while.

"I could use some good news, Lester," I replied with a half laugh, then I paused. "Lester before you tell your findings I have a question about Ateara."

"Have ya seen her Miss Alex?" He asked excitedly.

"No, Lester. I haven't, and I'm sorry," I said soberly. "Lester, if Ateara cast a spell, will it be only on Nick?"

"Not necessarily, Miss Alex. It could extend to people who work for him or are close to him. Why ya asking, has something happened?"

"Yes, Lester. One of Nicks workers was killed by a venomous snake yesterday. When they did the autopsy, they said this species of snake isn't found in the United States. The doctor said the body had enough venom to kill ten people. The young man had repeatedly been beaten."

"Oh no, Miss Alex. It's started. I be thinking she'll try to get him to give up the job first. You stay away from him. You don't want his scent on you," Lester said, his voice a higher pitch than usual.

"I'll do my best, now what did your friend find out for us?"

Lester gave me the information his informant had found. I thought my stomach would retch.

"Lester, I need to know one more thing?"

"Sure, Miss Alex, what information would that be?"

"I need to know why the infiltration. It has to be something big, I'm thinking. We have to find out Lester," I said urgently, afraid of things to come I couldn't do anything about or could I?

"I be on it right away," Lester said. "And in the meantime you be extra careful."

I sat back and took a deep breath, my chest rising and falling slowly. How many men would die before Nick would give it up? How can I stop this? My mind raced looking for direction. However, none formed in my mind. Feeling at a loss, I felt Sadie rub against my leg.

"You seem to know when something is wrong, don't you girl." Reaching down I pulled the dog back onto my lap, and gave her a hug. "We need to call Terry. Hope she can send some sunshine our way." Dialing the number Mr. Oshler had given me for Saint Ann's Hospital and asks for Terry Rodger's room.

"Hello," a familiar voice answered.

"Some people will do about anything to get out of work," I said laughing. "How are you?"

"I'm doing much better, thanks. How's the job going?" Terry asked.

"I didn't call to give you updates on the field. I want to know how you are doing? What are the doctors saying?"

"I have a concussion, and my left leg was fractured in two places. One above the knee, the other below.

Also my left shoulder, along with cuts and bruises," she started crying. "I'm so sorry Alex. I know you were counting on me," She sniffled and blew her nose.

"Hey, I'm managing. I just need you to take care of yourself. That's all you need to worry about. What do the doctors say?" I asked trying to hold back the tears.

"They said I should heal well. The breaks were clean. I might have a couple of small scars on my face," she added.

"Terry that's great news," I paused a pregnant moment. "Terry what happened that night?"

"I was sitting at Fourth and Broadway waiting for the light to change. I saw a truck come to a stop. The light changed, and I started across. I heard the truck's engine race and came right at me. I heard after if I'd been in a smaller car, it would have killed me. The police officer said it was probably a drunken driver, but they have never found him. Alex, I can't shake the feeling that it wasn't a drunk driver. I think it was intentional." Terry started crying again.

"Don't cry. I can't imagine anyone hitting you on purpose," I murmured, lying.

"You're probably right. I'm just paranoid."

"You concentrate on healing, and I'll talk to you soon." I hung up the receiver. *Somehow I'm going to get to the bottom of this. Hopefully without getting myself killed.*

It was five o'clock Thursday night. I was going over last minute instructions with Rod Perry when the trailer door opened, and Gary walked in.

"What are you doing up here?" I asked surprised, and not happy at seeing him.

"Is that any way to greet your assistant," Gary laughed walking over to me.

"I'm just surprised to see you. Let me introduce you to the crew." I did the introduction. "You will at some time be up here, and Rod will be your contact for information. Sometimes it's 'nice to have a face to go with a name. How are things in Watertown?" I asked sitting down on the chair behind me.

"They're doing well. The stringing has started, as the pipe keeps rolling in. Oh, this must be the famous Sadie," Gary said, kneeling down to pet her. A low growl was the response he received. "She must be very protective," he said, standing back up. "I thought they were joking about you finding a mutt. Didn't take you for a dog person"

"Some mutts are great to have around." I came back, my tone neutral as I patted Sadie's side.

"Are you about finished?" Gary asked, sitting on the edge of the desk. "I thought we could go to dinner. I have some things to talk to you about."

"I think so. Rod, I'll stop by on my way out of town for any last minute questions or concerns you may have," I told him. "Come on Sadie. Gary, you can follow me. I'll take you where home-style cooking is at its best."

I drove to Molly Brown's. Putting a leash on Sadie I tied her to the post outside the window table we would sit at. Feeling better having her where no one would bother her.

"You're actually attached to her aren't you?" He asked looking at the dog and then to me.

"Some things are worth getting attached to," I replied. "What's so important that you had to come up instead of calling me?" Sitting back in the chair my hands folded on the table, I asked. The waitress brought water and menus to their table. "I'll have a coffee and a French dip, please." I looked at Gary.

"I'll have the same." Handing the menu back to her.

"I was bored. It's not that long of a drive. Seeing how things were going here will help with my education." He smiled, his hand reaching for mine. In a flash, I put my hands back in my lap.

"Have they found out anything else on the young man that died?"

"All I know is he was repeatedly bitten by a snake, but what's crazy, they couldn't find one or any signs of one," I told him. I wasn't going to give him any more information. "I thought there would be enough to keep you busy and occupied in Watertown."

"One of the gals in the office has been helping me, so things are caught up. I told you they started stringing pipe. It's been an experience to see how they maneuver forty-two-inch pipe out the yard and down the road," he said amused. "What do you for fun up here?"

"Fun? I haven't had time for fun. We work up here," I said annoyed. The waitress brought out their meal.

"Where do you go to have fun around here?" Gary asked the waitress.

"The best place is Uncle Tom's. They have a band Thursday through Saturday," she told him.

"How would one find this Uncle Tom's?" She drew directions on a napkin for him.

"Okay Alex, you're leaving in the morning, so tonight we're going to have some fun. I won't take no for an answer," he stated.

"All right, Gary. I want to take Sadie back to the fifth wheeler. Then I will follow you to this Uncle Tom's." I noticed his smile slipped. However, he agreed.

When they arrived at Uncle Tom's, the parking lot had slim pickings for parking. *This must be a popular place.* I met Gary at the door. He took my arm, and we strolled in through a large wooden door into an entry where a guy stood near a pair of swinging doors. He looked like a body builder. Well suited for the job he was doing. Stepping aside he let us enter. A few feet inside we both scanned the room taking in the Western décor. The long black shiny bar was the only item that gave a modern aspect to the room.

I spotted the familiar face of Rod Perry before I noticed more people from the pipe yard sitting together. Rod saw me at the same time and motioned them over making room at the table. Rod asked what they were drinking and ordered ours and another round for the table.

"I was told you didn't do this sort of thing," Rod said grinning. "Gald to see they were wrong." He looked over at Gary.

"Goes to show you, you can't believe everything you hear," I said, looking at Gary. "Sounds like they have a great western band. Do you dance, Rod?"

"Yes, mam. Would you like to dance?" He asked and put out his hand to take mine.

"I'd love to," I replied. We went to the dance floor dancing through three songs. I noticed that Gary had watched us all three songs that Rod had kept me on the dance floor. When we returned, Gary had three beers sitting in front of him. He went to stand up to ask me to dance and was again ignored when I took another hand that was offered. I didn't leave the dance floor until the band's break. Returning to the table, Gary's mood had changed considerably

"I think boy's I've had enough. You've worn me out," I said, and they all laughed. "I'll see you in the morning. Gary, you have some fun." I was out the door not waiting for a response.

Pulling into the KOA, I parked in my usual spot. Unlocking the door, Sadie was there to greet me.

"You've missed me, huh?" I asked lifting her up giving her a hug. I had started to take off my boots when someone knocked on the door, and Sadie barked. "Who's there?" I asked, taking out the gun from my purse.

"It's Gary, let me in Alex," he shouted his words slurred.

"Gary, I think you need to go sleep it off," I responded.

"Alex open the door, or I'll wake everyone up," he continued.

"All right, just a minute and I'll be out." I put back on the one boot I'd taken off. "Stay Sadie," I said before stepping out of the trailer.

"It's about time," his words slurred. "Why did you leave me like that?" He asked, stepping closer to me.

"Gary, I really think you need to go find a motel and sleep this off," I said firmly, taking a step back. Gary grabbed my wrists and held me against the fifth wheeler leaning into me.

"You told me if I needed anything to yet you know. I'm letting you know now. I need you." His mouth pressed hard to mine as he reached up tearing the front of my blouse open before groping at my breast.

"Think again," I said, bringing my knee up between his legs. He groaned and doubled over. I brought up my knee to connect with his chin. He dropped to the ground out cold.

"Don't you ever think of touching me again."

"You need some help, Miss Kendall?"

I looked up and saw Rod Perry. "He was upset when you left. Knocked over a chair getting up to follow you. I thought he might come over here. Are you hurt?"

"No," I said, moving my blouse over to cover my flesh. You can help me put Gary in his car, though."

"I think I can manage that by myself, mam." He picked up Gary and laid him across his car seat.

"Thanks, Rod. I'll see you in the morning."

"Your welcome."

Sadie was barking and quieted as soon as I walked back inside the trailer.

"Well, now maybe we can get some sleep," I said and locked the door again.

When I woke, the first thing I did was look out the window to see if Gary's car was sitting next to my truck. It was gone. I gave a sigh of relief. After fixing breakfast for Sadie and myself, I dressed, and hoped I wouldn't see Gary at the office.

Arriving at the yard, crews were already busy. The inspectors were out doing their job. I smiled to myself how efficient the pipe yard had become since I'd arrived.

"You know Sadie, most people just need a bit of direction and guidance to help them get started on the right track. That's what we do, help people go in the right direction," I said to myself more than to Sadie.

"Good morning, Miss Kendall," the guard said as I passed. I nodded. Looking at the parked cars, I didn't see Gary's. I was hoping he had returned to Watertown. I could keep tabs on him through the office manager. He needed to do his job.

I talked to Rod Perry, neither of us mentioned the night before. I felt confident leaving Rod in charge and that the yard would be run efficiently.

"Rod, I'll be back down in three or four weeks. Here are the phone numbers for the other yards, if you don't already have them. Also my handle, if you need to reach me you can through the truckers

CHAPTER 15

We arrived in Wishek around noon, and I stopped at the first restaurant coming into town about three miles past the pipe storage yard.

"Sadie, you'll be okay. I'll bring you something out." Entering the restaurant customers glanced my way and went back to eating or the conversation they were having. I'd left my ball cap in the truck, and my hair was pulled back in a ponytail. I was dressed in jeans, a short sleeve denim shirt, and cowboy boots. At first sight, you would take me for a local. The waitress seated me in a corner booth. I checked out everyone in the place and could tell who was local and who were pipe-liners. I was in hearing distance of two pipeline workers at the counter. They were talking about a freak accident in Aberdeen.

He was saying "One of the drivers said snakes came out of the grass, and the kid had bites all over his body."

The man was tall and lanky, with dark hair and a scruffy bread.

"I didn't know the grass snakes up here were poisonous." The chubby guy who's hair was gray and cut short replied. He also had a southern drawl. "We best be carrying a stick around with us walking along those wide sloping ditches."

I held in laughter, even knowing it wasn't a laughing matter. It was how the stories grew as they were passed on. Two farmers to my right caught my attention.

"This pipeline has brought in a lot of riff-raff," he complained, but business has been good. My cousin who owns a bar in town says his business has tripled. I just wish I'd had land that pipeline went through. They made a killing."

A strange breed pipe-liners, nomads, most people didn't like them in their communities. But, they loved the money they spent. I guess some things will never change. I order lunch and my attention moved back to the two men at the counter.

"We'd better get back. Some big boss is supposed to be here sometime today. We need to be on our best behavior until he's gone. That's what's nice about being out in the sticks, you can slip out for a drink, or two and nobody the wiser."

"I agree with that. Going all day in the heat and that dust bowl they've made out there is the only reason I stay."

I made a mental note of the two men as they passed my table. *As I was thinking, somethings never change.*

I found a place to park the fifth wheeler for the week before heading back out to the pipe storage yard. I put on the ball cap with Northern Lights Pipeline across the front and I and Sadie went inside the office trailer.

"Hey missy, there ain't no animals allowed in this yard." One of the men said. I had seen him at the restaurant.

"You'll need to go put him back in your truck," said the taller of the two inspectors.

"I didn't see a sign out there that said no animals allowed. In fact, I didn't see a guard at the gate." I stayed calm wondering how long until they asked about the cap I wore with the company logo on it.

"The guard had to go into town on business. We're watching the gate until he gets back. So go on and put that mutt back in your truck," he said, leaning back in his chair.

"Whom did you say you are?" I asked.

"I'm an inspector if you need to know," he expressed in a cocky tone.

"Aren't you supposed to be inspecting that pipe they're unloading?" I asked nonchalantly.

"Missy, I can see that pipe just fine from here. You lost or are you looking for somebody?" he asked, amused now looking me up and down. The others started to laugh.

"I'm looking for the office manager. Is he here?"

"No, but I'm sure one of us can take care of you just fine," he stated grinning. There was more laughter.

I just smiled at them. "Do you know where I can find him?"

"He went into town to check the phone for any messages," replied someone in the back reading a newspaper.

"So you have no phone service out here?"

"Do you see a phone in here, missy? Are you lost or something?"

The door to the trailer opened and in walked Nick Salva.

"I thought that was your truck, Alex," he said, smiling at me before looking at the others. "I see you still have the mutt." Looking at Sadie in my arms.

"Yes, Mr. Salva I still have the mutt."

"Hey, Nick, who's your sweetie? Did you ship her up here to keep you company? Do you share?" Laughter rang out in the trailer again.

"Boys you are walking on thin ice here. I suggest you zip it," Salva said, amused. Maybe I should introduce this young lady to ya all."

"Yeah, Nick we'd like to get to know her better." The inspector leaned forward in his chair. I let Nick continue, waiting for the response when they found out who I was.

"Gentlemen, this is Alex Kendall, Vice President of Logistics. I suggest you treat her with respect if you want to work here."

There was a moment of silence. Mouths hung open and then closed. I heard a truck pull up and went out the door and down the steps.

"Are you the office manager?" It looks like another Southern boy as the man about thirty-five walked up to me.

"Yes, mam I am. What can I be helping you with?"

"I'm Alex Kendall. I think you have been expecting me," I said, reaching my hand out to him.

"Brant Hogan, please to make your acquaintance," he said sincerely.

"Mr. Hogan I'd like to talk to you alone. Please."

"Yes, mam. Come inside the trailer," he gestured." Everyone cleared out, and I got down to business.

"First of all, I want the name of the third party of the inspector that was sitting at that desk when we come in. I want him replaced today. Second I don't know why the phone is hooked up in town, but I will have you one out here next week. Third, is this your first manager's job?" I already knew the answer.

"Yes mam," he said, but he didn't drop his eyes from mine. "I guess it shows."

"That's okay Mr. Hogan. I'll be giving you guidelines, and we'll put your files in order, and make this a great experience for you, and successful, one you can add to your resume."

At five o clock, I went to town and called the third party of the inspector and made arrangements to have him replaced. After I called Mr. Oshler, and gave my report, and let him know I had talked to Terry. After dialing, Watertown to speak to Gary, the warmth was gone from his voice. However, Gary didn't bring up the incident. Giving him the information to put in the reports, the conversation ended. Coming out of the office, Nick was leaning against my truck waiting for me. Sadie growled.

"That's enough Sadie," I said walking over to stand in front of Nick.

"You took a lot of shit back there. I was surprised you stayed so calm," he said, grinning taking me in. The jeans fit nicely and my blouse wasn't tight nor loose the way it fit.

"I see you have your crew started," I said, ignoring the way his eyes traveled over my body taking inventory. "I guess you wouldn't consider giving up this job?" Knowing the answer before it flew out of Nick's mouth.

"Hell no. Why would I do that?" The grin was gone his eyes brows nearly touching, eyes cold.

"Because what you did to Ateara and Lester," I paused. "She has sworn to kill you, Nick. I don't want to see anyone else die for what you did, and that will happen if you don't step down."

"You finally called me Nick." His smile crawled slowly back over his lips.

"It won't make a difference what I call you when you're dead. You deserve everything Ateara does to you, but not the people that work for you."

"Ateara might be good at Voodoo back home. She has no power up here." He smirked.

"You're going to pay for what you did Nick. I know more than what you think. I can't prove it right now, but that will change," I said, giving him a cold stare.

Nick clasped my wrist bringing it to his lips. "Then we should take pleasure in what time is left."

I pulled back my hand and shook my head, before stepping back.

"I'd see you in hell first," I said calmly.

"You've said that before Alex. Be careful what you wish for. You'll pleasure me before I go. I'll make sure of that. I always get what I want."

"That's what you keep saying, Nick. It scared me at one time, but not anymore. Soon you'll be dead! The only thing that breaks my heart is that you won't die first. And I can't do anything about the others. Come on Sadie we have things to do." I walked around Nick and got into my truck, and drove back to the pipe storage yard not looking back in the rear view mirror.

When I arrived at the pipe storage yard, the inspector was waiting for me.

"What the fuck you think you're doing bitch? You can't have me fired," he yelled at me.

"I already have. Call your third party. I've also instructed the guard you are not allowed back in the yard after you leave," I said, and walked away from him.

"You'll pay for this, bitch. You'll pay for this."

I continued to walk away from him and went inside the trailer. Listening to him drive out the yard his tires throwing rocks and dirt as he went that hit the front of the trailer.

"Sorry about that," Brant Hogan said, as I came inside.

"Don't worry about it. Part of the job and that kind of stuff comes with it." I looked out the window and saw the men packing up their things ready to call it a day. Further, to the back of the yard I saw four men walking up and guessed they were Salva's crew. My heart ached at the thought of something happening to them. What can I do? If I say something, they'll think I'm crazy with such a wild story. If only I knew where Ateara was and could reason with her. I could see the one thing that Nick and Ateara had in common, they were both stubborn and had the tenacity of a bull dog. Once they set their mind to something they didn't turn back. Even if it was destructive to themselves, or those around them.

I was going to stop at the bar, when I saw Salva and his men walk in. *Well, so much for that. I believe there is still rum in the fifth wheel. I'll stop for a coke.*

"Is there anything that you would like Sadie? I'll ask the butcher for a bone. How does that sound?" I asked as I rubbed behind Sadie's ears. I was glad no one had claimed the black fur ball as she had claimed my heart. Giving her up now would be very hard.

The weekend was uneventful. I spent most of my time with Brant Hogan setting up files, walking the yard showing him the difference between pipe. This made it easier to understand the different reports he needed to keep up to date.

I was looking forward to Joe flying up in the morning and calling Lester. Hoping Lester was able to find the information I needed. The night was long as I tossed and turned. Thoughts of black snakes and men dying crept into my dreams turning them into nightmares.

Five a.m. came early when I hadn't been able to sleep. Stepping down from the bed I made my way to the bathroom, splashed cold water on my face. I wasn't surprised by the dark circles under my eyes and hoped I'd packed concealer. Sadie barked.

"You need to go out, I take it." It was more of a statement than a question. "Ouch." Looking down at the floor and the dirt I couldn't remember seeing last night. "Come here, Sadie." I picked the black fur ball up and looked at her feet. "Clean. Guess that didn't come from you," I said as I opened the door for her to go out.

Taking out the broom and dustpan, made quick work of sweeping up the dirt, also did a quick mop, made the bed and tidied the place up knowing Joe would be staying with me while he was here, or at least hoping. My body tingled all over thinking of the last night we'd spent together. I hadn't realized how much I had missed him, needed him.

The waitress greeted me knowing my first name and seated me at the table I requested. Sadie was tied to her spot under the window seal. Excitement for Joe arriving and the new inspector, I didn't think anything could down my mood. I was wrong when the team from the storage yard walked in along with Nick Salva and his four-man crew. The waitress pushed tables together enabling them all to sit together. Nick sat across from me. My smile was forced, but I was polite, giving a more genuine smile to the rest of the group.

Lester said it had begun. *I hope none of these men with Salva would fall victim to his curse. They were just young men looking to make some money.*

It was noon when I heard the twin-engine plane fly overhead. The landing gear lowered and the craft landing smoothly.

"I'll be back in a minute," I said as the group watched the plane taxi down the lone strip to the building at the end. I pulled up, jumping out of the truck running to where Joe was securing the wheels. There was no hesitation when he stood up, I was in his arms.

"I like this greeting." He held me tight.

"It's so good to see you." I kissed him, and his hand moved down to the small of my back.

"What's this? Why are you carrying a gun in the back of your pants?" he looked surprised. "What's going on Alex that you feel you need to carry this?" he asked as lines formed across his forehead.

"I'll tell you later. Did you see the train car of wrapped pipe from up there?" I asked, excitedly. If I started to tell Joe what I knew, my barrier would fold and I'd cry. I had to wait, hold things together a little while longer.

"Yes, I saw it. Let's go take a look and see how it's holding up." He opened the truck door and Sadie came bouncing out licking Joe on the face. "This must be Sadie?" he said, rubbing her behind the ears. "Yes, I'd say she is a mutt, but a loveable one at that." Joe laughed.

We drove into the yard and parked, and I introduced Joe to everyone there. We walked over to the first train car and looked at the wrapping around the pipe.

"Banding is doing its job, and the pipe looks good," Joe said, feeling satisfied. We started toward the second train car, when they heard someone shouting. I looked toward the end of the yard and sighted two men running. Taking out my gun, I started to run toward the men, Joe right behind me. I was horrified when I saw two snakes slithering after the men, closing the distance at incredible speed.

I stopped, and aimed shooting the first, then aimed at the second as it raised it's head closing in on it's victim. So close to the man, but I took a chance and fired. The bullet went through the man's bellowing shirt hitting the snake as it went to strike. The men continued running toward the trailer. I ran in the direction from where the men had come. I looked over at Joe, eyes wide he was trying to comprehend what was happening.

They cornered the stack of pipe, and saw two other men on the ground. A snake was wrapped around one man striking at his neck. I shot, and the snake dropped over the man's body, but it was two late to save either of them. The men's faces were distorted in terror and pain, their eyes bulging. Blood and yellow mucus oozed from their nose and mouth. I turned away as their skin turned black.

Joe bent over one body and picked up the snake holding his hand over his nose and mouth. They could hear the police siren coming from town along with the ambulance.

"I'm sure they're going to want to take a look at this. I've not seen a snake like this before," he said, turning to face me.

"I'm not surprised, Joe. At least in the United States you wouldn't."

The sheriff pulled up a few feet away from me and Joe. He stepped out of his truck, and a few moments later, the medics arrived.

"What's happened here?" I received a report of a snake attack." His jaw fell when he saw the six foot snake Joe was holding up. The sheriff returned to his truck and retrieved a burlap sack and Joe put the snake inside.

"I believe you will find two more I shot up by the second pipe stack," I said, stopping my hand from trembling. The sheriff walked back up the way I pointed, and picked up the other two snakes putting them in the bag.

When the paramedics looked at the men laying on the ground, they had the same reaction I had the first time I'd seen snake victims.

"Oh my God, I'v never seen anything like this," one said, backing away from the smell. The two medics covered their nose and mouth when they put the bodies in body bags to take to the coroner's office.

The sheriff waved the medics on, and said, "I'm going to drop these off at the vet's. Who can tell me what happned?"

"The two men that saw what happened are up in the trailer," I replied. I still held the gun in my hand, put the safety on and placed it back in the waist band of my pants. Joe and I started walking back up to the trailer. I felt nauseated and swallowed the bile, fighting the sickening feeling in my stomach.

They were laughing at breakfast, and now two of them were dead. It could have been all four. It should have been Nick, I thought. Why take innocent lives, Ateara? I have to find you," I muttered under my breath.

The story told to the sheriff was the same as what happened in the other pipe storage yard. The officer's expression was that of disbelief. He was thinking what kind of drugs they were on with such a story, however he had the dead snakes in the back of his truck. He'd never heard of snakes chasing down their victims. The yard was shut down as the the sheriff looked for other evidence, which I knew they wouldn't discover if they looked for the next hundred years.

Joe and I drove to the office in town as I had to report two more deaths to Mr. Oshler. Also, I hoped Lester had more information for me. When we arrived I saw Nick coming out of the office.

"Wait here a minute, Joe. I need to talk to Nick alone," I said, the anger spilling over me, the hatred clogging my throat.

"What!" Joe exclaimed.

"Please, Joe, trust me." My eyes searched his as I opened the door of the truck and stepped down. Walking up to Nick, my fists so tight my nails bit into my palms.

"Did you hear about your men?" I asked, trying to stay calm.

"What about them," he shrugged, his eyes taking her in.

"You have two more dead! You need to back down from this job," trying to sound stern more than pleading.

"You're still blaming me for these deaths? Men die all the time on the pipeline," his anger rising.

"Not. Like. This. Nick. It's the curse Ateara put on you for what you did. You can't deny it anymore. It's also effecting anyone around you."

"Anyone?" he said, taking hold of my arm his expression darkened.

Sadie growled and Joe stepped out of the truck when he saw Nick grab me by the arm.

"I see you brought your bodyguard. You must be worried Alex," he said smugly.

"I can take care of myself, Nick. But, your time is running out. You're going to look just like your men when they find you," I said, pulling my arm back.

"We'll see Alex, who dies first," his face red from rage as he looked at Joe and then back at me before stomping away.   "Joe, grab Sadie please, I need to make some calls and I don't want to leave her in the truck." The three of us went inside and I rang Mr. Oshler.

"Hello, Alex. I heard from Watertown this morning, and things are going well up there," Mr. Oshler said.

"I hate to burst your bubble Sir, but they are not here in Wishek. Nicke Salva just had two more men die of snake bites; the same as before."

"My gosh Alex, where are they coming from?" he asked. concern wrapped around his voice."

"We don't know. I did shoot three of the snakes this time and the police took them to the Vets. So, hopefully we'll be able to add to what information we know, and give us a clue where they're coming from."

"You shot them. Why the hell were you close enough to shoot them? Where's the sucurity up there? I'm sorry Alex, I just worry about your safety," there was silence for a few moments before he continued, "Keep me posted Alex, and be careful."

"I will, Sir," I promised. I disconnected the phone and then called Watertown and asked for Gary.

"Hello, Miss Kendall. Gary isn't here. Isn't he with you?" the Watertown secretary asked.

"I thought he would be back by now," I said irritated.

"We've not seen Gary since Friday morning," she replied.

"Really? Okay. How are things going there?"

"So far so good. Pipe is rolling in and out on schedule," the young woman stated.

"Great, I'll keep in touch, and you know how to reach me." I hung up the receiver. "Gary hasn't been back to Watertown since Friday morning," I told Joe.

"Can't say that I'm sorry. That guy rubs me wrong.

"I have one more call to make, and then I'll tell you what I've found out," I said as I rang Lester's office, and to my surprise Lester answered the phone.

"Hello Lester, it's Alex."

"Miss Alxandra, I've been waiting for you to call me. What I be finding, ain't good news and I be afraid for you," he said anxiously.

"What have you found?" I asked as worry crossed my brow. I was standing, listening to Lester before reaching for a chair to sit down. "Are you sure of all this Lester?" Sighing heavily before closing my eyes for a few moments.

"Yes, Miss Alex. He be a dependable source a lot of years. Have you seen Ateara?"

"No, Lester, but two more men were killed this morning. The same manner as the first. I know she is following him. I even tried to talk him into giving up this job. Now, I understand why he won't. It won't matter how many men die." My stomach felt cold and empty. I'd be surprised if my stomach would ever be the same again with my emotions in constant turmoil.

"Miss Alex, if he finds out you know, he'll kill you. When Joe be coming up?"

"He's here now Lester. He arrived at noon."

"That be good. You be going to the police?"

"No," my voice harsher than I intended.

"Let the police take care of this, Miss Alex," Lester pleaded.

"I can't go to the police Lester. Who's going to believe this story? We don't have any proof. I have to gather proof, evidence to back this up. Listen Lester, I'll call you if I find Ateara. Take care." I hung the phone up and looked at Joe, wondering where to start.

Joe set Sadie down and crossed his arms. "What the hell is going on Alex? Men are dying around you, we can't find Ateara, and Lester wants you to go to the police? And now you need to look for evidence, evidence of what?"

I sat down and motion Joe to do the same. When Sadie rubbed against my leg, I picked her up and sat her on my lap.

"Okay, Joe. Here's what I've found out. Gary has been on Salva's payroll from the time he started working at Oshler and Marsh Construction. He tried getting close to me after we broke up, and when that didn't work he threatened Sharon. That's why she left. He found out Matt in human resources was having financial problems, and bribed him to destroy Terry's application. That put him in line for my assistant."

Joe stood up and looked out the window. "I never liked that guy. And now you don't know where he is?"

"Not at the moment," I said, rubbing my fingers behind Sadie's ears.

"What else did Lester tell you?"

"With Gary as my assistant, that would put in access of the bids, and securing Salva the contract for yard cleanup. However, neither new of my close relationship with Lester (Kierbow Construction) and Ateara until the banquet. Salva had to change his tactic, and when Gary learned I was bringing Terry up here instead of him," I paused, choking back tears. That's when they arranged the accident Terry was in. Gary had to be out in the field with me. He'd be helping close down the yards. There is millions of dollars of equipment in the field, and they were going to have it disappear as the job was ending. They already have a buyer."

"Wait a minute, just wait a minute," Joe said, pacing in front of the window. "You mean this started two years ago?"

"Yes. The only hitch was Lester. Nick, I believe, didn't realize Lester wouldn't sell him the patent. That's when he was desperate to break him."

"Then Nick had no idea that Ateara would react the way she did," Joe added.

"That's right. Nick has wanted Ateara since high school. That night she walked into Nick's home to plead for her dad, the only thing Nick was thinking with was his cock. He had no idea he was signing his own death warrant in blood," I said standing up and picked up my purse. "That has added pressure on Nick."

Opening the door, "we need to go to the police." Joe said, taking my hand he gave it a squeeze.

"With what Joe? Theory, conjunctures, we have no proof. That's why we can't go to the sheriff. We have to do it ourshelves," I said, closing the door.

"We can get killed, you realize that don't you?"

"We could. However, Nick didn't realize how much power Ateara really had until his men were killed. I think he will have his mind on her."

"And Gary?"

"We'll have to keep an eye out for Gary until we find out what he's up to."

"Where do we start?"

"The vets."

"The vets?" he asked, giving me a curious look.

"We need to find out if we can get a serum to counter act the venom from that snake."

"Makes sense, Alex, but why would we need an antidote? From what I saw, you wouldn't have time to save anyone as fast as that venom works."

"No, Joe, we need it for us. Lester said we are as vulnerable as Nick's worker's."

"This is crazy Alex! You best keep your gun handy. What about Sadie? I could see from Nick's expression, she's not on his happy list," he laughed, and shook his head. "I think we could use some voodoo of our own right now. Where's this vet? He should have had time to examine the snake and at least found out it's orgin."

"On the outksirts of town. We passed it coming in.

&&&&&

Joe and I walked into the small white building.. a buzzard sounded. The inside was neat and clean and it looked to be empty.

"Be with you in just a minute," someone yelled from the back. A few minutes later a man in his late twenties came into the office area. "Can I help you?" he asked, looking around for an injured animal.

"We were looking for the Vet." I said, looking at the blonde, curly headed guy.

"You found him," he said grinning. "Neil Hawks. What can I help you with?" He knelt down and rubbed Sadie behind her ears.

"I'm Alex Kendall. I'm over the pipe storage yard. The sheriff was bringing three snakes in for you to examine. Have you had time to look at them yet?"

"Yeah, I have. Those are some big Mumbos. I can't imagine anyone having them as pets as deadly as they are. In fact, you don't find them in the United States, and we are in troulbe if they're breeding," he answered me.

"I've heard and saw that they're deadly," I replied.

"It's a Black Mumbo. You find them in Africa. They're called that because of the black color inside their mouths. You've seen what they can do. I have a friend that specializes in reptiles that I called a while ago. He's going to get back to me in a couple of hours, if you want to call or come back around five; I'll have more information. Right now I need to go help deliver a calf just up the way," he said, opening the door for them and following them out.

"Thank you. We'll see you in a couple of hours."

"Let's get something to eat while we're waiting. All this intrigue has made me hungry," Joe stated, pulling me close giving me a quick kiss before getting out of the truck.

Entering the restaurant, we saw the sheriff sitting at a table with local residents. The waitress nodded her head, and then walked us to a table in the back. It was only a few minutes before the sheriff rose, and walked to where we were sitting.

"May I sit down?" he asked, placing his hat on the empty table behind him.

"Of course," Joe gestured.

"I've heard this isn't the first killing like this," he said solemnly.

"No, it's not," I said. "The first one was in Aberdeen last week. He was reported bitten, but there was never a trace of a snake found. However, the body looked the same as the men today," I paused, while Joe ordered us something to eat.

"We didn't have a clue then or now where the snakes came from." I laid my hand over Joe's, giving me comfort with his presence.

"Could they have come in on the pipe?" the sheriff asked.

I thought, *if he only knew.*

"No. I don't believe so. That pipe is coming from my plant in Texas, and its made there. I don't import any raw material from Africa."Joe said in a steady low pitched voice.

"How do you know the snakes are from Africa?" the sheriff's face tightened looking from Joe to me.

"We stopped by the vet, Neil Hawks, I believe that's the name he gave us. He told us," Joe answered.

"I see. This is a small town and news travels fast. People are scared. The boss of that crew didn't stay around long, did he? Thanks, May," the sheriff said as the waitress set his coffee in front of him.

"What do you mean he left?" I asked, sitting up straighter in the booth. *But I could see Nick doing something like that, as he only looked out for one person, himself.*

"He told the two workers on the crew they would be on their own, and he would be in touch with them in a couple of weeks. Said they could pick up their checks each week at the post office general delivery. No respect for his people or their families. Even asked the office manager at the yard to telegraph the men's family. The other man was from here in town. He said he had to be up in Williston," the sheriff said, his words brass and his eyes cold looking at me and Joe.

"Sheriff, I'm as concerned, if not more than you. I can't have a panic on the line. We have deadlines to meet. However, I don't want anyone else killed either, so the faster we can get to the bottom of this the better. I just don't know where to start," I stated. *I did but I couldn't explain to him I had to find a black girl who had put a voodoo curse on Nick Salva. And finding Ateara right now was like finding a needle in a haystack.*

"I was told you were the one who shot the snakes, Miss Kendall."

"Please, call me Alex, and yes I was the one who killed them."

That was good shooting, if what they told me was true. One of the men showed me where the bullet went through the side of his shirt and killed the snake that was almost upon him. The young man said, if he'd had a choice he'd rather have taken your bullet than the bite from the snake. I saw where your bullet hit each snake, you're quite the marksman," he smiled stiffly. "How long have you been using a gun?"

"I've been shooting a gun since I was able to hold one properly. My dad is an avid hunter, and I've had my permit to carry for about fifteen years."

"I saw that," he said standing. Most farmers carry a rifle in their trucks up here, but I don't know of any that carry a gun in the back of their pants," he said, his smile softening. "You did save two young men today, so I guess it doesn't matter where you carry it. Enjoy your dinner."

&&&&&

It was fifteen after five when we returned back to the vet's office. I was eager to find out more about the snake, but especially if there was an antidote. We needed it before we left for Williston. Hopefully, the crew at Dickson wouldn't come to any harm, if Nick went straight to Williston. I could hope. Doing my job in pursuit of Nick, I might stumble onto whoever else Nick had hired on the line. I was thankful Joe was with me, as it gave me courage. I'd be more careful than if I were alone.

The vet was coming out of his office when we arrived. He was carrying a bag over his shoulder.

"Hi," he said, setting the bag on the back of his truck.

"Did you receive your call?" I asked, walking over to him.

"Sure did. My friend was in awe as much as I am, about how those snakes got up here, or even in this country. Getting an antidote for the venom is hard to come by, and as you know, the poison is swift to kill." He kicked a rock in front of him, and his hands fisted.

"I was going to try a get a sample of the venom to ship to my friend to analyze, but someone is playing a deadly game. If they were pets, but I doubt it from what my friend tells me, someone has a sick sense of humor."

I looked over at Joe, "Why, what's happened?"

"I told you I went back to get the venom samples. I didn't see any forced entry, but the snakes were gone and in their place was three pieces of banding. The banding I've seen come in on the train cars in your yard. I'm taking them to the sheriff. Maybe he can get fingerprints or something from the banding. Sorry, I couldn't be more help," he said, getting in his truck.

I felt empty, my only hope gone to save me and Joe if we were bitten. That meant they had to find Ateara. She had to be following Nick, which would mean she must be close enough to watch his movement. A black woman couldn't be that hard to find up in this country. I was missing something. If Ateara were close enough to watch Nick, she'd be close enough to see Joe and I. I had to think of a way to get Ateara to contact us, but how? A headache was growing more painful in the back of my head. I needed to relax, knowing it was the stress building, and I was losing my focus on what needed to be done.

"Are you okay," Joe asked, kneading the back of my neck.

"Just stress. I need to unwind so I can think. Ateara has to be close, Joe. I just know it," I sighed heavily and moaned under the pressure of Joe's massaging hands.

We turned into the pipe storage yard as Brant Hogan was getting in his truck. He stepped down and waited for my truck to come to a stop. Joe and I met him in the shade of the trailer. Brant was the first to speak.

"Some day we've had, huh?"

"Yeah. How are things with the crew?" I asked, looking over the yard.

"They're still shaking. Afraid to walk out in the yard, and I can't say that I blame them. Do you?"

"No, but I don't think they'll have to worry about another attack. There hasn't been another one in Aberdeen."

"Who'd be crazy enough to bring a snake like that on a pipeline job? I've heard of some weird pets, but nothing that was deadly to humans."

"Brant, how you feeling about the office and the yard?" I asked, changing the subject. "Do you think you have a handle on it now?"

"Yeah, I'm feeling okay, now that you helped me with some things. The waters aren't as muddy."

"Good. We're leaving in the morning for Dickinson. I haven't heard how the office manager is doing up there, have you?" It would be good to have some knowledge of what I was walking into.

"Miss Kendall, in the manager's class I attended, all the managers I talked to said this would be their first manager's job in the field. So I'll leave it at that," Brant laughed. "Drive carefully and keep in touch as I'm not invincible yet."

We waved goodbye and drove back to the fifth wheeler.

CHAPTER 16

"Alex, why don't you go take a hot shower, and after I'll give you a massage. That will help loosen up those muscles in your back that are strung tighter than a fiddle."

"That does sound nice. There's coke in the fridge and Rum in the cupboard, that should also help."

I stepped out of the bathroom wearing only a towel. Joe handed me a glass which I took a large swallow. The liquid warming my stomach. Taking another swallow, I was feeling more relaxed.

"Lay down here."

I let the towel drop and laid down on my stomach across the bed. I felt Joe's hands move up and down my spine, a little extra pressure with his thumbs around my shoulder area. I moaned softly. His hands maneuvered down my sides, fingertips brushing my breast. My mind slipped into nothingness taking pleasure from his hands on my body. Joe slid one hand between my thighs. Gentle lips brushed against my ear and worked down.

My breathing escalated as he worked my body. Time seemed to stand still as our love making continued into the late night hours.

&&&&&

We left Wishek for Dickinson early the next morning, deciding to have breakfast on the road. A couple of hours later we pulled into a truck stop outside of Bismark to gas up and eat.

"Joe, don't turn around, but the guy that just walked in and sat at the other end of the counter, is the inspector I fired last week. He followed us from Wishek. His truck is parked in between two big rigs."

"He's probably on the way to another job."

"I don't think so, Joe. Guess we'll find out when we move out."

Forty-five minutes later we were back on the road. We had traveled about hundred miles when I spotted the truck behind us. It was the inspector's vehicle, I recognized the lights across the front of the cab when the sun reflected off the chrome. Nothing I could do now but wait and see.

"Joe, I'm glad you changed your mind about not making love to me until after we were married."

"I was going to be firm with that decision Alex, after you left the ranch. I decided if you didn't love me more than your job, I needed to move on. I want a family Alex, and I'm not getting any younger."

"Then why last night?"

"The way I see it, we may not get out of this alive. You do realize that don't you? If we're going to die, I'd rather do it with you than without you. And right now, I wouldn't put any money on our chances coming out of this is one piece. Especially when Nick finds out what we know."

"I think Ateara will kill Nick before he finds out what we know," I said, gliding my fingers through his hair.

"I don't know, Alex. I just don't know."

We passed the sign for Dickinson twenty miles back. Brant had told me about a place to park the fifth wheeler that was just outside of Dickinson. A farmer had taken a small portion of land and turned it into a camp with all the hook ups. *One farmer was a visionary*, I thought. *Free enterprise, in more ways than one.*

Joe spotted the turn off to the camp and slowed making the turn off the highway onto the dirt road.

"This is nice, at least there are trees," I said as Joe turned in to park in front of the office. Sadie enjoyed the time to run around while I took care of the formalities. Half an hour later we were on the way to the Dickinson pipe storage yard.

&&&&&

Pulling into the Dickinson Pipe storage yard, we were greeted by the security guard.

That's a plus, I thought, and grinned at Joe. "They are ahead of the other yards. Perhaps the word had been passed along helping the other managers get a better hold on what was expected of them."

"You didn't think they've been talking back in forth, Alex? After what has happened, I bet they know all the way to the Canadian border. I bet you dinner that you'll find things more in order here than the other two yards."

Once through the gate, Joe parked in front of the office trailer. Getting out I noticed the inspectors were carrying four-foot sticks, and looking to the far end of the yard, someone was standing by the banding pile with a shotgun.

"You're right. The news has reached here, Joe." *What was I thinking?* I paused, looking at the organized yard. "This is a pipeline, and news spreads as fast as the gas will in the line. Hope everything else is in order."

Before I stepped up on the cinder-blocks to the trailer, the door swung open, and a burly gentleman stood in the doorway.

"Come in Miss Kendall. We've been expecting you." His voice the deep and his smile broad. "I'm Jeremy Clackson." He stood to the side so we could enter. "Brant called, and said you were on your way up here."

Joe gave me a wink. *He'd been right about them talking to each other. I knew from past experience, how fast things travel on the line. Too much on my mind, not good.*

"Glad to meet you Mr. Clackson. This is Joe Larkin. The pipe coming into the yard is manufactured at Joe's plant."

"Happy to make your acquaintance Mr. Larkin." Shaking Joe's hand before he introduced us to the others in the trailer.

"How are the crews doing?" I asked, sitting on the corner of a nearby desk.

"They're nervous, but we're taking precautions. Nick Salva has one of his own men standing guard with a shotgun. I guess the killings have only happened to his crews. He had to pay them extra to even get them to hire on." Jeremy pushed a chair over to Joe before he sat down at his desk. "Everything so far is on schedule. Brant and I were in the same class in Nebraska, so he's been calling and helping me set up the filling system the way you like Miss Kendall."

"He's a good man, Brant. I'm sure then you are doing a great job. We're going to inspect a couple of the train cars. Nice meeting all of you," I said, before walking out of the trailer with Sadie and Joe behind me.

We walked along the rail tracks a few hundred feet before reaching the first rail car.

"Remember that truck I suspected was following us?" I reached up as if I was checking the banding, "in a minute, look past the last rail car at the truck parked off the road."

Joe climbed up on the rail car and inspected the coating on the forty-two-inch pipe in several places along its length.

"I believe you're right, Alex. He's not a professional spy, however, that will make it easier to keep track of him. You're thinking that Nick hired him to keep tabs on you?" he asked, getting down from the car. He put his arm around my shoulders and we continued down the line until Joe had checked nine train cars. Sadie growled and moved closer to me.

"We meet again, Alex, Joe," Nick said, his eyes dancing with amusement.

"You think that shotgun will save your men, Nick?"

Nick looked at the man cradling the rifle. "Probably not, but it does give them comfort."

"Give it up Nick." I had to keep asking, my thoughts on those that had died. "If anymore of your men die working on this line, I'll come after you myself Nick, and I'll be more prepared than Ateara was." My anger getting the best of me.

Joe squeezed my hand attempting to calm me.

"Ah, Alex," Nick's smiled widened as he looked me over ignoring Joe, "I would kill one myself if I thought that would bring you to me."

I stepped forward to strike Nick, and Joe grabbed my arm.

"You touch her Nick, and it will be the last woman you'll ever touch," Joe said confidently. "I know you're tough at killing dogs and raping women, and if I could prove it, I'd take you in myself," the anger flowing off Joe in waves.

Nick just stood grinning at Joe, and I picked up Sadie.

"But, that's the catch isn't it Joe, finding the proof? All you have is a story from an old man and some crazed woman. Stick to making your pipe and stay out of other people's business. People get killed on pipelines, and not just by snakes. Some even get buried," Nick glared at both of us as if we were pebbles he could kick out of his way.

Sadie growled.

"That goes for dogs, too," and then Nick walked away.

"I have more on you than that, Nick," outrage flowed from my lips.

Nick stopped for an instant, and then hastened back toward the trailer.

"Alex," Joe scolded, yanking me back, "what the hell were you thinking?"

"I'm sorry Joe. He just makes me so angry, and it comes out out of my mouth before I think of the consequences," I said again.

"You best hope to hell he doesn't make anything out of that. Our lives are already dangling by a thread having contact with him. Come on, let's go look at the rest of the cars, and you can walk off some of that steam." Holding my hand, we preceded down the line, Sadie trotting ahead of us.

When we the reached the last car, the truck that had been following us was gone. I was sure he was working for Nick. Walking over to the banding pile, I said hello to the workers. They were all in their twenties.

I smiled at the guard, "you expecting trouble?"

"Mam, I hope not," he said, grinning back. "You've heard the rumors. Boss is just taking precautions to protect the workers."

"Have you worked for Mr. Salva long?"

"Just a year, mam. I was working for him on the docks back home." His smile grew wider. "Mr. Salva said, it was time for me to step up to bigger things, so he brought me up here to help out."

"Be careful what you're shooting at," I said, walking away, a sickening feeling crept into my stomach. *I don't get it why his people are loyal to him.*

"You okay, Alex?" Joe asked, turning me to look at him.

"Yes." I let out a heavy sigh. "How do nice people get involved with scum like Nick?"

"Nicks always had a way with people. He makes them feel good about themselves, and receives their loyalty before using them. Ateara was the only woman I know that never fell under his spell that way. I think because she grew up with him in the same town and went to the same school, she knew him well. She has watched him use people and disguard them."

&&&&&

We took a ride up the line and watched the pipe unloaded from the stringing trucks, placed on skids where they would be butted together, welded, and x-rayed. It was around five o'clock when we stopped back at the yard. I went inside the office.

"Is anyone hungry? I'm buying." I looked at Jeremy and asked, "where is is the best place in town to eat?"

Jeremy smiled. "Follow me," giving me a wink.

We arrived at a place called Zippy's Bar and Grill. The four that had accepted my offer were two veterans to pipe-lining. We talked about prior jobs, a few that my company had contracted. The pros and cons of being a gypsy moving from one line to another. But all agreed on one thing, they liked the money. Eventually, the conversation turned to the killings. No one had heard the likes of it. They asked me what I knew, and what was being done about it.

If only I could tell them the truth, I thought, *but then again who would believe me.* I told them what I could, and that was sufficient for the time being.

"We heard you saved two lives down in Wiskek with some fancy shooting Miss Kendall," Jeremy commented.

"I don't know how fancy Jeremy, but there are two young men alive that would have died."

I couldn't rid myself of the anxiety that crept over my body. The feeling that someone would die tonight. I had never felt so utterly helpless. Thinking of the four young men that were working on Salva's crew, and Salva's man thinking he could make a difference with the shotgun. Maybe he could if he wasn't close and fear didn't make him panic or hesitate. I knew there was nothing that could stop the supernatural. Seeing spells that Ateara had done, I'd made the choice to stay away from voodoo. If there was something out there, I couldn't stop it until I found Ateara. What was I thinking, we couldn't talk her out of vengeance before we left Louisiana, why believe I could now?

It was dusk when we arrived back at the fifth wheeler. Some of the pipe-liners were just getting back in from the lines. I let Sadie out to run, and we pulled out the camp chairs to enjoy conversations with the new arrivals.

"We have our tail back on watch, and there is someone riding shotgun. Did you see them?" Joe asked, handing me a bottled water.

"Up the dirt road quarter mile back, I saw them." Taking the water, I took a long swallow. "At least we know where they are. If they come snooping around, Sadie will let us know. Won't you girl?" I ruffled the dog's ears lovingly.

It was ten-thirty when the last of our company left, and we decided to turn in. I was exhausted, and sleep came shortly after laying my head on the pillow. I sensed Joe lay listening for intruders but soon drifted off as well.

I awoke first as dawn was breaking. After taking a shower, and dressing, I made coffee.

"Ouch," I squawked, walking on the dirt near the sink. Backing up to take a better look. *paw prints*, I thought. Looking up on the bed, Sadie lay watching me.

"Come here, you little stinker." Puting my arms out, Sadie jumped off the bed and into my waiting arms. "Are these your paw prints? Let me look at your paws." Sadie's paws were clean and before putting her down, she licked my cheek.

"I smell the coffee." Joe stretched and raised up on his elbow. "Can I have it in bed or do I have to get up, and dress?"

I loved the way Joe looked in the morning. His walnut colored hair going in many directions, and waking up next to him gave me second thoughts on staying single.

"You want this, huh?" I smiled pouring the cup of coffee. "And I get what in return?" I was feeling full mischief. After putting Sadie down, I took him the cup.

"I'm sure I can think of something that would satisfy you," he said, putting one of my fingers in his mouth his eyes never leaving mine. "Maybe I'll drink this later."

"No, drink it now. I'm already dressed, and I really don't want a quickie." My sex clenched with the thoughts of him in me, but, they still had to meet the guys for breakfast, and they had miles of line to check. "By the way, did you let Sadie out after I went to sleep?" I asked before giving him a kiss.

"You sure you want to wait until later?" He rubbed my nipple through the thin blouse and watched me as my eyes closed before taking a step back, not wanting to. "Okay, later. No, I didn't. She didn't act like she wanted to go out. Why?" he asked, flipping the covers back to get out of bed.

I started to answer and then there was a knock at the door. "Best get your pants on." I teased, throwing them at him. Opening the door, the Dickinson Sheriff was standing there. My chest tightened, choking off my breath as I looked at the expression on his face.

"Mam, can you step outside, I'd like to ask you some questions?" His expression steeled his features.

"Sure let me get my boots on, and I'll be right out," I replied. I gave Joe a look as he hurried to dress. Putting on socks and boots I stepped outside with Sadie and Joe behind me.

"You are Alex Kendall?" His voice stern, but his posture somewhat relaxed.

"Yes, I am sheriff. Is there a problem?"

"And you are sir?"

"Joe Larkin. What's going on sheriff?"

"Miss Kendall, Mr. Larkin I have two murders that took place last night. Can you tell me where you were around two a.m. this morning?"

"We were right here. We haven't left since we came back from dinner last night. You can ask anyone here," Joe answered briskly.

"Who's been murdered?" I asked, picking up Sadie.

"Do you both know Nick Salva?"

"Yes. Mr. Salva is one of the contractors on the pipeline," I replied. *It finally happened,* I thought. *Ateara has killed him.*

"I was told you had an argument with him yesterday," the sheriff scoffed never taking his eyes off Me.

"We had a disagreement. Has something happened to Mr. Salva?"

"No mam. But, we did find the bodies of two of his men just up the road a bit in a tan truck. I was also told you fired one of his men down at the Wishek pipe storage yard, and that was one of the guys murdered. It seems Mam, that his men have been mysterious killed when you show up at each yard facility."

"The man I fired was an inspector on the yard and was not working for Mr. Salva at the time. I didn't know that he'd hired the inspector after he left the yard. I have no say who Nick Salva hires or fires, sheriff."

Joe's jaw tightened. "Are you saying you think Alex had something to do with these killings?"

"I'm just saying that it's strange that each pipe storage yard she has visited his men have ended up dead. Also, we've been told that there is a lot of hostility between you and Mr. Salva."

Joe's angry grew and I put a hand on his arm to calm him.

"Sheriff, how did these men die?" I asked, keeping my voice steady.

"Snake bites, and from my information the same as the others."

"You think I'm carrying around deadly snakes in my trailer? Would you like to search it?" I stood straighter my confidence back. I wondered if Nick had bought off the sheriff.

"Sheriff, I want to get to the bottom of this as much as you do. I don't want a panic on this pipeline, I have a schedule to keep. Besides, Killing Nick Salva's men is not on my agenda," I said, the anger starting to bubble up.

Most people in the camp were awake and had gathered around listening to the conversation. Two killings had spread fast.

"Did any of you hear anyone leave here in the early morning hours?" the sheriff gave a questioning look at those who had gathered.

"No, I didn't," were most of the responses.

"I don't know about leaving, but, I thought I saw someone go back in around three, when I went to the bathroom. But, I could be wrong as I didn't have my glasses on to tell for sure," said an old-timer.

"Did you find any snakes or signs of snakes when you found them?" Joe asked, putting his arm around my waist.

"No, Sir, all we found were a couple pieces of that banding."

A rugged looking pipe-liner spoke up, "Did you find any footprints around the truck?"

"Yes. We found three sets. Two we believe to be the victims, and a smaller set of a child or woman."

A truck drove up. It was one of the line foreman.

"You men on a holiday or are you wanting to make some money today?" he asked, getting out of his truck. "If you're planning on having breakfast and out on the line in an hour, you best be hauling ass, or looking for another job." The group scattered.

"Morning, Miss Kendall, Joe, Sheriff. Anything I can help you with?"

"Good morning Jake," I replied. "No were fine. How are things out on the line?"

"We're still on schedule. Heard we might have some rain tomorrow night, which might put a damper on things. I'll talk to you later." Jake retreated back to his truck and drove away.

"Sheriff, is there anything else I can help you with?"

"No, Miss Kendall. Not right now." The sheriff tipped his hat and backed away.

Joe, Sadie and I went back into the trailer where I paced in the small area.

"I can't believe they would think I had something to do with these killings. Ateara has to be close. They weren't the men on the cleanup crew, thank God. But, both men worked for Salva. It just wasn't in the yard this time. Ateara had to know they were watching us, Joe."

"Do you want some coffee," he asked. "It's still hot." He poured another cup for himself and looked over at me, I nodded, and gave him my cup.

"I bet you a dollar to donuts that Nick isn't even around here now." I slid over so Joe could sit down.

"Probably not."

"Joe, I'm going to ask his crew to lunch. You can find out valuable information from people when they're in a relaxed atmosphere." I sipped the hot coffee pressing my thigh tightly against his.

"I believe you're right, Alex. At least it's a place to start. I don't like the feeling you're a target, and that's just how I'm feeling right now. Someone had to talk to the sheriff to cast suspicion on you."

We both sat for a few minutes in our own thoughts, me rolling the cup between my palms.

Joe broke the silence. "Maybe it was Nick. He's good at that. Thinking if he kept you away you couldn't call Ateara, and that would slow her finding him. When she realizes he's not going to give this job up, she won't mess with his workers anymore. She'll go straight for Nick. That's why you won't find him here or Williston either, I bet."

Joe sipped his coffee laying his hand on my thigh. He was concentrating so hard, I doubted if he even realized it. That one motion set electricity rolling through me and gathered in my lower stomach. *Stop it*, I scolded. *We have more important things to do right now.*

"If this plan of Nick's has already been in the works for some time, Alex, Nick would have a base camp off the pipeline. He'd have to. Somewhere he could coordinate the operation after the lines were finished."

&&&&&

It was early afternoon when Joe and I drove into the pipe storage yard. Jeremy came out to meet us.

"Guess you heard about those two guys of Salva's?" Jeremy asked, his hands on the lowered window.

"Yes, Jeremy. Early this morning we had a visit from the sheriff." I admitted with a heavy sigh. "He was here I take it?"

"Yep. I think he came out here after he talked to you it sounds."

"You haven't seen Nick Salva have you?" Joe asked, turning off the truck.

"Not since he left yesterday, and I haven't heard from him today, nor anyone else that I know of. You'd think he would be more concerned about the people that work for him. Here comes his crew now." Jeremy stepped away from the truck.

"Hi, guys. Sorry to hear about your friend," I paused a minute waiting for a response. None came. "You on your way to lunch?"

"Yeah, after the sheriff left we were behind," said the young man carrying the shotgun.

"How would you like to go to lunch with me?"

"Sure," they responded.

"Jump in the back," I smiled over at Joe, and he turned the truck back on."

"Wait, I need to put my gun in the trailer. Don't want to take that with us.

Sitting at the round table at the Pizza House, and after they ordered, the conversation was not about the pipeline. However, it wasn't long before one of them brought up the name of the dead guard. I was hoping one of them would know him, making it easier to ask a question. And I was right.

"Did you know him very long?" I asked, twirling the straw in my coke.

"Only about two weeks," one of them answered as his eyes grew large when the big pizza sheet was set in the middle of the table. "He was going to take us to Mr. Salva's cabin in the Bad Lands one weekend to party. Said he had an in with Mr. Salva and he wouldn't care if we went up."

"Yeah, it's hard to party up here as the sheriff keeps an eye on us in Dickinson. If not him, the deputies," the red-head said.

"They walk through the bars at night to see who's in there," the youngest one commented, before taking a large bite of pizza.

"Would have been fun to have a place to go. Have you ever been to the Bad Lands?" I asked.

"No, I haven't. That's why we had to wait for Jimbo to take us," another one said.

"Beautiful country up there, you could get lost without a guide," said Joe.

"That's what we've heard. I doubt now Mr. Salva would let us go up without Jimbo. Jimbo said we would have a real good time cause it's out of the way so we wouldn't have to worry about the cops. Said we could go swimming in the dam. No hopes of doing that now," they all agreed.

"It's probably by the Williston pipe storage yard," I suggested.

"No Mam, I think Jimbo said it was about twenty miles out of Williston, close to a place called Alexander, I think that was it," another man answered.

"Well, if you guys do a good job for Mr. Salva, he might still take you up there himself," Joe stated. Knowing full well it would be a cold day in hell. If it didn't gain Nick something, you were like an ant squashed or killed. Nick had no regard for life if it wasn't his own.

They finished eating, and after went right back to the yard.

"I wish we had another guard," said the youngest of the group.

"I think you'll be alright. I haven't heard of a second attack at any of the yards," I assured them.

"Thanks for lunch." They walked back down to the banding pile.

"You were right, Joe. Nick has a place that's out of the way. In the Bad Lands, it could be anywhere. You could easily find a place to hide out up there." I shrugged my shoulders letting out a heavy sigh.

"We have a couple of clues," Joe said, lifting my chin and gazing into those green eyes he could so easily get lost in.

"Leland Dam!" I exclaimed. "That's up by Alexander, and the dam has a lot of shoreline."

"I think Nick would go in far enough to stay out of prying eyes, but not too far if he had to get away in a hurry," Joe stated.

"At least we have a direction. I need to talk to Jeremy, and make some calls," I said, heading over to the trailer.

"I need to call the plant, also." He followed me into the trailer Sadie on his heels.

I went to the back desk that was unoccupied and sat down. Joe used the phone in the front. Dialing, I tapped my fingers on the desk waiting for someone to answer.

"Dave Oshler."

"Hi, this is Alex."

"Alex, what going on up there? Gary called me and told me about two more deaths. That makes five in all, and he said the sheriff has you on the list of suspects. Told me you'd been arguing with Nick Salva and requested he back out of his contract. Is it true that only his men have been killed?" he took a breath finally, giving me a chance to respond.

"Gary told you this? When did you talk to him?"

"Around ten this morning. Gary said he had not been able to reach you. I was worried they'd put you in jail the way he talked. So what's the story, Alex."

"Yes, we had two more deaths, and they were Salva's men. They died of snake bites, also. We have no idea where the snakes are coming from. We've actually seen three, and the ones I managed to kill, disappeared from the vets' clinic."

"How do snakes disappear?"

"I don't know sir, that's just what's happened."

"And what's this about you being a suspect?" he continued.

"The sheriff did come out and talk to me early this morning, and asked Joe and I a few questions. I didn't have anything new to tell him, other than I was as concerned as he was. Getting to the bottom of these killings was a priority with any information I could gather on the pipeline."

"Alex, I know there is tension between you and Salva. Has he threatened you in any way, and do I need to take action from here?"

My teethed bit into my bottom lip, if only I could say yes, how many lives could I save. But what proof did I have that could revoke Nick's contract, none. Who would believe such a wild story? If I hadn't seen it myself, I wouldn't believe it. No one heard the conversation between me and Salva other than Joe. Gary had to have talked to Salva to know I'd asked him to give up this job.

"No, Salva has not threatened me. Did Gary say where he was when he called you?"

"He said he was in Watertown. Isn't that where you told him to coordinate all the records?"

"Yes. I guess we've just missed each other. I'll try again in a while."

"Alex, try and stay away from Nick Salva. I don't need something happening to you. I'm glad Joe is with you, how long is he staying?"

"I'm not sure, sir. I'll keep in touch."

I looked over at Joe and he was still on the phone. It was a good time to call Gary. I wanted to wring his neck, and to think I'd been attracted to him. Gary had played me all along. I wonder now if it had been Gary who had switched the security wires on my home alarm. The more I think about it, the madder I got. Second thought, I'd better wait a while to call him when my anger has simmered. I need to act like nothing is wrong.

It would depend on what Nick had told him to do next. If Nick lost Gary off the line, it would put a damper on his plans. If Nick were dead, hopefully, his plans would die with him. I sat back in the chair and closed my eyes. What had Mr. Oshler asked, how do snakes disappear? How do snakes disappear? Three were killed in the yards, two in the truck and what did the sheriff say was in the truck with them? Banding. That's it!

"Joe, I know what it is," I exclaimed.

Joe hung up the receiver, stood up and walked over to me. "What do you know?" he looked at me as his brows knitted together.

"Ateara put a curse on the banding! It's the banding that's turning into snakes! That's why when we went back to retrieve the poison, the snake was gone and only the banding was there. When I shot it, it took longer to tranform, and the police couldn't find any sign of a snake in Wishek."

"You could be right, Alex."

"Joe it makes sense. Remember the sheriff said there were three set of footprints around the truck. The two men and a woman's or a child's. Joe, it was Ateara who put the banding in the truck with the two men."

"That means Ateara is close. That means she is following you to get to Nick. But that doesn't make sense. She's had plenty of opportunities to kill Nick, Alex. You've talked to him, been around him. I don't get it." Joe sat down on the edge of the desk, his arms crossed over his chest.

"Remember Lester said, she would try to get him to give up the contract first. Ateara doesn't know he can't give it up with what he has in the works. He doesn't care how many die, when it comes to the money they'll make stealing from the pipeline."

"Maybe she does Alex. Look at the first three, they were new hires. The last two from last night were in a closer circle with Nick. I think she's closing in, making him sweat. I don't think Nick has ever known fear, but I believe he is starting to wear it now, and he doesn't like the fit."

Jeremy came back inside the trailer and sat down at his desk, glancing at me before he spoke.

"The sheriff is hot to trot, and he's not one to let something pass without getting to the bottom of it. I think he has interrogated every pipe-liner in Dickinson from what I've heard. I don't know what has his feathers ruffled, but he's trying awfully hard to find something on you Alex, from what they're saying."

"Really, just me?"

"He's been back to your fifth wheel twice snooping around."

"I wonder what the sheriff thinks he will find? I don't know anything more than anyone else, Jeremy. We are going back out on the line. Joe wants to check the coating on the pipe. Here's my handle if you need to reach me," I said, handing him her card.

He looked at her and smiled.

"I know, you thought it would be more feminine. I hear it all the time," my laughter filled the trailer.

&&&&&

The truck rolled along the temporary road along the pipeline both of us mulling over the conversation we had in the trailer. Or I assumed that was what Joe was thinking about.

"We have to find Nick before we go to the Williston pipe storage yard. I don't want to show up there and have someone else get killed."

"If that happened you would know that Nick was in the vicinity."

"That's true, and I killed two of the snakes. I can't understand how the blame has been put on my shoulders." I looked down as Sadie licked my hand.

"Let's see I might have a treat in the glove box for you Sadie." Opening the glove box, I pulled out a dog treat which Sadie happily took.

"Alex, perhaps Nick has padded the sheriff's pockets to keep the limelight on you. After your comments in Wishek, he may believe now you know more about what's going on besides killing Lester's dog, and raping Ateara in Louisiana. If so, you are more of a threat than Ateara since he cares nothing for the lives lost on his crews. I also think at this point we have more to worry about than snakes," Joe took my hand and gave it a light squeeze before bringing it to his lips.

"I'll have to say Ateara is doing a damn good job of disguise because I haven't seen anyone that resembles a small black girl. What is she capable of?"

"I don't know Joe, and Listening to what Lester has learned, Nick has ties with the Mofia. Damn Ateara and damn Nick for what he did to her," I started to cry, and then choked back the tears. "I try to find a happy ending to all of this, and I can't find one. I think Ateara knew there would be no turning back once things were set in motion. Poor Lester, he doesn't deserve this either," I sobbed again, hugging Sadie close. "Roxy was gone and now Ateara, it isn't fair."

Joe watching tears run down Alex's cheeks reminded him just how vulnerable she was under the tough exterior she showed to the world. He did know if he found Nick before Ateara, she could have what was left of him.

The men started moving off the line for the day, so they turned and headed back to the camp site. Joe had looked at most of the pipe laid out and was satisfied how well the coating was holding up. He was feeling the stress himself, and overall, Alex was handling the stress of the job, Nick, and Ateara. Maybe the pressure helped keep the smell of death away, not knowing how close it really could be.

When they reached the campsite, a few had arrived before them and had the barbecues out and fired up. They waved Joe and I to come down, so instead of parking in our usual parking spot we drove down to the gathering.

"I'm going to grab the lawn chairs and a coke. Would you like one, Joe?" I asked before walking away.

"No, but if there is a beer I'd like that."

Sadie and I were close to the fifth-wheeler when Sadie started biting and pulling on my pant leg.

"Sadie, stop it. I see you want to play. Come here you little stinker," I yelled, chasing after her. "That's far enough Sadie, come---. The blast threw her to the ground. Turning around I saw her fifth-wheeler in flames and debris flying in the air. I screamed and stayed down covering my head with my arms.

Joe and the others ran toward the explosion, Joe coming to me as the others tried to move the trailer next to mine, three stalls down so it wouldn't catch fire.

"Are you alright, Alex?" Helping me up he gave me a quick once over, satisfied I wasn't bleeding anywhere.

"Yea, I think so. Sadie, come here and let me look at you. My God Joe, what happened?"

"My guess, I'd say Nick knows you're more a threat than he thought."

"Joe, if Sadie hadn't wanted to play that would have killed me."

"I'm sure that was the intent, Alex. I believe Sadie sensed something wrong and drew you out of harm's way," Joe said, scratching Sadie behind her ears. "Good girl."

"Damn, Joe, look at my fifth-wheeler. It's utterly destroyed, that son-of-a-bitch!" *If Ateara doesn't kill him, I will, I thought.* "Nick Salva has wreaked havoc ever since he came into my life. He's stressed me out, hurt my friends, destroyed my property and put panic on the pipeline, all for money. He'll never see a dime of it. Never!"

Joe pulled me close and kissed my forehead. I was still shaking. If they'd park where they usually did, it would have destroyed my truck, also.

"Joe, the black truck up the road, that's it isn't it?"

The truck was creeping along until whoever was in it saw them running down to my truck, and sped away.

"Come on, let's go see who that is. You still have your gun under the seat?"

"Yes, but what about my fifth-wheeler? We're just going to leave it like this?"

"Alex there's not much left. We'll worry about it later, come on." They jumped in the truck, backed out of the park but before they could pull onto the highway, the Iriff stopped them.

The Iriff took his time strolling up the side of the truck. "You're in an awfully big hurry. What's going on? I heard an explosion," he said, too casually.

"There was an explosion in Alex's fifth-wheeler," Joe said rather impatiently. *You could see the flames from here, was the Iriff daft?*

"Hold up a minute and I'll call the fire department," the Iriff said, looking down at the camp site, before hurrying back to his vehicle. A few moments later the Iriff approached them. "Can I have you folks drive back down to the campsite? We need to determine what happened.

"What happened, it blew up and burned down," *and you're letting the ones that did it get away,* I hissed.

"Damn, we'll never catch them at this rate," Joe said aggravated, and drove back to the burning rubble.

"Strange he just happened to be coming this way when this happened."

"Let's keep our cool Alex, and we'll get out of here faster." Joe parked a short distance away. The heat was still intense.

"You were going to take off and leave it burning?" the Iriff asked, taking out a pad and pencil.

"We were on our way to find you," I lied. *I hope these white lies won't catch up with me.* Looking over at Joe, I waited for him to concur.

"Why didn't you call on your CB? We've been monitoring channel five for emergencies since those two men were killed.

"If we'd know that sheriff, we'd have done just that," Joe responded, looking back at me.

"Here comes the fire department now. You two stay here until we can take down your statement to what happened."

"We might as well relax, Alex. We wouldn't be able to catch them now anyway." We went over to the picnic table that was close and sat down and watched the firemen hose down the remaining flames.

"All my clothes were in there along with my hair brush," I said leaning over and putting my elbows on my thighs, my face in my hands.

Joe started to laugh.

"What are you laughing about, it's not funny."

"You, Alex. You almost get blown up, the fifth wheeler is destroyed, and you're worried about clothes and a hairbrush," he pulled me close and then added, "this isn't a funny situation, but I can't help but laugh. Our lives are hanging by a thread, and you're upset about incidentals."

I sighed leaning into Joe as we watched the last embers fade and die leaving only ash. There would be nothing salvageable looking at it from where we were.

"Damn Alex, we're in deep shit here. We don't know who or when Ateara will strike again, and now we have Nick trying to take us out. The odds are not in our favor."

"I'm sorry. It's my fault that Nick is after us. We'll just have to get to him first."

"And then what?"

I looked up at him, "I guess we'll have to figure that out when we find him."

"Come on, let's go take a look." He tightened his arm around my waist as we walked over to the fire chief

"There's not much left, it burnt extremely hot," said the fire chief. "The fire is out, and it may smolder for a while. That aluminum melts quite fast and like I said it was hot. The boys will investigate, see if we can tell you where it started from. Mam, I'm very sorry."

"Thanks, Chief." I walked closer to the rubble. Sadie smelled around what little was left. *Nick tried to kill us, or maybe just me. No, the men in that truck would have seen me chase after Sadie. This was a warning.*

"You okay Miss Kendall?" asked a couple of the pipeline guys.

"Yah, I'm still here to listen to some of your wild tales," I tried to laugh, but it caught in my throat. Looking down at Sadie, she held my hairbrush in her mouth. "Joe, Sadie found my hair brush. It's burned a bit on the handle but perhaps usable if the smell goes away. Thanks, Sadie," I said, picking up the little dog I hugged her to me. "Thanks for saving my life."

"They also found one of Sadie's steel bowls and a few odds and ends but for the most part, everything was destroyed.

"Do you want to tell me what happened," the sheriff asked, looking down at me from his six-foot frame.

"I don't know what happened. I was playing with Sadie, I heard a blast, and was thrown to the ground. Getting up, I saw my trailer in flames."

"You didn't touch anything on the fifth-wheeler, like the propane?"

"No. I wasn't even close to it. I was running after Sadie."

"I see, and where were you, Mr. Larkin?"

"I was down there talking to these gentlemen," Joe said looking at the men that came up to look at was left of Alex's rig.

"By the way, Sheriff, what were you looking for both times you were looking around the fifth-wheeler today?" I quizzed, not taking my eyes off the man in uniform.

The sheriff looked at me in surprise, for a moment.

"That's police business, Mam."

"Did you think you'd find snakes hidden in my wheel wells?" my voice raised accusingly.

"That's enough Alex. I'm sure the sheriff was just doing his job," Joe squeezed my arm giving her a warning. He needed to find another spot to squeeze as that one was getting tender. I wouldn't be surprised if I had a bruise.

"Maybe you'd like to come to the station for a while? I'm sure we have more question that haven't been answered yet," the sheriff said with a cocky attitude to go along with the smirk on his face.

One that I wanted to smack off his face. My jaw tightening, I counted to five slowly. "I've told you all I know." I crossed my arms instead of tightening my fist.

"Sheriff, are you there? Come on back," the voice yelled over the radio from the sheriff's truck.

He strolled over to his truck and pick up the hand receiver. "Yes, I'm here. Go ahead."

"We have a fight at Pet's Bar and Jay has gone home for supper."

"Alright, I'm on my way." He tipped his hat and stepped up into his pickup, and drove back down the road toward town.

"Miss Kendall," the fire chief called, walking up to me. "I know a couple of men that can take care of this mess. If you'd like, I could call them for you?"

"Thank you, Chief. That's very thoughtful of you."

The fire chief nodded, and added, "if there is anything salvageable, I'll ask them to set it aside."

I nodded in agreement, picked up Sadie and walked back to my own truck.

Looking at those still huddled in a group, I saw one of the foremen and motioned him over.

"Will you be seeing Jeremy today?"

"Yes mam, in about forty minutes."

"Will you let him know we are leaving for Williston, and that I will call him tomorrow."

"Sure will, Miss Kendall. You two be careful," said the foreman opening the truck door for me to get in.

Joe felt under the seat for the gun Alex usually keep there, his hand tightened around the leather holster positioning it where he could grab it swiftly if need be.

CHAPTER 17

"We can stay the night in Belfield and pick up a map. I believe it's only about sixty miles."

"That's good news, my stomach is starting to rumble," Joe said, glancing over at me.

"How can you think of eating right now?" That was the last thing on my mind. My stomach was in knots, and didn't know if there would be room for food. Thinking of the lives Nick Salva had destroyed, hatred burned hot.

Joe laid his hand over one of mine. "Very easily. If I might die, I'd like to do it on a full stomach. I don't run on nerves as you do, and my brain doesn't function that well on things when my belly is empty.

Aren't you hungry Sadie?" Sadie gave him two barks. "See, I'm not the only one."

I looked out the side window across the fields and watched the sun as it slid behind the small rolling hills. Colors of purple, gold, and pinks had curtained the horizon before shadows would swallowed them. There would be a full moon rising the next three nights. Hopefully, that would be to their advantage finding Nick's cabin.

"Joe, I bet at the truck stop there would be locals that could tell us about Leland Dam."

"I bet you're right, especially if they are fishermen. People up here seem to do a lot of that, listening to them talk." They read the sign, Belfield fifteen miles.

Joe looked in the rear view mirror and saw a black truck about a half mile back. *It could be someone else. But not likely.* Looking over at Alex, she was somewhere in thought and hadn't noticed the truck. Hoping it might be someone else, he didn't mention it.

"Did Mr. Oshler say how Terry was doing?"

Bringing me back to the present, I leaned my head back against the seat before answering.

"She'll be able to go home in a couple more days, and will be staying at her parent's for a while."

I slipped back into the recesses of my mind, and Joe had learned when I did that, it was better to leave me alone. I'd almost gotten Terry killed, and now I might get Joe killed. That was enough guilt. I wasn't going to take on the guilt for Nick's men. That was all him. I heard the blinker when Joe signaled to exit the highway bringing me back to the present. The lights of the truck stop was a welcome sight. Joe pulled up to a gas pump, a good strategy in case we needed to make a quick get-a-way.

"Alex, will you go inside and find us a table? I'm going to fill gas first and then I'll be in," he said, squeezing my hand.

"Okay. Sadie, we'll bring you something out." Stepping out of the truck, I gave a quick scan around the parking lot before going inside.

The black truck didn't roll in until Alex had entered the restaurant. The truck went to the last pump. Joe couldn't see who got out.

I watched Joe park in front in a well-lighted space, cracked the window for Sadie and locked the doors before coming inside. He stopped inside the doors watching something that had caught his interest. Could it be the black truck?

"What were you looking at?" I'd picked a corner booth where we could keep an eye on the truck, and watch who came in.

"A black pickup that pulled in." He sat down and picked up the coffee I ordered for him. "Did you order food or just coffee?"

"You didn't say what you wanted, but she'll be back in a minute. Joe, do you think they meant to kill me, or just scare me when they blew up the fifth-wheeler?"

"The truth? I believe they intended to kill you. From where they were they could see you headed up to the trailer, but lost sight the closer you were. They couldn't see Sadie lead you away. What do you think?" We looked over at the door and watched five guys walk in. Three went to a booth, and two sat at the counter.

"I believe you're right. If it hadn't been for Sadie, I wouldn't be sitting here right now. I never thought Nick would actually have someone kill me. Looking death in the face and walking away, that doesn't happen to everyone. I thought they could see me run after Sadie, but you're right."

The waitress walked back to our table, filled the cups and took our order. I decided I'd better eat, not knowing for sure when the next time would be.

"Okay, who are you watching?" I lifted my cup and cautiously looked around. I didn't recognize anyone.

"What do you mean?"

"I say that you have been glancing around the whole time I've been talking to you," I said, setting my cup down. "I don't see anyone familiar."

Joe looked at her deciding whether to tell her about the truck or let it slide for a while. Then again, he knew she'd be more upset if he didn't tell her.

"I think we are being followed. It's the same black truck. They were following us the last fifteen minutes before we arrived here, and pulled into the truck stop after you went inside. Staying behind the pump when they filled gas, I couldn't get a look at them."

Two more guys walked in and sat down at the bar.

"They all look like truck drivers to me, Joe. Maybe they are still out there."

"Perhaps they are already at Nick's cabin. We'll see in the morning if the black truck is still parked between the two semi trucks," Joe said, hoping it would be gone. Our food had come, and we ate in silence, after which we went back out to the truck.

"Sadie, here you go." I set the food on the floorboard. "I'll go see about a room." I looked around when I left the office and walked back to the truck. "The only room available was on the lower level and in the middle of the motel. It wasn't a well-lit area, but at least they weren't on the second level or at the end."

"I doubt they will try anything with the motel full," Joe said, moving the dish to the side so I was able to step inside the truck.

Joe drove around the motel and backed into the parking space in front of their room.

"Come on Sadie, let's get some sleep. Tomorrow Joe, we need to find a clothing store and buy a change of clothes." Watching Joe unlock the door, he pushed it open, and we went inside. He locked it and secured the chain to the door.

"I think that is a great idea," he commented, pushing aside the curtain to look outside.

"I'm sleeping in my clothes." I pulled down the comforter.

"That's not a bad idea." We laid down, and Sadie jumped up on the bed cuddling next to me. I tried to keep my eyes open, but soon they closed. Dreams bombarded my mind as snakes crawled in and out of the fifth-wheel. Then I felt Sadie stand. She was growling. I rolled over and saw Joe standing by the door. The door knob moved from side to side. I looked at the security chain. Yes, Joe had secured it. They heard a click, and the door opened to the point the chain allowed. Joe put his finger to his lips, and I sat up on the bed holding Sadie to keep her from growling.

The adrenaline surged through me as I watched the black rubber band pushed through the narrow slit in the door and then another. Joe motioned to the bathroom.

My heart was pounding in my chest as I watched the door close again. Joe released the chain and followed me to the bathroom. We took one more look and saw the banding start to move before we closed the door. Joe opened the bathroom window, looked out to see if anyone was watching the backside of the motel. At the far end, he saw movement. Someone was walking along the back wall. Joe closed the window again and locked it.

I took the towels and laid them along the bottom of the door. A shadow passed the window. I hoped that whoever was out back wouldn't be able to tell which room was theirs. In the silence, I could hear the ticking of Joe's watch. How long would they wait? I looked at the bottom of the door and watched the towel move. I grabbed Joe's arm. He took another chance and opened the window. Looking along the wall, he saw nothing. Taking my hand, he helped me out the window and then gave me Sadie.

Sadie growled, and I felt someone grab my arm. Instinct took over as I dropped Sadie to the ground and come around with a punch to my assailants throat, knocking him backward. He came at me again as I whirled around with a round kick connecting to the man's head. He dropped to the ground. Joe finished climbing out the window and closed it. Looking at the guy on the ground and then at me, he said.

"I knew there was a reason I liked having you around. Let's see if we can get to the truck."

I picked up Sadie, and we clung to the back wall like a second skin inching our way to the far end. Joe looked around the corner, and it was clear. We moved silently along the end of the building and looked around at the front side. There was a guy in front of the room leaning against the back of my truck.

"We need to think of something fast, Joe. The other one will be waking up soon."

"Around here." He led me crouched down along the back of the parked cars trying to stay as quiet as we could. When we reached the truck, Joe walked up along the side.

"You looking for someone?" Joe asked. The guy turned around and met with Joe's fist. The man went down. "Get in Alex. We need to get out of here."

Joe reached for the door and felt a jab to his ribs. As he turned around the man delivered a blow to

Joe's head. Joe staggered. Shaking his head to clear his vision the guy threw another punch. Joe ducked and come up with a fist to the guys gut followed by one to his chin. The man went down, again. They heard someone running toward them.

"Joe, get in," I yelled turning the ignition. The motor roared to life as Joe jumped inside the cab. Shifting into gear, I drove out of the parking lot and into the night.

An hour later we pulled off the highway onto a gravel road. I drove up the road about a mile and turned around before stopping.

"I think we'll be safe to sleep here for a while."

"How's your head? That was some punch he gave you."

"My eye hurts, but I'll feel better after I can get some sleep. Those were definitely Nick's men." Watching Joe move his head in a circle to ease the tension in his neck, I wished we had an ice pack.

"I'm sorry I got you involved in this Joe," I said, moving my hand gently up and down the side of his face.

"I knew loving you would be an adventure, but I didn't expect this," he whispered and kissed my hand. He laid his head back on the seat, his eyes closing.

I slept, but the images of the banding transforming, the faces of the victims, Lester's gaunt face, and Ateara's carved breast, streamed in and out of my dreams. No, they weren't dreams, they were nightmares. I woke with a gasp, my heart pounding. Looking over at Joe, surprised I hadn't woke him. He looked peaceful even with the bruising on his face. How could I have thought this job was worth more than a lifetime with Joe. I didn't know why I was such a control freak. That trait has our lives hanging on a thin web. Twice today I had stared death in the face and walked away. God must have an angel on my shoulder.

I looked at the moon crossing to the far side of the world dressed in orange flame, running from the sun. Is that like life running from death, excaping just beyond it's reach. That's how I felt, cheating death. How many times would I escape before the sand in my hour glass ran out? I wouldn't let it run out until seeing Nick Salva dead.

I closed my eyes, mind weary, thoughts chaotic, searching for a peaceful place to hide from the entanglements of nightmares, and fear.

We both woke to Sadies barking, sat up and looked around for the danger. All we saw was a John Deer tractor pulling a bailer down the dusty road toward them.

"Goodness sake, it's ten thirty," I exclaimed. "You need out Sadie?" Sadie barked and I opened the truck door stepping out with the dog. "Sleeping in this truck is not the most comfortable bed for a body." Putting Sadie down, and stretching as I walked around to the front of the truck.

The tractor slowed and then stopped next to the truck.

"Morning, Mam," was the farmers greeting.

"Good morning," I replied. "We're kinda lost. Could you tell us how to reach LeLand Dam?"

"Why yes Mam. You keep driving, the direction your going for about another mile, and that will put back on higway 85. Head north going through Grassy Butte, Watford City, there you'll turn west to Alexander. There are signs from Alexander to get you to the dam."

"Thank you."

He nodded his head, and started back up the road.

"Ouch!" Joe winced holding his side. "I think that guy may have cracked my rib."

"Here, let me see it," I lifted his shirt. "You do have a nice bruise. When we reach Grassy Butte, we'll pick up an ace banage, and wrap this."

"Yes, and Grassey Butte is on the way." I pulled back onto the road, turned on the radio humming along to Let's Dance by David Bowie.

"Isn't that approperate," Joe started to laugh, stopped, gritting his teeth.

Turning on to 85 just when the news followed the song.

"Good morning, this is KXWZ. This is the update on our top story today. The two men found dead at the Belfield Truck Stop this morning, the coroner said died of snake bites. Information we received is this is the seventh death in three weeks caused by snake bites. When we have more information we will be updating you as it comes in. Grain prices.." I turned off the radio.

"They're dead. We left them alive, Joe. How is she doing this. That would mean she was at the truck stop." My hands flew off the stirring wheel exasperated.

"Slow down, Alex. How do we know she has to be there when a death occures?"

"I don't know, Joe. I'll call Lester when we stop at Grassey Butte. It's eleven fifteen, hopfully he's still in his office. I've seen Ateara do spells for other people and she didn't have to be there, however, they were in her area. She's into magic that I know nothing about."

"She can't go invisiable can she? I know that sounds like something out of a science fiction book, and I wouldn't even entertain the idea, if wasn't for what I've seen."

"Are you serious. How can someone be invisible?"

"I don't know. You explain it then. I haven't seen a black person since we come up here. And she would stand out, black and beautiful. You know how guys on the pipeline talk. If they'd seen her.."

"Look, there's the sign for Grassey Butte." I turned on to the frontage road. After two miles we entered the small town. Parking in front of the drug store for an ace bandage, took me all of five minutes to go in and come out with what was needed.

"I'm hungry, let's go eat and you can call Lester." They walked down the block to the front window of the Grassey Butte Café. I led us inside and took a booth near the back. Joe took the sack from the drug store, and went back to the men's restroom.

I looked up at the pretty young waitress and smiled as she set two glasses of water on the table with the menus.

"I'll give you a few minutes. Would you like coffee?" she asked. I nodded and the girl left. Returning she filled both cups and left.

It was a few more minutes before Joe emerged from the back. I noticed the pain had eased from his face.

"The ace bandage must have helped?"

"Yeah, it does. Did you call Lester yet?"

"I thought we would order first, and then I'll call." We looked over the menu and then gave the waitress our order. Watching the girl walk away, I went to the phone in the corner. Deposited the coins, and listened to the ring tone three times before it was picked up.

"Hello, is Mr. Kierbow in?"

"No, Mam. Not at the moment. He be gone to the post offfice. Shoud be back right shortly, can he call ya back?"

I gave her the number to the pay phone, and sat down on the small bench to wait. Joe brought my coffee over knowing I would stay there until Lester returned my call. Five minutes later the phone rang.

"Hello, Lester." I sat the coffee cup down on the small table, the tightness leaving my features.

"Miss Alexandra, I be waiting for days for you to call. What be happening, and have ya seen Atera?" I could hear the worry in his voice.

"I be reading in the paper about the killings up there."

"The killings are in the paper down there?"

"It seams anything unnatural anywhere in the country makes its way into our paper. And it's not everyday you have seven killing by snake bite nobody can explain in North Dakota."

"That's why I'm calling, Lester. Does Ateara have to be in the area when this curse kills? I know you said anyone connected with Nick. All the men killed have been Nick's men, but two weren't in the pipe storeage yard, and the last two weren't even on the pipeline. However, I've been in the vinicinity when all have taken place. Has Ateara connected me with this curse?"

"Oh, Miss Alex, she be there. You might not recognize her, but she be there. You stay away from Nick and his men." His commanding tone filtered through the line.

"That's kinda of hard right now, Lester. Nick knows I'm aware of his plans. He's already tried to have me killed, and I'm sure it was him who gave the orders to blow up my fifth-wheel. They thought I was inside."

"I was afraid of this. Telling you what I be finding out has only put you in more danger."

"We found out Nick has a cabin up by Leland Dam. He must have known he couldn't pull this off if all his men worked on the line."

"Miss Alex, you not be going up there! You be putting your life in danger twice over. Ateara had gone past the point of no return with those that be dead. You be like a daughter to me, Miss Alexandra. I don't want to be losing you too. You let her be, and get away as far as possible. There ain't nothing you can be doing anyway to stop him. Honest child, what can you do at this point? What can you prove? You stick close to your job and you be keeping people close around you."

"I'm being careful, I have Joe with me. I'll keep in touch, Lester, bye." I hung the phone up, picked up my coffee and made my way back to the table.

"What did he say? You look like your color has been siphoned from your face." Joe reached out and took my hand, but let it go when our meal was delivered.

"He said we wouldn't recognize Ateara, but she is up here and has been at each one of the murders. He said if we go find Nick, first, we have no proof of what he's doing or going to do. And second it puts us in double jeapardy of getting ourselves killed. So where we at, you want to know? Seven murders, and we couldn't stop them. Don't know how many more there could be. We're like leaves being tossed in the wind, hoping a tornado doesn't tear us apart. And right now I don't even see a soft landing."

"Alex, your tried, but Lester is right. We have no proof that Nick is doing anything illegal and until something comes up missing, that's pipeline property, your hands are tied. As for Ateara, I think that is hopeless. We have no idea what to look for." He smiled and squeezed my hand again. "Doesn't make sense Alex to get ourselves killed. Myself, I'm not ready to check out and I hope you aren't either."

"I know, your right," I sighed, and took a bite of toast. "I just feel so helpless knowing what's happening and I can't do a damn thing about it." I took the extra sausages and wrapped them in a napkin for Sadie, putting them in my purse.

"If we're lucky we can get back to work and Nick will drop things for a while. He's had four men killed trying to take you out. I would think that would be enough incentive to leave you alone." Joe kissed her knuckles. "I love you." Joe wished they were somewhere else. A place he could make love to her. They finished eating and were getting ready to leave, when they looked up.

"You are hard to catch up to," Gary said, sliding across the seat making room for the guy with him.

"Gary, what are you doing up here?" Looking at him, and the guy next to him made my stomach queasy.

"Let's say I'm working a side job for a bit. Nick wants to see you both. You should have minded your own business Joe, you'd have lived longer." A smirk crossed Gary's face.

"So I see your true colors unfold Gary. What about Mr. Oshler, you don't think he'll find out you've been working for Nick?"

"Got it covered. I've been checking in everyday with Oshler. Told him I haven't been able to find you, so when they do find you and Joe dead from snake bites; things will go on as usual. Our plans will run smooth. There will be two more unexplained snake bite deaths. Let's go."

They all slid out of the booth and walked to the cashier. The door opened and in walked a sheriff and his deputy. They looked around, and strolled over to the cashier.

"Excuse me Mam, are you Alex Kendall?" he asked, looking at me and then the others.

"I am. Can I help you with something?" Taking Joe's hand when he finished paying for their meal.

"Would you please come down to the police station, we have some question we'd like to ask you," he said politely.

"You can't ask her here?" Gary spoke up.

"Are you with Miss Kendall?"

"No, Sheriff, he is not. Only Mr. Larkin." I answered quickly before Gary could answer. "I'd be happy to come down to the police station with you. Can I follow you in my truck?"

Gary gave me a dirty look and walked out of the café.

"That would be fine Mam." Joe and I walked the block to the truck and got in. I first laid the napkin with the sausages on the floorboard for Sadie. Joe backed out of the parking spot and went up the street to fall in behind the sheriff's truck. I saw Gary get into a black 4-x-4 truck and he glared at me as they passed by. The wheels started to spin in my mind. *The person in the black truck parked across the street from my home had been Gary all along or his friend. What a set-up and I fell for it, hook, line, and sinker. What a fool I've been. Nick the aggressor, and Gary the hero.*

"So much for Nick letting things go."

"Yeah," I agreed.

"We can't stay at the police station forever, so we better start thinking of a plan to get away when we walk out. You know they will be waiting."

Joe parked right in front of the police station. I picked up Sadie and took her with us. I didn't think Gary would do anything there, but I wasn't taking any chances of something happening to Sadie. As much as I had fought about having a dog, I'd come to love the small black haired one she'd hurt on the right-a-way.

"Back this way please," they were directed. I had never seen the inside of an interrogation room other than on TV or the movies. This room was much the same, a table, four chairs, gray walls, certainly not anything you'd write home about. Joe and I sat on one side of the table, Sadie on my lap.

"Miss Kendall, we understand that you and Mr. Larkin stayed at the Belfield Motel last night. Is that true?"

"Yes, we did."

"Did you see anything out of the ordinary?" The deputy asked, twirling a pencil between his fingers.

"No, Sir."

"Mr. Larkin that's quite a bruise you have on the side of your eye. Do you want to explain how you received that?" asked the sheriff this time.

"Sheriff, what's this all about?" Joe stayed calm, but he didn't take his eyes from the sheriff.

"Well, Mr.Larkin, we've had seven deaths in the state since Miss Kendall arrived up here. She has been in the vicinity when each one of the murders have taken place."

"There have been a lot of people around when they took place. Why are you singling Alex out?"

"From our information all the vitims were associates of a Mr. Nick Salva. We've been told that he and Miss Kendall on several occasions had heated arguments."

"Are you accusing Alex of having something to do with these deaths?" Joe felt his anger stirring inside.

"Mr. Larkin, I'm not accusing anyone, Just trying to get some answers," the sheriff spoke in a mild manner.

"We had reports of a disturbance last night at a motel around three in the morning. Some said there was a fight outside their room. When we looked at the register, you had paid for the room next to that room. They said there was a fight, and after one of the men was knocked out, the truck parked there left in a hurry. However, they weren't able to describe the man, however they said a woman was in the truck with him."

Joe sat back in the chair and I continued to comb my fingers through Sadies coat.

"Around seven this morning, two men were found in a truck parked at the motel by an employee. Both men were dead from snake bites. Now Miss Kendall will you tell me why you're up here and what you know about these deaths?

It was around six pm when all the information was verified and they were allowed to leave. The sheriff walked out and down three doors to a café. Joe and I scanned the street and saw the black 4x4 parked two blocks up. Joe took my arm and we followed after the sheriff.

"I think we'll have a better chance getting away after dark. Follow my lead."

"Joe let me put Sadie in the truck first. I don't think they would try to kill her this close to the police station.

"We won't be to long Sadie," I said as if the dog could understand me, giving her a kiss between her ears I locked the truck door and followed Joe inside the café.

"Sheriff do you mind if we sit with you? Joe stepped to the side allowing me access to the booth. When they sat down they would be facing the window.

"No, not at all. I have question about the pipeline maybe you could answer for me, just out of curiosity."

"Sure, what would you like to know, sheriff? I'd be glad to give you any information your interested in." I relaxed and Joe ordered coffee and pie.

The three of us sat at the table for two hours talking about the pipeline, farming, fishing and the large rock piles that seamed to be off in the corner of fields. They were back on the subject of the pipeline when Joe saw Gary look into the café and then entered when he saw Joe and I sitting at a booth. The two men sat down at a booth and gave the waitress their order after she approached them.

"You know sheriff, one of the men from home office is sitting at the booth on the other side of the room. I'm sure he could answer your questions about the stringing. His name is Gary Spindle and he actually worked on the pipe stringing.

"That would be great. I'll ask them to join us," the sheriff said enthusiastically.

"It would be better if you joined them. I was supposed to be in Williston three hours ago. I have enjoyed chatting with you."

The sheriff walked over and sat down next to Gary. Joe paid for their pie and coffee and left the café without a backward glance knowing Gary would not be happy that he'd been tricked.

When we walked out of the café, black clouds drew across the heavens extinguishing what little light was left. The air drew heavy with the smell of rain. When it started to sprinkle, we ran to the truck.

They reached highway 85 and turned north. Lightening stretched out it's fingers and lit up the sky. Joe wasn't sure how long the sheriff would keep Gary talking and he wasn't going to take his time finding out. Williston was an hour and a half away. With luck they would make it. The rain came down in torrents and Joe did have to slow down. Black clouds curtained the full moon, and the trucks headlights dwindled almost down to nothing in the storm.

"This must be the storm the line foreman mentioned," I stated holding Sadie more for comfort than anything else. "It will indeed raise havoc on the line."

CHAPTER 18

They spotted the sign for Watford City Ten miles, when they were jolted forward. I hit the windshield.

"What the hell was that?" Looking in the the rear view mirror Joe saw the headlights. "Hang on Alex, here they come again!"

I screamed as the impact on the truck swerved us on the slippery black top. Joe brought it back under control. He saw the truck start up along side and swerved to knock it off the road. The other truck pulled back as lightning lit up the sky. Joe and I saw the bridge along with the other driver of the truck behind ours. The other vehicle raced up along side us, swerved, forcing our truck through the barrier.

"Oh my God, Joe!" I screamed looking down at the angry river.

"Jump out Alex! Jump out!" I forced the door open and jumped with Sadie just before the truck hit the water and disappeared out of sight. I lost sense of direction as the water carried me away. The rain felt like pellets beating down on me. I went under and came back up gasping for air while the angry water pulled me along in its wrath. I was tossed into a fallen tree and hung on tight as the tree was swept down stream. I looked for Joe and Sadie, seeing neither one my tears blended with the rain.

I wasn't sure how far I'd been swept down stream. Feeling the tree catch on something I reached out and felt a another tree that its roots still clung to the earth. Pulling my bruised body along until my feet made purchase with the bank. Clutching anything my hands could use to pull me out of the raging river. The grass clump was wet and slippery and my weight pulled it lose and I slid back toward the swells, catching myself before falling back into the water. Sobbing, afraid to call out for Joe, not knowing if the other truck had stopped or kept going.

"Joe where are you?" I continued to cry. Remembering I'd jumped with Sadie. "Oh Sadie." I stared up the bank hearing someone running, and saw the beam a light. *Joe didn't have a light, oh my God what should I do.* Taking hold of the tree branch I eased myself back into the river pulling myself into the the tree roots as tight as I could, fighting the current. Something clasp over my mouth.

"Alex," Joe whispered. I started to cry again. 'Shhh."

"I can't see anything down here. We'll have to wait until it stops raining," Gary yelled.

"I think they went down with the truck," his partner spouted.

"You're not paid to think, and we're not leaving until I find that bitch," Gary growled. "Come on let's get back to the truck and we'll drive down when it's light."

Joe watched the light go back the way the two men had come, giving them a few minutes before he helped Alex and himself out of the water.

"Are you hurt." Joe pushed my hair from my face.

"I don't think so. Just cold." He wiped the tears and raindrops from my face. "I've lost my fifth wheeler and my truck in three days."

"Be grateful it wasn't your life, because it very well could have been." Joe rubbed my arms, and kissed my forehead. "We can't stay here, Alex, and if we start moving it will warm you." Joe didn't know which direction they were headed, only that he wanted to put as much distance between them and Gary Spindel.

"Alex, this looks like a good road that runs along the river. Stay on the grass so we don't leave boot prints."

"Did you see Sadie?" I rubbed my arms as I followed in Joe's bootprints waiting for him to answer.

"No, but dogs are good swimmers. I'm sure she's fine," he told me. But doubt was in his words.

We ran until I thought my lungs would burst. The rain was sprinkles now and the black clouds that had hid the moon were thinning.

"Joe, I've got to rest for a little bit," I pleaded, my legs felt like rubber and I had a sitch in my side.

Joe looked around and found an overhang along the bank from a prior flooding. It looked like we'd be able to stay out of the water and out of sight, at least until first light. Sliding down the embankment rounding the grassy wall, I saw something in my peripheral vision. Looking back under the overhang was Sadie.

"Sadie," I cried out, and hurried over to the small dog. "I can feel a heart beat, Joe. Sadie. The little dog lifted its head and licked my hand, and then laid her head back down. "I think she's just exhausted." I pushed back under the overhang as far as I could go and put Sadie on my lap. At this point I didn't worry about the sand and grass that mingled with strands of my hair. We were all alive and that's all I cared about.

"We can stay here an hour, maybe two. I think they will wait until daylight to come looking for us. I wish I'd thought to grab your gun." Joe snuggled up to me putting his arm around my shoulders.

The two hours they sat huddled together gave them time too gain their strength for the next run.

"Joe, we have to cross the river." The flash flood had slowed. They could make it across, maybe.

"I think your right, Alex. It's finding a place to cross. Stay here. I'm going to check around the bend." Joe used a broken tree branch to sweep away the tracks going down to the overhang and away from it. He was gone for fifteen minutes which seemed like eternity to me. When he came back down the embankment Sadie was sitting up.

"I found a boat ramp and there's a canoe hidden in the overgrowth along the bank. Come on, the sun will be rising soon." Joe reach down to help me up and brushed the tracks away again.

It didn't take them long to reach the boat ramp. They pulled the canoe out of it's hiding place and turned it over.

"I thought we would stay dry. We'll have to use it like a log looking at the hole in the bow. At least the river isn't as wide here. We can place Sadie on top."

They eased the canoe and themselves into the river, Sadie seemed to know exactly where she needed to be, and didn't take long to get there. Pushing off, we let the current carry us along for a while, until we saw a landing place up ahead. Kicking in that direction to reach the other side, there wasn't a place to hide the canoe so we sank it.

"Sorry," I mumbled under my breath, and thanking the canoe for getting them across the river.

"Come on, let's go. At least on this side we have places to hide if we have to."

There were trees, tall grasses and taller shrubs. If we chose to leave the river, there were plenty of ravines where one could hide.

"This is beautiful country. I'm sorry we can't enjoy it," Joe said wistfully.

"Joe there's a campground that should be up ahead. It's the North Unit of Roosevelt Park. We might find a park ranger that could help us. We can go to the police now, and press charges against Gary for attemped murder."

"One thing at a time, Alex. Let's look for the Ranger station, we're not out of danger, yet."

We started out keeping an eye on the other side of the river for Gary. The sun was up and our clothes were drying as we walked down the grassy hump of the road.

"I think we were lucky to have that storm last night," I said, looking down the river.

"Why's that?"

"If the river hadn't risen with the rain, we'd have died going over that bridge. I'll bet now you can see my truck. Come on Sadie, don't chase things too far away from me."

"You're probably right."

We'd been walking about an hour, and had rounded a bend when an engine motor could be heard. Sinking down in the tall grasses along the river, the black 4x4 was moving slowly along on the other side of the river. We waited. Gary was cussing standing in the back of the pickup looking for our bodies along the side. The truck stopped directly across from us.

"Damn it Gary, that river was running in torrents last night in that down pour. Their bodies are long gone by now. We couldn't even see the truck in the water then, but now you can and it won't be long until someone sees it and calls the police."

"Alright. Nick is going to mad as hell not getting his candy. Don't blame him though, I wanted some of that too," Gary growled.

"Hey you had your chance and blew it." The other man stated laughing.

"Knock it off. I still have a feeling she's alive and if she is.."

"If she is, and you touch her, Nick will kill you."

"You going to tell Charlie?" Gary sneered.

"I won't need to. I've known Nick long enough he'll know Gary. Come on, let's go"

Gary climbed back inside the truck and they turned around and went back the way they'd come.

"That means it will take them time to get back to the bridge as it couldn't be seen. But then they had also gone around a bend in the river," I whispered, and held Sadie a little tighter until the truck was out of sight.

Starting out at a slow trot for about forty-five minutes we slowed to a fast walk, and continued till the sun was above us when we saw the campground.

"Thank goodness, I don't know how much longer I can walk in these boots." Sitting down on the first picnic table we came to, Sadie lay down breathing heavily, her tongue hanging out.

"I feel the same way, Sadie." Glad the picnic table was under a tree, and feeling the suns extraction of their body fluids.

"Look Joe! A water spicket three camp sites down." As tired as I was, we needed water. The three of us staggered over to replenish. After turning on the water, I cuped my hands for Sadie to drink, after Joe and I drank our fill.

"I'm surprised the campground is empty." Turning in a circle taking in the campground, there were no signs of anyone.

"That rain storm deterred many from coming yesterday, I bet. And those that were here left hearing of its coming," Joe gestured at the puddles everywhere. Wouldn't be much fun playing in the mud."

"What do you mean? Kids love playing in the mud, maybe not their parents.. Joe, even with the rain, if there had been campers, there would have been something to show for their stay. Look the restrooms."

Running over to the small square building, I pulled on the handle of the door, it was locked.

"It's locked," I exclaimed.

Looking down the river, the road continued to the north. Grassy ravines, small shrubs, trees, and rocks we hoped would lead to civilization.

"Do you know how to eat off the land? Because, my stomach is saying it's starving."

"Is that the rumbling I've been hearing?" Joe laughed and kissed my forehead. "If we were in Texas, I could help you with that hunger. But, up here, your guess is as good as mine. Should we start up that road? Maybe we might even discover the pipeline.

Venturing up the road, it lead away from the river. Small pine trees shaded some areas, but the further from the river the trees were smaller and the intervals longer in between. The grasses were lush after the rain, a place I would have liked to hike and explored.

"Joe, look buffalo." I started to count to keep my mind off my feet and empty stomach. Sadie had stopped chasing the small critters, and walked along beside me.

I stopped counting and stood still. "Listen, it sounds like a truck, or a jeep coming down the road. Maybe it's the ranger." I smiled at Joe, but before I could explore that idea Joe grabbed my hand.

"Just in case its not, let's get off the road. Up there between those rocks." Joe pointed to a cluster and we scrambled up and slid behind the rocky shield as the black truck came around the corner followed by a brown one. The trucks stopped a few feet from them and one of the men jumped out with a rifle.

"Buffalo! I think I can shoot one from here," the tall, thin, thirtish man cried out putting his gun to his shoulder.

Gary climbed out of the other truck and ran up to the man grabbing the gun away.

"Are you crazy? They'll be able to hear that shot for miles. You'll have the ranger down on us and you'll warn those other two,"he said, shoving the gun back into the man's chest.

"But I've never shot a buffalo before," he whined. Gary sneered, shaking his head angrily. "You're not going to start acting like Buffalo Bill. I hear shooting anything but those two, and I'll kill you myself. Now get back in the truck."

"What makes you think they are still alive, anyway?"

"Because I saw footprints at the river. Nobody is going far in this country barefoot, and Joe can't carry Alex all the time. That's why I think they'll come this way to the campground hoping to find someone here."

"You don't think they'll know the campground is shut down for improvements?

"No. And there won't be anyone coming here for months. Now let's go up a ways more and wait." Gary put his own rifle in his truck before they rolled further down the dirt road. One truck went fifty yards and stopped, while the other truck kept going.

Joe and I couldn't see the front truck, however, a few minutes later the engine went silent.

"What we going to do now, Joe?" I tried silently to soften a place to sit, knowing we would be here a while.

"Right now, stay put," watching me settling in to our hiding place. "We haven't a chance with the four of them. If the black truck leaves, we could probably overpower the two in the brown truck, and then we'd have wheels and a weapon."

"Joe, I wonder what they meant by me being barefoot?

"I have no idea, since we are both wearing boots. Might as well relax. I think we will be here for a while."

I turned over on my back, closed my eyes to the sun as it made its way across the sky. My body ached and my stomach growled as sleep crept over me.

Joe watched for movement below, but all he heard was the muttered sound from the two men in the truck just up the road. He fought to keep his eyes open, but soon lost the battle as sleep washed over him.

I was the first to wake. Looking at the sun, two hours had passed maybe more. I saw Sadie coming up the hill with a limp.

"Come here girl. Where have you been? You found a sticker on your round about?" I whispered. "Let me see." I sat Sadie on my lap, leaning up against the rock to stay hidden. "How did you cut your front leg? I don't have anything to doctor it with Sadie." My whispering woke Joe.

"How long have I been asleep?" he questioned, looking at me and then the dog.

"About two hours, maybe more. Look Sadie has a cut on her leg."

"Where did she get that?"

"I have no idea Joe. I saw her coming up the hill and she was limping on her left leg."

I need to see what's going on down there. Have you heard any noise?"

I shook my head no.

"The rest did some good, my ribs don't hurt as much. I'll be back in a minute."

"Oh no, you don't. I'm coming with you," I glared at him, challenging him to tell me to stay.

"Okay, come on. Stay down," he motioned.

We worked our way down until the brown truck was in sight. One door was open. We saw no movement, nor heard a sound other than the wildlife around us. He motioned to stay put for a minute and made his way up behind the truck. I edged my way through the tall grass keeping an eye on the road up ahead. Joe stopped and looked along the side of the truck and waved me forward.

I noticed how pale Joe's face looked when he waved me down. Coming up behind him, I looked over his shoulder and knew even with an empty stomach I was going to retch. What had been there blind side of the truck, lay the wannabe Buffalo Bill, part way under the vehicle. His eyes bulging, mouth held in a silent scream of terror, skin blackened, with blood, and yellow mucus oozing from his nose, eyes, and mouth.

Joe reached for the rifle and pulled it to him. Looking under the truck and in the grass for any movement before he went around to the other side. Opening the door, the driver fell out looking the same as his friend. There on the seat lay a bloody knife.

"Much good that did him," I moaned holding my stomach. "Look at the floor board," I pointed at the banding.

Joe slipped the two banding over the end of the rifle, and flung them as far as he could. After he put the knife under the seat, and pulled out the blanket seat covering, tossing it over one of the men.

"Get in Alex, we need to get out of here."

I put Sadie in the truck, and slid into the drivers seat. Joe on the other side, shut his door.

"How am I going to get around the body?" I asked, trying to hold down the bile.

"Back over him, there's no other way Alex. He's dead and he won't feel a thing."

"Oh God, Joe," I whimpered.

"Move it before we get caught. I can't see anyone in the campground, but if they hear the engine start up you can't dally. Now go!"

I started the engine and shoved it into reverse. I heard the bones break and the body explode from the weight of the truck. Blood and guts hit the side. I kept looking backwards for a place a to turn around, not wanting to see what I'd left. It was a quarter of a mile before the road widened. Turning the truck they heard the hum of the other truck coming. I put the gear into drive and pressed on the pedal. The truck sprang forward on the grassy road. The road when dry would have been easily maneuvered, but after the rain fall, was slick and dangerous.

I saw the other truck coming up fast behind us almost sliding off the road. They slowed and punched it again closing the distance.

Joe broke out the rear window with the butt of the gun. Trying to shoot bouncing and slipping all over the road was almost impossible.

"Joe look ahead!" my eyes widened and fear took the place of the bile.

Joe turned. The road led into the stream, but gave no indication how deep it was. "Floor it Alex!"
I looked at the gear box and it was already in four wheel drive, maybe it would get us across. Putting my foot to the floor just before we hit the water. The truck slowed, the wheels churring up the river bed as it struggled to cross.

"Come on, you can do it. Keep going, keep going," I cheered the truck on. We felt the tires hit the slippery grass coming out of the wter and lurched forward. I didn't look back. All I cared about was what was ahead. The road became more rocky, the curves sharper. *Please God let there be a way out of here.*

"Oh no, Joe!" I shouted as I applied both feet to the breaks. The road came to a dead end. The sign read, Scenic View Trail Head. The truck slid to a stop and we both jumped out and had started down the trail when we heard the gun shot.

"I think that's far enough!" Gary yelled. "Put the rifle down Joe. Now walk back up here. I don't think we need that black little mutt around anymore. I picked up Sadie and held her close. "Put her down Alex or I'll make it a slow death." Anger sprurred every word out of his mouth.

I turned around and threw Sadie ahead of me. "Run Sadie, run." I knew I was in the line of fire and could hear Gary running up behind me. *Just a little further and the little dog would drop out of sight.* I crossed my fingers. Gary knocked me to the ground. When Gary shot, Sadie was already out of sight.

"You Bitch." Gary raised his hand gun to hit me again and Joe tackled him.

"That's enough. We've already wasted too much time," said the guy standing at the trail head. "Pick up your gun Gary, and you two get back up here. Joe you drive, and Gary you go with him." He watched as the three of us made it back to the trucks. "Alex get in," he said, pointing to the truck I'd been driving.

Looking back down the trail, I saw nothing of Sadie before stepping back inside the truck. Joe pulled back onto the road and I followed. The return trip wasn't as hurried. They crossed back over the river, and twenty feet pass it   Joe turned onto another unpaved road. I hadn't seen this road, nor was it well traveled. I was thankful for that as we wouldn't drive past the bodies left on the other road.

"You've given us one hell of a time catching up with you Alex. Looking at you, I can see why the boss wants you. Maybe when he's done, he'll share. He has done that on occasion," he smiled. I ignored the comment, and kept driving staying a truck length behind Joe.

"I take it you've been with Nick a long time. What did you say your name was?" I asked.

"I didn't. It's Charlie, and yes I grew up with Nick."

"Has Nick shared other things with you besides his women?"

"Most things. Nick takes care of us."

"Really. You willing to die with him Charlie?" I asked, looking over at him. He was average built, didn't have the looks that Gary had. However, Charlie seemed not to have the temper Gary unleashed. I wondered why I'd never felt it beneath his cool exterior. I'd have to give Gary one thing, he was a damn good actor.

"Everyone has to die sometime. Your time will be up before mine Alex."

"Haven't you heard the saying, those that run together, die together? Nick's time is very close to being at an end. Didn't he tell you about the curse?" I mused.

"What curse?" he asked suspiciously.

"I see he doesn't share the most important things with you," I smiled feeling a little more confident. "You haven't seen how some of your other friends have died up here, like Jimbo?"

"What are you talking about? I talked to Jimbo last week."

"That was last week. Jimbo is dead and he died like Nick is going to die," I concluded.

"I think you need to shut the hell up now, bitch. I don't need to listen to you lies,' he said ruffled.

"You think I'm lying? Ask Nick what happened to nine of his employees. Ask him how they died. You drove past two of them. Didn't you see them splattered on the road or did Gary keep you busy till you passed them. Didn't the smell sicken your stomach?

"Shut up, just shut up until we get to camp," Charlie growled.

I didn't say anything else. Seeing that Charlie was thinking about what I said. The little beads of sweat across his forehead, the deeper creases around his eyes gave it away.

CHAPTER 19

As slow as we drove, I hoped that Sadie wasn't far behind. I kept looking for her in the side mirror with no success. Seeing the camp ahead, however, knowing what I knew of Nick, this camp must be for his men. I couln't see Nick at any time staying in a tent. There were four sleeping tents and a galley tent, besides a large supply tent. The sleeping ones didn't look like there was room for more than two. All I could see was Gary, Charlie, and the cook. This made the odds better for an escape.

Gary and Joe stepped out of the truck, Gary still held a gun on Joe.

"Get out and no funny business," Charlie said, giving me a push. I walked over and stood beside Joe.

"You'd better go radio Nick," Gary told Charlie. "Let him know we have them and we're down two more."

"What do you mean we're down two more?" Charlie yelled.

"Go do what I told you," Gary ordered.

"You haven't told him the others are dead, have you Gary?" I mocked.

"Shut up Alex," he snorted.

"Alex, that's enough. Don't agitate him," Joe urged.

"Shut up Alex, or I'll shut you up," Gary responded, his face going an ugly shade of red.

"That's the way you're going to die Gary." I pushed. Gary cocked his gun and pointed it at me. Joe pushed me out of the way as the gun went off hitting him in the arm.

"Joe," I screamed, jumping up to run to him.

"Get away from him, or I'll shoot him again." The blood ran down Joe's arm and he tried to take off his shirt to wrap it. I backed away moving out of Gary's vision. "Stop right there Alex," pointing the gun at me.

Charlie walked around Gary and bent over Joe, helped him wrap his shirt around the wound, slowing the bleeding.

"Get away from him Charlie. If he bleeds to death, he bleeds to death. Turn around Alex and lean up against that tree and put your hands behind you. Charlie throw me that rope on the table," Gary ordered.

Charlie handed him the rope and took a step back.

"Here, take my gun. Make sure he doesn't move and if he does shoot him." Gary pulled my wrist together tying them with the rope, then roughy turned me around pushing me up against the tree. "I've waited two years to have some of this." He ran his hand down the front of my Levis and clutched my crotch.

Joe tried to get up, but Charlie pushed him back down.

"You're not man enough to have any of this, Gary," I said, smiling at him.

"We'll see about that," reaching out and tearing my blouse open.

"That's enough Gary," Charlie warned. I came up with my knee and delivered a hard hit to his groin. When I brought my knee up the second time Gary managed to move away.

"You little bitch," he swore, and then back handed me, knocking me to the ground. He went after me, and a gun shot ripped through the air.

"That's enough Gary. She's Nick's and you've already damaged her," Charlie said, looking at the blood running from my mouth. "You touch her one more time and I'll kill ya." From the look on Gary's face, he knew Charlie would do it, he sneered backing down.

The cook came running out of the galley tent when he heard the second gun shot. "What's going on?"

"Nothing right now. Would you bring them something to eat, and some bandages to wrap his arm?" Charlie asked, as he helped me up.

"Sure, Charlie, right away," the cook said, going back into the tent.

"I think you Gary, ought to go radio Nick, and lelt him know we have his prize." Gary left in his truck leaving the same direction the truck was faced.

There must be another way out of here. I eased back against the tree. Charlie might seem like an oaf, however, he was loyal to Nick, and he did help get Joe's arm tended and them something to eat. I'd forgot how hungry I was pushing Gary to his limit. He was walking a tightrope, as he had seen what the others looked like when they'd died. He's afraid. I had no sympathy for Gary, and hoped when Ateara came that somehow Charlie wasn't here.

"How you doing, Joe," I asked trying to get up.

"You stay right where you are, Alex. You can talk to him from there," Charlie said, softly.

I wasn't going to aggravate the only somewhat ally we had so I sat back down against the tree. "Can I put my hands in front of me? It will be easier to eat that way, unless you're going to feed me."

"If you can do it, go ahead. I'm not untying you."

I pushed up with my hands and lifted my butt over them, and brought my legs back through before I sat back up against the tree.

"Considering I'm alright and will be much better with food in my belly, I thank you Charlie," Joe said. Charlie didn't smile but nodded his head at Joe.

A half hour later the cook had us fed and Joe's arm bandaged and his wrists tied in front of him. It didn't hurt my feelings one bit at Gary absence. Charlie, however, didn't waver his watch nor did he talk to them. I looked back down the road hoping to see Sadie. *Where are you girl.* Not knowing what kind of animals were out there, hoping none that would have her for breakfast. Oh, Sadie. Be careful. Not knowing how many miles we'd traveled to this camp, I hadn't thought to look at the odometer. I knew Sadie would follow, and hoped the little dog would stay out of sight.

Alex Think, I thought. *You have to get out of this before Nick comes.* The sound of a a truck coming up the road brought me out of thought. I looked over at Joe and shrugged my shoulders.

"Get up both of you and get inside the tent," Charlie ordered. He gave the cook the gun. "If either of them moves, kill'em. I think it's the ranger, so if you don't want his death on your conscious, I'd keep your mouths shut." He walked back outside and pulled the flap down with one hand and held a cup of coffee in the other. They heard the truck come to a stop, and the engine cut.

"Good evening Tom. How's the ranger business?" Charlie asked, handing him the cup of coffee. "I thought it might be you."

"Thanks, Charlie. Not so good tonight," the ranger said, taking a sip. "Found something down by the camp sites I've never seen in all my years of being a ranger. Almost lost my stomach with the smell and the sight of the bodies."

"Bodies?" Charlie asked.

"Yeah, two bodies. One looked like he had exploded. Guts and blood all around it, hole in the belly as big as a cannon ball. Their skin was black, but they were white men." The ranger shivered. "Ugly mess, an ugly mess."

"What happened to them?" The anxiety crossed over Charlie's face, his stomach churning as he took a quick look at the tent.

"They had snake bites around the neck and face. Looked like the other seven victims that come over the fax." The ranger took another sip of coffee.

"The other seven?"

"Don't you listen to the radio? It started around the time you set up camp here."

"Do you know who they were?" Charlie's hands were clammy and he pushed them inside his jean's pockets.

The ranger swallowed the rest of the coffee in his cup and set it on the make-shift table. "Not by names, but they said they all worked for a guy by the name of Nick Salva. One of the contractors on the pipeline. Don't know if it's the same Nick Salva that bought land up here a couple of years ago. Don't see much of him. Built a cabin by Leland Dam, not too far from here. Anyway, I wanted to tell you to keep your eyes open for snakes while you're here. You don't want to end up like those fellows."

"What kind of snake we looking for?"

"I'm not sure Charlie. I do know it's not a rattler. I need to go. See you later." The ranger stepped into his truck, turned it around and headed back the way he'd come.

Charlie stood there another five minutes considering what he'd heard.

The three in the tent heard every word the ranger had spoken, refreshing the memory Joe and I were trying to block out. My stomach churned, again, and wasn't sure the food would stay down this time. The cook sat down resting the gun on his lap, looking at the opening in the tent.

"Come on you two, outside," the cook said, standing back up. Charlie turned toward the tent and looked questioningly at me when I parted the flaps.

"I tried to tell you Charlie. There's a curse on Nick, and right now his peple are dying because of him."

"Who would do such a thing?"

"Ateara," I answered. "Black magic. Nick hurt her bad, Charlie."

"No! Nick wouldn't hurt Ateara. He loves her, and she loves Nick. Been that way since school. Yeah, I know Nick lust after other women and he's had more than his share, but he only loves one. Ateara."

"Well Charlie, that love is going to get us all killed. You gotta let us go," I pleaded.

"I can't do that. Nick said to keep you here until he came. That's what I gotta do."

"But Charlie..."

I could leave you here with Gary? He hasn't seen Nick when his orders haven't been carried out, and I wouldn't care if Nick killed him. Nick said no one was to touch you, and I'll make sure of that. Now go back over there and sit down." He pointed to where they'd been sitting before the ranger came into the camp.

&&&&&

The sun was setting in the west when Gary came back. He parked in front of the brown truck. After getting out, he walked over and stood in front of Charlie.

"What took you so long?" Charlie asked him.

"I stayed and had a couple of beers. I also called Oshler and let him know that Alex was still missing," he said, looking directly at me.

"Nick isn't going to like that. The police will be getting involved," Charlie said scowling.

"Don't worry Charlie, Nick will have his fun with her, and then they'll find her and Joe in a couple of days. Victims of snake bites like the others," he laughed.

"I know why Pete and Elmer aren't back. You thought they just knocked them out and took the truck. Ranger found them and what he described wasn't pretty. They had snake bites on their neck and faces.

"NO! Dammit it can't be," Gary swore and kicked the tire on the truck.

"Don't act upset with me, Gary. You had me picking up bullets off the floorboard of the truck when you drove past the bodies, before we started the chase. You didn't want me to see them."

"Guess I can't fool you any longer, Charlie," Gary said, leaning against the truck.

"That's what happened to the others that haven't come back to camp, isn't it," Charlie raised his voice up a notch.

"Alright! It's true," Gary responded.

"My nephew's dead!" he yelled. "And you didn't tell me?"

"I'm sorry, Charlie. Nick told me not to," Gary shouted back.

"When's Nick supposed to be here?"

"He said it would be around midnight. He's flying back up. He wants Joe tied back up and Alex taken to the cabin," Gary sneered.

"Alex stays here with me," Joe spat, standing up.

"Well, aren't we the hero," Gary laughed, walking up to Joe, he hit him in the head with the butt of his gun. Joe fell to the ground and didn't move.

"Joe!" I screamed. Gary grabbed my arm pulling me away from Joe's unconscious body.

"Come on, we have plans boss," Gary said, shoving me toward his truck. He stopped when he heard a gun cock.

"She's not going anywhere with you Gary. She needs to go to the cabin, I'll take her." Charlie stormed. Gary pushed me ahead of him and turned around when he heard the second gun cock.

"Alright, boys. We'll do it your way, for now. I know Nick shares his spoils, I can wait."

"You'll be dead Gary," I taunted. Gary turned to back hand me, I ducked, and Charlie caught his wrist.

"Get in the truck Alex," Charlie urged. They both got inside the truck and drove around Gary's black one and vanished up the road.

The drive was a short one, maybe half a mile maybe three quarters. Neither one spoke as they rode the distance. I looked around when we pulled up in front of the cabin. It was nice as I knew it would be. As we walked around to the side, I could see a tool shed set back from the house and further down and to the right a boat ramp the ranger had mentioned. A large rock fire pit was six feet from the large deck where padded chairs surrounded it.

Charlie escorted me up the back stairs and through the French doors into the kitchen.

"Can I use the bathroom?" I asked.

"Down the hall second door on the right."

I walked down the hall looking into the rooms I passed. *Nothing special*, I thought. The room at the end of the hall was Nick's. Very plush for a mountain cabin. The comforter was purple velvet, and as my eyes continued to the headboard I saw a shiny object attached. *I see his sexual pleasures haven't changed even here.* Checking the bathroom for a window, a heavy sigh left her lungs, there wasn't one and went back into the kitchen. Charlie was standing looking out the French doors. The moon would soon be up and cast its spell over the water.

"I'm sorry anbout your nephew, Charlie. I'm sorry about all the men that have been killed over this."

"You might as well make yourself comfortable. It will be a few hours before Nick gets here." I sat on the couch that faced the stone fireplace, tried to get my wrist untied. The rope cutting into my flesh, didn't give.

What a mess I made of things, Joe. I hope Gary doesn't take his anger out on you. I should never have involved you. What was I thinking? What have I been thinking these years? Now at the end, I realize what I really want, and if we get out of this I will let him know. Maybe there is still hope and maybe Ateara is close, and maybe she'd finish Nick tonight.

"Charlie, you said you've been with Nick since high school. Has he always been this way, on the wrong side of the law?"

"Not always. Nick grew up poor. It's an old love story. He fell head over heels for Ateara. He was afraid she wouldn't love him back when he had nothing. He wanted to give her everything. He learned with his chrisma, people would do his bidding. He was likeable, fun to be around. When Ateara saw how he used people she grew distant, even though she loved him. The further she drew away, the more he used and hurt people. I think he was taking his pain out on others, until it became a way of life for him. Bitter, hateful. He just couldn't see that she loved him for just him. Neither one ever married, but I guess you know that being friends with Ateara. Nick grew a lust for women and he used them. I think he was looking for a way to rid himself of the pain. Which isn't an excuse. I believe that's what he was doing." Charlie walked over to where I was sitting.

"Nick has always treated me well, taken care of me. I love him like a brother. I don't condone all the things he's done, and I guess it was easier for me to look the other way. I don't much know about curses, but I do believe in black magic. I don't know how this will end, but I feel they'll be together in the end." He walked back into the kitchen and stood looking out the French doors.

*****

I heard a truck pull up, a door open and shut. My heart raced. *Stay strong, don't let him know you're afraid.* I stood up when the French doors opened. Nick walked in sat a bottle of wine on the counter, with a sack, after which both men walked out on the deck. I could hear voices, but couldn't make out what was being said. Their voices heated and then softened. Five, ten, fifteen minutes passed.

I looked for another way out, and remember the door in Nick's bedroom, and ran to it. Turning the knob I pulled and then saw the chain and lock on the other side. I turned around, and Nick was standing in the doorway.

The moonlight through the window danced across my white breast. Buttons gone from when Gary had torn my shirt open. My chest rose and fell at a quicker pace as panic reached for me threatening to take control.

His eyes scanned my body stopping at my exposed breast, the lust emitting from his body. A brush hadn't touched my hair since the swim in the river, and the natural curl gave me a wild look. My clothes had dried, mud caked to the material. All signs of makeup were gone, the cut on my lip Gary had given me, and the dirt across my cheek did nothing to lessen the blood surge to his cock.

Dropping my arms down, there was no reason to hide what he'd already seen, and by no means was I going to act coy with him. I stepped away from the door, took a dozen steps before standing in front of him.

"Alex, you're here with me at last," he said, pushing a stray lock of hair from my face. His finger slipped gently across my swollen mouth before he bent down lightly kissing my lips. His tongue toured the outline tasting the dried blood.

"We have time for this and I want this to be a night you'll remember. Looking at you, and those dirty clothes you could use a shower." He took my wrist and backed us up until I stood in front of the bathroom door. He pushed it open. I remembered there were no window to escape from. Looking down at my tied wrist, and the blood stains on the rope, I looked back up at him still not saying a word.

"I will cut these bands so you can shower. Consider this," he said, as he leaned down and ran his tongue along my ear. "I know you have a black belt, but so do I. I consider it passionate foreplay if you want to indugle." He cut the ropes from my wrist, and let them fall to the floor. Bringing my wrist to his lips, he kissed each one before backing away and leaving the entrance to the bathroom open.

I walked in and shut the door, not bothering to lock it. If Nick wanted in, a lock wouldn't stop him. Taking off my clothes, letting them fall to the floor, stepping out of them. I ran the water until it was the right temperature before stepping inside and pulling the curtain over. I'd almost forgotten how good a shower felt as the water cascaded down my body. After washing my hair and body I noticed bruises I didn't know were there. Stepping out a large soft towel had been laid out with a pair of soft pants, a tee-shirt and a pair of socks. Next to them was a brush and a decorative barrette. I knew it wouldn't have made a difference to lock the door. Taking my time dressing and pulling my hair up, I walked into the hall. Candles were lit on the table, and there was a bottle of wine on ice. Nick was standing looking out the French door. He was wearing a pair of silk pants drawn at the waist.

CHAPTER 20

Joe tried to sit up straighter, stretching out the kink in his back. His mouth was bloody, and he had a headache the size of Gibraltor where Gary had hit him with the butt of his rifle. He heard the truck coming back down the road, which meant Nick was at the cabin with Alex. He tried to loosen the rope for the hundredth time that held his hands, but the rope held tight. He hoped Alex would be able to take care of herself, because sitting here tied to this tree, there wasn't a damn thing he could do and he hated Gary that much more for it.

He didn't say anything to Gary, afraid of getting knocked out again or worse, so he just watched him. Gary was getting skittish. He was like a time bomb ready to go off. The camp fire cast ghostly shadows across the landscape, leaving Gary searching for anything that moved and his gun was at the ready.

Charlie parked the truck, stepped out, and walked over to the fire.

"Want some coffee, Charlie?" the cook asked.

"That would be great," he replied. "Nick gave me a list of things he wants you to go pick up tonight," he told the cook.

"It's past midnight, why would Nick want him to go tonight? He can go in the morning," Gary grumbled.

"Unlike some, when Nick tells us to do something, we do it, when he says to do it." Charlie threw the keys to the cook. "I left the list on the seat. Make sure you get everything before you come back."

"Yes Charlie," the cook said, handing him the coffee and giving him an odd look. He watched Gary go inside the tent. "Drive slow past the cabin without your lights. You don't want to disturb Nick with his pleasures. Go!" Charlie urged him. The cook jumped inside the truck, turned it around and headed back up the road at a slow pace.

"Charlie, Nick isn't going to hurt her is he?" Joe asked waiting for reassurance.

"Joe, he isn't going to do anything that she doesn't want, and the rest is left up to the magic of the night.

"I didn't tell you did I Joe," Gary said, coming out of the tent. "When Nick's finishes having his fun with your little girlfriend, I get her," Gary laughed. "Maybe

I can talk Nick into lettting you watch." Joe scythed. He tried the knots again. All he felt was wetness around his wrist.

Half an hour they heard a truck coming back down the road. Stopped for a minute by the tall tress and then continued on until it stopped thirty feet away.

"What's going on?" Gary asked, walking toward the truck.

"I'll see what he needs," Charlie said. "You stay right here. Charlie put his hand in his pocket, and pulled something out handing it to the cook. He talked to him a minute, before the truck turned around and went back the way it had came.

Joe felt a hand on his shoulder. "Be still, Joe. Be keeping your hands behind you."

"Lester?" Joe whispered.

"Don't be talking," Lester said, his voice almost non-audible cutting through the rope binding Joe's wrist. "When you see da fire leap high in the pit you cut da rope around your feet, run to the black truck and get in. Lock the door, stay out of sight, and don't get out until I tell ya it's clear.

"What's that all about?" Gary growled.

"He needed more money. I thought about it after he left. I wasn't surprised to see him come back. Gary, let's go sit by the fire. Would you like a beer?"

"Now you're talking. Get me loosened up for that little bitch. I've waited two years to get some of that. Took a hell of a lot of acting working around Miss High and Mighty. Shouldn't be much longer before Nick is through with her," Gary smiled wickedly at

Joe. It took everything Joe had not to jump up, and punch the bastard in the face.

"Here, Ill trade you." Charlie reached for Gary's rifle

Gary sneered. "Hell no, I don't think so."

"Your choice, beer or the rifle. I'll set it here on the other side of the fire," Charlie said, reaching for the gun in Gary's hand.

"Alright," Gary said, taking the beer. You might as well bring me another one. Two should do it," looking at Joe, while he rubbed his crotch.

Joe cursed under his breath, wanting so bad to get his hands on that son-of-a-bitch. He knew without a distraction he wouldn't have time to cut the rope on his ankles and make over to Gary before Gary shot him. Besides, Lester said to get inside the truck. He held the knife tighter.

Five, ten, fifteen minutes passed. Gary had finished his second beer. Hissss, hissss, came from the fire before blue flames shot up. It looked light a torch had been lit. Joe cut the ropes around his feet and hesitated a second before he jumped to his feet and raced to the truck. Gary saw him, and reached for his gun. He picked it up and shot hitting the front tire. He lifted it up to shoot again, and click. The gun was empty.

Joe looked over the dash and wondered if he was seeing an mirage.

Gary stood staring into flames of blue and white, a woman standing in the center. She spoke to him, but he heard nothing. Her hair was blowing away from her face, and her dress whipped around her body. Gary could feel no breeze, no wind. He heard the sound, like it was coming from a tunnel, a hissss. It grew louder. Where one woman stood, now there was two swaying within the flame. Fear grabbed Gary's gut and he tried to step back. His feet wouldn't move. A scream tore from his throat as he watched the women transform into snakes. The eyes held him in place until one hissed and struck him in the neck, and then the other wrapped its way around his body tightening till no sound came forth. His eyes bulged, his face distorted as he fell to the ground his last breath escaping into the night air.

&&&&&

"Ahh, Alex, I'm sure you feel much better after a warm shower. Come sit down, have a glass of wine," Nick said, taking the bottle from the ice, and popping the cork. Picking up a glass, he filled it half way and handed it to me.

"What is all this, Nick?" I asked, trying to keep my voice calm.

"Consider it a last supper, before your death. I really didn't want it to end this way Alex," he paused, smiling at me as his fingers slid softly down my cheek. "you wouldn't leave it alone. We could have had great sex, did our work on the pipeline and gone home. We still will have great sex and then..."

Taking a sip of the wine, I asked, "Then what, Nick. A very good year."

"I like the best. I have a surprise for you in the shed. But we won't talk about that right now." Nick picked up two large pieces of meat and tossed them onto the back porch. I watched as the meat was torn apart and swallowed in three gulps by the two Rottweilers. "As you can see, I won't need to lock the door. You wouldn't make it off the porch."

Nick closed the door before walking over to the table. I took a large gulp of wine trying to stay calm, and set the glass down when Nick moved around the table. He raised his arm to put his hand on me, and I put up an arm blocking him, and backed away, his eyes laughing. I came up with a kick to his chest, it connected. The laughter faltered in his eyes for a moment. I staggered, feeling light headed. Making it around the couch, just before Nick jumped over it landing in front of me. I came around with another kick just missing him as he jumped back. He was playing with me as a cat would stalk a mouse waiting to pounce. Coming at him with a jab to his ribs, and another kick, but he caught my leg and threw me to the floor.

I stood up slowly, stretching, eyeing my enemy keeping eye contact. My head was swimming. I looked over at the glass of wine and then at Nick. He smiled.

"You put something in the wine, didn't you?"

"How you feeling Alex? Are you feeling warm between your legs? Are your breast starting to tingle?" he asked, moving towards me. "Physical activity moves it through your blood stream faster, Alex."

"Nick, stay where you are. If you don't, I'll scream."

"Scream Alex, no one will hear you."

"Is this what you do to all your women Nick? Drug them and knock them out?" I asked, feeling for the closest chair without losing eye contact with Nick.

"Only women who need persuasion, and it doesn't knock you out Alex. Another minute you'll want me as much as I want you." His smile broadened. I could feel my body temperature rising. My shirt was so warm around my body. My breast ached, and I fought the urge to take my shirt off.

No, I won't give in. I won't. I felt my shirt rise over my body, and Nick's hands covered my breasts. His thumbs dipped beneath my lacy bra tearing the fabric apart. His head dipped, taking my nipple into his mouth he groaned. I put my arms around him feeling the ecstasy of his flesh against my own. Picking me up, he carried me to the bed not breaking the kiss as he laid me down. The heat between my legs was becoming wet and demanding, I arched my body upward. My body needing to be sated.

Nick's hand caressed my inner thigh before slipping under the sweat pants tightening on my sex. I moaned as two fingers slipped between my wet lips.

"Ateara, Ateara," he whispered.

"What did you say?" I asked, trying to clear my head. "Stop, Nick!" I shouted, pushing him away. My body wanting sex, my mind screaming for me to stop.

"Not this time. I won't stop this time," he said, pressing me down.

"I'm not Ateara, Nick."

He struggled to push down his pants holding my hands above my head. I pressed upward and rolled us over so I was on top and pulled my hands free when I jumped to the floor. My head was still spinning. Nick grabbed my arm to pull me back down, and I doubled up my fist and swung catching him under the jaw. Struggling to the front room my hands giving me balance from one side of the wall to the other. Finding my shirt, pulled it over my head and thrust my feet into the tennis shoes. I ran to the patio door and stopped.

"Go ahead and open it," he said, walking up to me. Grabbing me by the hair he kissed me again, and fondled my breast. Nick let me go when we heard the gun shot. "I guess Alex that's all the time we have," he said, running back to his room, he came back with his shirt and shoes on.

My head felt like fog was moving in and out of it. Nick grasped my arm, tuned me before throwing me over his shoulder. I didn't have the strength to fight him and the blows to his back must have felt like nothing to Nick as he didn't even flinch. Carrying me through the door way and down the steps he trekked to the shed. Opening the door wide he walked in sitting me on a chair.

"You're not going to spoil my plan's Alex. You should have kept to the pipeline. Now you can die like the others," he said, looking over at the lumpy bag laying on the floor that the moon light settled on. "You have your choice snakes or dogs?" he grinned pulling me to him giving me a hard kiss.

"No Nick!" You can't do this," I cried, clinging to him.

"You should have thought of that before you got in my business. By now your boyfriend is dead. To bad I can't tell him you made love to me." He pushed me away shutting the door and locking it. I heard him walk away. Looking at the bag on the floor the fear filled every fiber of my being. I saw the window and opened it. Growls were heard, before the large beasts jumped at the window. I quickly shut it. I took a deep breath clearing my head with each intake. Looking around the room I saw a table, and pushed it under the window and climbed up on it.

"Oh God, please help me, please," I sobbed. Watching the bag starting to move, perhaps my eyes were playing tricks. No. It moved again. "Oh God, what am I going to do?" Tears rolled down my cheeks, heart pounded, and sweat beaded my forehead. There was no where else to escape. I saw the split tongue lash out at the opening of the bag. My stomach, and my throat tightened to the point no sound would emerge. One snake slithered out and two more followed moving toward me, drawn to my body heat.

I was pressing against the window when the window open and I fell backward. A hand closed over mouth and someone closed the window.

"Shhh, be quiet," Ateara whispered in my ear.

"Ateara," I put my arms around her and held tight. "The dogs?"

"Dead. Did Nick be drugging you?" Ateara asked.

"Yes. I'm so sorry Ateara," I sobbed, trying to control the relief of excaping the shed.

"You have nothing to be sorry for. Here take this. It will clear you head.

"What about Joe? Is he alright?"

"Pas' with Joe, and he be fine."

"Lesters here? How?"

"Not be time for questions. You see that road over there? You run and it be taking you to Joe. Go!" she said, pushing me away. "Go!" I started to run down the road still feeling dizzy, slowed, stumbled and fell.

"Nick come out," Ateara called, walking over to the fire pit. "Come out my love."

The French doors opened and Nick walked out onto the porch. Looking at her as the silver rays of the moon shone down on her. Long black strands fell over her shoulders and down her back. A slight smile touched her lips. Nick walked down the steps, and over to her drinking in her beauty. The love he had for her was like a torch lighting his very soul, consuming. He looked into the depth of her eyes, and what he saw was not love. He pushed it aside not wanting to believe the image reflecting back at him.

"Ateara, I love you," Nick cried out, pulling her to him kissing her, feeling her softness against him. Wanting this moment to last forever.

"You don't brand people you love, Nick. The Nick I loved, died along time ago. Now the evil that lives in his body will die tonight," she said.

"What are you talking about?" backing away from her. "You still love me, and you won't kill me. I'm going to walk down to the boat ramp, get in my boat and leave." Nick backed up a few more steps.

"No. You won't run away this time Nick. You will pay for all the horrid things you've done," Ateara said, tears running down her cheeks.

"I don't think so Ateara," he replied, retrieving the gun from his jacket pocket. "Don't make me use this." He backed up a few more steps, and turned walking to the boat ramp.

"Nick!"

He turned around as she raised her hands, a light few out of her fingertips and fire shot from Nick's gun. He started running to the boat ramp snakes slithered behind him. When he turned to take one last look at Ateara they were upon him, smothering him completely. His very soul sucked out, until all that was left was an empty shell.

I raised my head when the gun shot echoed.

"Ateara, Ateara," tears raced down my face, again. I got to my feet, and ran back to the cabin. Ateara was laying by the firepit. Reaching for her, great sobs racked my body as I looked down at the body of my friend. Looking down at the boat dock, Nick stood or what I could see of him, was engulfed in the black snakes.

I knelt over Ateara, picked up her head and shoulders and held her to me. Ateara was holding her stomach, blood ran under and through her fingers.

"Ateara you can't die. You need to hold on," I cried.

"It be my time," she choked. "Alex, the bag around my neck you need be need be taking it, and empty the contents into the water before I die," she said coughing up more blood.

"I don't want to leave you."

"You must break the spell, hurry," she begged. I took the bag hanging around Ateara's neck and ran to the water. Opening it up before I emptied it all. Stepping back as the water began to hiss and boil and a blue white mist rose catching the last moon beans before the moon sunk out of sight behind the hills of the Badlands. I ran back to Ateara and there lay Sadie. No sign of Ateara.

The cries rose from me and were carried in the wind. My body exhausted sank beside the lifeless form of my friend. When I opened my eyes, Joe and Lester were running toward me.

"Ateara, where be my Ateara, Alex?" Lester looked around them.

"She's gone Lester."

"Did you be doing what she asked before she went?" he asked, silent tears running down his face.

"Yes Lester, I did as she asked," I said, standing up reaching for Joe. "Joe," I whispered, and held him tight. "Joe." Joe tightened his arms around me like he'd never let me ago. They heard a wine and Lester looked down and saw Sadie.

"My Ateara," Lester's quiet crying turned to ragged cries that racked his body.

"Ateara." I looked at Lester questionably.

"She left a little bit of her soul in Sadie so she wouldn't be be lost," he said, picking her up gently.

"Sadie was Ateara?" Joe asked surprised.

"Yes," was Lester's only reply. My mind flashed back. The muddy paw prints on the floor of the fifth-wheel, the foot prints beside the truck and along the river. Sadie's cut leg, the bloody knife in the truck.

"It was always there in front of me, and I didn't see it." They heard a truck coming up the road and stopped behind Nick's. Out stepped Charlie. "Charlie where is Gary?"

"Gary got pretty much what Nick got," he said.

"Charlie had sent the cook to town to keep him out of harms way after he brought Lester into camp," Joe explained. They watched Charlie go over and hugged Lester, tears ran down both their cheeks.

"I see," I said "Charlie was your informant wasn't he Lester?"

"Yes. A friend flew me up when I heard Nick had left for up here. I think it be time we be going home,"

Lester said, cuddling Sadie in his arms as he and Charlie made their way to the truck.

I looked to the boat dock, and all I could see was a heap of banding. Grateful not to see Nick's body. My hand closed around the small empty satin bag and tears welled up again thinking of the two of them. The years Ateara and Nick could have had, if Nick had realized that his love was all Ateara wanted and needed. I looked up at Joe.

"Joe," I said, putting my arms around his neck, "if you still want to marry me, my answer's yes."

The End.